REBECCA
of Sunnybrook Farm

BY

KATE DOUGLAS WIGGIN

LONDON

ADAM & CHARLES BLACK

FIRST PUBLISHED 1903, REPRINTED 1903, 1904, 1905
ILLUSTRATED EDITION 1907
CHEAPER ILLUSTRATED EDITION 1908, REPRINTED 1912
POPULAR EDITION 1911
REPRINTED 1911, 1912, 1913, 1914, 1915, 1917, 1918
1919, 1920, 1921, 1923 (27TH PRINTING)
NEW EDITION (RESET) 1929, REPRINTED 1932, 1933
1935, 1937, 1939, 1940, 1942, 1946, 1948,
1950, 1952, 1955, 1957, 1962 AND 1966

A. AND C. BLACK LTD
4, 5, AND 6, SOHO SQUARE, LONDON, W.1

Printed & bound by the Hollen Street Press, Ltd.
London W.1

REBECCA
OF SUNNYBROOK FARM

CONTENTS

REBECCA
OF SUNNYBROOK FARM

I

"WE ARE SEVEN"

THE old stage-coach was rumbling along the dusty road that runs from Maplewood to Riverboro. The day was as warm as midsummer, though it was only the middle of May, and Mr. Jeremiah Cobb was favouring the horses as much as possible, yet never losing sight of the fact that he carried the mail. The hills were many, and the reins lay loosely in his hands as he lolled back in his seat and extended one foot and leg luxuriously over the dashboard. His brimmed hat of worn felt was well pulled over his eyes, and he revolved a quid of tobacco in his left cheek.

There was one passenger in the coach, a small dark-haired person in a glossy buff calico dress. She was so slender and so stiffly starched that she slid from space to space on the leather cushions, though she braced herself against the middle seat with her feet, and extended her cotton-gloved hands on each side, in order to maintain some sort of balance. Whenever the wheels sank farther than usual into a rut, or jolted suddenly over a stone, she bounded involuntarily into the air, came down again, pushed back her funny little straw hat, and picked up or settled more firmly a small

pink sunshade, which seemed to be her chief responsibility, unless we accept a bead purse, into which she
looked whenever the condition of the roads would
permit, finding great apparent satisfaction in that its
precious contents neither disappeared nor grew less.
Mr. Cobb guessed nothing of these harassing details
of travel, his business being to carry people to their
destinations, not, necessarily, to make them comfortable on the way. Indeed, he had forgotten the very
existence of this one unnoteworthy little passenger.

When he was about to leave the post-office in
Maplewood that morning, a woman had alighted from
a waggon, and coming up to him, inquired whether
this were the Riverboro stage, and if he were Mr.
Cobb. Being answered in the affirmative, she nodded to
a child who was eagerly waiting for the answer, and
who ran towards her as if she feared to be a moment
too late. The child might have been ten or eleven
years old, perhaps, but whatever the number of her
summers, she had an air of being small for her age.
Her mother helped her into the stage-coach, deposited
a bundle and a bouquet of lilacs beside her, super-
intended the " roping on " behind of an old hair-
trunk, and finally paid the fare, counting out the silver
with great care.

" I want you should take her to my sisters' in Riverboro," she said. " Do you know Mirandy and Jane
Sawyer? They live in the brick house."

Lord bless your soul, he knew 'em as well as if
he'd made 'em!

" Well, she's going there, and they're expecting her.
Will you keep an eye on her, please? If she can get
out anywhere and get with folks, or get anybody in to

keep her company, she'll do it. Good-bye, Rebecca; try not to get into any mischief, and sit quiet, so you'll look neat an' nice when you get there. Don't be any trouble to Mr. Cobb. You see, she's kind of excited. We came on the cars from Temperance yesterday, slept all night at my cousin's, and drove from her house—eight miles it is—this morning."

"Good-bye, mother; don't worry. You know, it isn't as if I hadn't travelled before."

The woman gave a short sardonic laugh and said in an explanatory way to Mr. Cobb: "She's been to Wareham and stayed overnight; that isn't much to be journey-proud on!"

"It *was travelling*, mother," said the child eagerly and wilfully. "It was leaving the farm, and putting up lunch in a basket, and a little riding and a little steam-cars, and we carried our nightgowns."

"Don't tell the whole village about it, if we did," said the mother, interrupting the reminiscences of this experienced voyager. "Haven't I told you before," she whispered, in a last attempt at discipline, "that you shouldn't talk about nightgowns and stockings and—things like that, in a loud tone of voice, and especially when there's menfolks round?"

"I know, mother, I know, and I won't. All I want to say is"—here Mr. Cobb gave a cluck, slapped the reins, and the horses started sedately on their daily task—"all I want to say is that is a journey when"—the stage was really under way now, and Rebecca had to put her head out of the window over the door in order to finish her sentence—"it *is* a journey when you carry a nightgown!"

The objectionable word, uttered in a high treble,

floated back to the offended ears of Mrs. Randall, who watched the stage out of sight, gathered up her packages from the bench at the store-door, and stepped into the waggon that had been standing at the hitching-post. As she turned the horse's head towards home she rose to her feet for a moment, and, shading her eyes with her hand, looked at a cloud of dust in the dim distance.

"Mirandy 'll have her hands full, I guess," she said to herself; "but I shouldn't wonder if it would be the making of Rebecca."

All this had been half an hour ago, and the sun, the heat, the dust, the contemplation of errands to be done in the great metropolis of Milltown, had lulled Mr. Cobb's never active mind into complete oblivion as to his promise of keeping an eye on Rebecca.

Suddenly he heard a small voice above the rattle and rumble of the wheels and the creaking of the harness. At first he thought it was a cricket, a tree toad, or a bird, but having determined the direction from which it came, he turned his head over his shoulder and saw a small shape hanging as far out of the window as safety would allow. A long black braid of hair swung with the motion of the coach; the child held her hat in one hand and with the other made ineffectual attempts to stab the driver with her microscopic sunshade.

"Please let me speak!" she called.

Mr. Cobb drew up the horses obediently.

"Does it cost any more to ride up there with you?" she asked. "It's so slippery and shiny down here, and the stage is so much too big for me, that I rattle round in it till I'm most black and blue. And the windows are so small I can only see pieces of things, and I've most broken my neck stretching round to find out whether my trunk has fallen off the back. It's my mother's trunk, and she's very choice of it."

Mr. Cobb waited until this flow of conversation, or more properly speaking this flood of criticism, had ceased, and then said jocularly :

"You can come up if you want to; there ain't no extry charge to sit side o' me." Whereupon he helped her out, "boosted" her up to the front seat, and resumed his own place.

Rebecca sat down carefully, smoothing her dress under her with painstaking precision, and putting her sunshade under its extended folds between the driver and herself. This done, she pushed back her hat, pulled up her darned white cotton gloves, and said delightedly :

"Oh, this is better! This is like travelling! I am a real passenger now, and down there I felt like our setting hen when we shut her up in a coop. I hope we have a long, long ways to go?"

"Oh, we've only just started on it," Mr. Cobb responded genially; "it's more'n two hours."

"Only two hours!" she sighed. "That will be half-past one; mother will be at Cousin Ann's, the children at home will have had their dinner, and Hannah cleared all away. I have some lunch, because mother said it would be a bad beginning to get to the brick house hungry, and have Aunt Mirandy have to get me something to eat the first thing. It's a good growing day, isn't it?"

"It is, certain; too hot, most. Why don't you put up your parasol?"

She extended her dress still farther over the article

in question as she said: "Oh dear no! I never put it up when the sun shines. Pink fades awfully, you know; and I only carry it to meetin' cloudy Sundays. Sometimes the sun comes out all of a sudden, and I have a dreadful time covering it up. It's the dearest thing in life to me; but it's an awful care."

At this moment the thought gradually permeated Mr. Jeremiah Cobb's slow-moving mind that the bird perched by his side was a bird of very different feather from those to which he was accustomed in his daily drives. He put the whip back in its socket, took his foot from the dashboard, pushed his hat back, blew his quid of tobacco into the road, and, having thus cleared his mental decks for action, he took his first good look at the passenger—a look which she met with a grave, childlike stare of friendly curiosity.

The buff calico was faded, but scrupulously clean, and starched within an inch of its life. From the little standing ruffle at the neck the child's slender throat rose very brown and thin, and the head looked small to bear the weight of dark hair that hung in a thick braid to her waist. She wore an odd little visored cap of white Leghorn, which may either have been the latest thing in children's hats, or some bit of ancient finery furbished up for the occasion. It was trimmed with a twist of buff ribbon and a cluster of black and orange porcupine quills, which hung or bristled stiffly over one ear, giving her the quaintest and most unusual appearance. Her face was without colour and sharp in outline. As to features, she must have had the usual number, though Mr. Cobb's attention never proceeded so far as nose, forehead, or chin, being caught on the way and held fast by the eyes. Rebecca's eyes were like faith—" the substance of things hoped for, the evidence of things not seen." Under her delicately etched brows they glowed like two stars, their dancing lights half hidden in lustrous darkness. Their glance was eager and full of interest, yet never satisfied; their steadfast gaze was brilliant and mysterious, and had the effect of looking directly through the obvious to something beyond—in the object, in the landscape, in you. They had never been accounted for, Rebecca's eyes. The school-teacher and the minister at Temperance had tried and failed; the young artist who came for the summer to sketch the red barn, the ruined mill, and the bridge, ended by giving up all these local beauties and devoting herself to the face of a child—a small, plain face, illuminated by a pair of eyes carrying such messages, such suggestions, such hints of sleeping power and insight, that one never tired of looking into their shining depths, nor of fancying that what one saw there was the reflection of one's own thought.

Mr. Cobb made none of these generalizations; his remark to his wife that night was simply to the effect that whenever the child looked at him she knocked him galley west.

"Miss Ross, a lady that paints, gave me the sunshade," said Rebecca, when she had exchanged looks with Mr. Cobb and learned his face by heart. "Did you notice the pinked double ruffle and the white tip and handle? They're ivory. The handle is scarred, you see. That's because Fanny sucked and chewed it in meeting when I wasn't looking. I've never felt the same to Fanny since."

"Is Fanny your sister?"

"She's one of them."

"How many are there of you?"

"Seven. There's verses written about seven children :

> " ' Quick was the little maid's reply—
> "O master, we are seven !" ' "

I learned it to speak in school, but the scholars were hateful and laughed. Hannah is the oldest; I come next, then John, then Jenny, then Mark, then Fanny, then Mira."

"Well, that *is* a big family !"

"Far too big, everybody says," replied Rebecca, with an unexpected and thoroughly grown-up candour that induced Mr. Cobb to murmur, "I swan!" and insert more tobacco in his left cheek.

"They're dear, but such a bother, and cost so much to feed, you see," she rippled on. "Hannah and I haven't done anything but put babies to bed at night and take them up in the morning for years and years. But it's finished, that's one comfort; and we'll have a lovely time when we're all grown up and the mortgage is paid off."

"All finished? Oh, you mean you've come away?"

"No; I mean they're all over and done with—our family's finished. Mother says so, and she always keeps her promises. There hasn't been any since Mira, and she's three. She was born the day father died. Aunt Miranda wanted Hannah to come to Riverboro instead of me, but mother couldn't spare her; she takes hold of housework better than I do, Hannah does. I told mother last night if there was likely to be any more children while I was away I'd have to be sent for,

for when there's a baby it always takes Hannah and
me both, for mother has the cooking and the farm."

"Oh, you live on a farm, do ye? Where is it?
Near to where you got on?"

"Near? Why, it must be thousands of miles! We
came from Temperance in the cars. Then we drove
a long ways to Cousin Ann's and went to bed. Then
we got up and drove ever so far to Maplewood, where
the stage was. Our farm is away off from everywheres,
but our school and meeting-house is at Temperance,
and that's only two miles. Sitting up here with you is
most as good as climbing the meeting-house steeple.
I know a boy who's been up on our steeple. He said
the people and cows looked like flies. We haven't
met any people yet, but I'm *kind* of disappointed
in the cows; they don't look so little as I hoped they
would, still "—brightening—" they don't look quite
as big as if we were down side of them, do they?
Boys always do the nice splendid things, and girls can
only do the nasty dull ones that get left over. They
can't climb so high, or go so far, or stay out so late,
or run so fast, or anything."

Mr. Cobb wiped his mouth on the back of his
hand and gasped. He had a feeling that he was being
hurried from peak to peak of a mountain range without time to take a good breath in between.

"I can't seem to locate your farm," he said,
"though I've been to Temperance, and used to live
up that way. What's your folk's name?"

"Randall. My mother's name is Aurelia Randall.
Our names are Hannah Lucy Randall, Rebecca
Rowena Randall, John Halifax Randall, Jenny Lind
Randall, Marquis Randall, Fanny Ellsler Randall,

and Miranda Randall. Mother named half of us and
father the other half; but we didn't come out even,
so they both thought it would be nice to name Mira
after Aunt Miranda, in Riverboro. They hoped it
might do some good; but it didn't, and now we call
her Mira. We are all named after somebody in par
ticular. Hannah is Hannah at the Window Binding
Shoes, and I am taken out of 'Ivanhoe'; John Halifax
was a gentleman in a book; Mark is after his uncle,
Marquis de Lafayette, that died a twin. (Twins very
often don't live to grow up, and triplets almost never.
Did you know that, Mr. Cobb?) We don't call him
Marquis, only Mark. Jenny is named for a singer and
Fanny for a beautiful dancer; but mother says they're
both misfits, for Jenny can't carry a tune, and Fanny's
kind of stiff-leggèd. Mother would like to call them
Jane and Frances and give up their middle names, but
she says it wouldn't be fair to father. She says we
must always stand up for father, because everything
was against him, and he wouldn't have died if he
hadn't had such bad luck. I think that's all there is
to tell about us," she finished seriously.

"Land o' liberty! I should think it was enough,"
ejaculated Mr. Cobb. "There wa'n't many names left
when your mother got through choosin'. You've got
a powerful good memory. I guess it ain't no trouble
for you to learn your lessons, is it?"

"Not much; the trouble is to get the shoes to go
and learn 'em. These are spandy new I've got on, and
they have to last six months. Mother always says to
save my shoes. There don't seem to be any way of
saving shoes but taking 'em off and going barefoot;
but I can't do that in Riverboro without shaming

Aunt Mirandy. I'm going to school right along now when I'm living with Aunt Mirandy, and in two years I'm going to the seminary at Wareham. Mother says it ought to be the making of me. I'm going to be a painter, like Miss Ross, when I get through school. At any rate, that's what *I* think I'm going to be. Mother thinks I'd better teach."

"Your farm ain't the old Hobbs' place, is it?"

"No, it's just Randall's Farm—at least, that's what mother calls it. I call it Sunnybrook Farm."

"I guess it don't make no difference what you call it so long as you know where it is," remarked Mr. Cobb sententiously.

Rebecca turned the full light of her eyes upon him reproachfully, almost severely, as she answered:

"Oh, don't say that and be like all the rest! It does make a difference what you call things. When I say Randall's Farm, do you see how it looks?"

"No, I can't say I do," responded Mr. Cobb uneasily.

"Now, when I say Sunnybrook Farm, what does it make you think of?"

Mr. Cobb felt like a fish removed from his native element and left panting on the sand. There was no evading the awful responsibility of a reply, for Rebecca's eyes were searchlights that pierced the fiction of his brain and perceived the bald spot on the back of his head.

"I s'pose there's a brook somewhere near it," he said timorously.

Rebecca looked disappointed, but not quite disheartened. "That's pretty good," she said encouragingly. "You're warm, but not hot. There's a brook,

B

but not a common brook. It has young trees and baby bushes on each side of it, and it's a shallow, chattering little brook, with a white sandy bottom and lots of little shiny pebbles. Whenever there's a bit of sunshine the brook catches it, and it's always full of sparkles the livelong day. Don't your stomach feel hollow? Mine does. I was so 'fraid I'd miss the stage I couldn't eat any breakfast."

"You'd better have your lunch, then. I don't eat nothin' till I get to Milltown, then I get a piece o' pie and cup o' coffee."

"I wish I could see Milltown. I suppose it's bigger and grander even than Wareham—more like Paris? Miss Ross told me about Paris; she bought my pink sunshade there and my bead purse. You see how it opens with a snap. I've twenty cents in it, and it's got to last three months—for stamps and paper and ink. Mother says Aunt Mirandy won't want to buy things like those when she's feeding and clothing me and paying for my school-books."

"Paris ain't no great," said Mr. Cobb disparagingly. "It's the dullest place in the State o' Maine. I've druv there many a time."

Again Rebecca was obliged to reprove Mr. Cobb, tacitly and quietly, but none the less surely, though the reproof was dealt with one glance, quickly sent and as quickly withdrawn.

"Paris is the capital of France, and you have to go to it on a boat," she said instructively. "It's in my geography, and it says: 'The French are a gay and polite people, fond of dancing and light wines.' I asked the teacher what light wines were, and he thought it was something like new cider, or, maybe, ginger-pop. I can see Paris as plain as day by just shutting my eyes. The beautiful ladies are always gaily dancing around, with pink sunshades and bead purses, and the grand gentlemen are politely dancing and drinking ginger-pop. But you can see Milltown most every day with your eyes wide open," Rebecca said wistfully.

"Milltown ain't no great neither," replied Mr. Cobb with the air of having visited all the cities of the earth, and found them as naught. "Now, you watch me heave this newspaper right on to Miss Brown's doorstep."

Piff! and the packet landed exactly as it was intended—on the corn-husk mat in front of the screen door.

"Oh, how splendid that was!" cried Rebecca with enthusiasm—"just like the knife-thrower Mark saw at the circus. I wish there was a long, long row of houses, each with a corn-husk mat and a screen door in the middle, and a newspaper to throw on every one!"

"I might fail on some of 'em, you know," said Mr. Cobb, beaming with modest pride. "If your Aunt Mirandy 'll let you, I'll take you down to Milltown some day this summer when the stage ain't full."

A thrill of delicious excitement ran through Rebecca's frame, from her new shoes up, up to the Leghorn cap and down the black braid. She pressed Mr. Cobb's knee ardently, and said in a voice choking with tears of joy and astonishment: "Oh, it can't be true—it can't! To think I should see Milltown! It's like having a fairy godmother, who asks you your wish and then gives it to you. Did you ever read 'Cinderella,' or 'The Yellow Dwarf,' or 'The Enchanted Frog,' or 'The Fair One with Golden Locks'?"

"No," said Mr. Cobb cautiously after a moment's reflection. "I don't seem to think I ever did read jest those partic'lar ones. Where'd you get a chance at so much readin'?"

"Oh, I've read lots of books," answered Rebecca casually—"father's, and Miss Ross's, and all the dif'rent school-teachers', and all in the Sunday-school library. I've read 'The Lamplighter,' and 'Scottish Chiefs,' and 'Ivanhoe,' and 'The Heir of Redclyffe,' and 'Cora, the Doctor's Wife,' and 'David Copperfield,' and 'The Gold of Chickaree,' and Plutarch's 'Lives,' and 'Thaddeus of Warsaw,' and 'Pilgrim's Progress,' and lots more. What have you read?"

"I've never happened to read those partic'lar books; but land! I've read a sight in my time! Nowadays I'm so drove I get along with the Almanac, the *Weekly Argus*, and the *Maine State Agriculturist*. There's the river again; this is the last long hill, and when we get to the top of it we'll see the chimbleys of Riverboro in the distance. 'Tain't fur. I live 'bout half a mile beyond the brick house myself."

Rebecca's hand stirred nervously in her lap and she moved in her seat. "I didn't think I was going to be afraid," she said almost under her breath; "but I guess I am, just a little mite—when you say it's coming so near."

"Would you go back?" asked Mr. Cobb curiously.

She flashed him an intrepid look and then said proudly, "I'd never go back—I might be frightened,

but I'd be ashamed to run. Going to Aunt Mirandy's
is like going down cellar in the dark. There might
be ogres and giants under the stairs, but, as I tell
Hannah, there *might* be elves and fairies and enchanted frogs! Is there a main street to the village,
like that in Wareham?"

"I s'pose you might call it main street, an' your
Aunt Sawyer lives on it, but there ain't no stores nor
mills, an' it's an awful one-horse village! You have
to go 'cross the river an' get on to our side if you
want to see anything goin' on."

"I'm almost sorry," she sighed, "because it would
be so grand to drive down a real main street sitting
high up like this behind two splendid horses, with my
pink sunshade up, and everybody in town wondering
who the bunch of lilacs and the hair-trunk belongs to.
It would be just like the beautiful lady in the parade.
Last summer the circus came to Temperance, and they
had a procession in the morning. Mother let us all
walk in and wheel Mira in the baby-carriage, because
we couldn't afford to go to the circus in the afternoon.
And there were lovely horses and animals in cages,
and clowns on horseback; and at the very end
came a little red-and-gold chariot drawn by two
ponies, and in it, sitting on a velvet cushion, was the
snake-charmer, all dressed in satin and spangles. She
was so beautiful beyond compare, Mr. Cobb, that you
had to swallow lumps in your throat when you looked
at her, and little cold feelings crept up and down your
back. Don't you know what I mean? Didn't you ever
see anybody that made you feel like that?"

Mr. Cobb was more distinctly uncomfortable at
this moment than he had been at any one time during

the eventful morning, but he evaded the point dex-
terously by saying: "There ain't no harm, as I can
see, in our makin' the grand entry in the biggest style
we can. I'll take the whip out, set up straight, an'
drive fast; you hold your bo'quet in your lap, an'
open your little red parasol, an' we'll jest make the
natives stare!"

The child's face was radiant for a moment, but the
glow faded just as quickly as she said: "I forgot—
mother put me inside, and maybe she'd want me to
be there when I got to Aunt Mirandy's. Maybe I'd be
more genteel inside, and then I wouldn't have to be
jumped down and my clothes fly up, but could open
the door and step down like a lady passenger. Would
you please stop a minute, Mr. Cobb, and let me
change?"

The stage-driver good-naturedly pulled up his
horses, lifted the excited little creature down, opened
the door, and helped her in, putting the lilacs and
pink sunshade beside her.

"We've had a great trip," he said, "and we've got
real well acquainted, haven't we? You won't forget
about Milltown?"

"Never!" she exclaimed fervently; "and you're
sure you won't either?"

"Never! Cross my heart!" vowed Mr. Cobb
solemnly, as he remounted his perch; and as the stage
rumbled down the village street between the green
maples, those who looked from their windows saw
a little brown elf in buff calico sitting primly on the
back-seat holding a great bouquet tightly in one hand,
and a pink parasol in the other. Had they been far-
sighted enough they might have seen, when the stage

turned into the side doorway of the old brick house, a calico yoke rising and falling tempestuously over the beating heart beneath, the red colour coming and going in two pale cheeks, and a mist of tears swimming in two brilliant dark eyes—Rebecca's journey had ended.

" There's the stage turnin' into the Sawyer girls' dooryard," said Mrs. Perkins to her husband. " That must be the niece from up Temperance way. It seems they wrote to Aurelia and invited Hannah, the oldest, but Aurelia said she could spare Rebecca better, if 'twas all the same to Mirandy 'n' Jane; so it's Rebecca that's come. She'll be good comp'ny for our Emma Jane; but I don't believe they'll keep her three months! She looks black as an Injun, what I can see of her—black and kind of up-an'-comin'. They used to say that one o' the Randalls married a Spanish woman—somebody that was teachin' music and languages at a boardin'-school. Lorenzo was dark complected, you remember; and this child is, too. Well, I don't know as Spanish blood is any real disgrace, not if it's a good ways back and the woman was respectable."

II

THEY had been called the Sawyer girls when Miranda at eighteen, Jane at twelve, and Aurelia at eight, participated in the various activities of village life; and when Riverboro fell into a habit of thought or speech, it saw no reason for falling out of it—at any rate, in the same century. So, although Miranda and Jane were between fifty and sixty at the time this story opens, Riverboro still called them the Sawyer girls. They were spinsters, but Aurelia, the youngest, had made what she called a romantic marriage, and what her sisters termed a mighty poor speculation. "There's worse things than bein' old maids," they said; whether they thought so is quite another matter.

The element of romance in Aurelia's marriage existed chiefly in the fact that Mr. L. D. M. Randall had a soul above farming or trading, and was a votary of the Muses. He taught the weekly singing-school (then a feature of village life) in half a dozen neighbouring towns; he played the violin, and "called off" at dances, or evoked rich harmonies from church melodeons on Sundays. He taught certain uncouth lads, when they were of an age to enter society, the intricacies of contra dances, or the steps of the schottische and mazurka; and he was a marked figure in all social assemblies, though conspicuously absent from town meetings, and the purely masculine gatherings at the store, or tavern, or bridge.

His hair was a little longer, his hands a little whiter,

his shoes a little thinner, his manner a trifle more polished, than that of his soberer mates; indeed, the only department of life in which he failed to shine was the making of sufficient money to live upon. Luckily, he had no responsibilities; his father and his twin brother had died when he was yet a boy, and his mother, whose only noteworthy achievement had been the naming of her twin sons Marquis de Lafayette and Lorenzo de Medici Randall, had supported herself and educated her child by making coats up to the very day of her death. She was wont to say plaintively: "I'm afraid the faculties was too much divided up between my twins. L. D. M. is awful talented; but I guess M. D. L. would 'a' be'n the practical one if he'd 'a' lived."

"L. D. M. was practical enough to get the richest girl in the village," replied Mrs. Robinson.

"Yes," sighed his mother; "there it is again. If the twins could 'a' married Aurelia Sawyer, 'twould 'a' been all right. L. D. M. was talented 'nough to *get* Reely's money, but M. D. L. would 'a' be'n practical 'nough to have *kep*' it."

Aurelia's share of the modest Sawyer property had been put into one thing after another by the handsome and luckless Lorenzo de Medici. He had a graceful and poetic way of making an investment for each new son and daughter that blessed their union. "A birthday present for our child, Aurelia," he would say; "a little nest-egg for the future." But Aurelia once remarked in a moment of bitterness that the hen never lived that could sit on those eggs and hatch anything out of them.

Miranda and Jane had virtually washed their hands

of Aurelia when she married Lorenzo de Medici Randall. Having exhausted the resources of Riverboro and its immediate vicinity, the unfortunate couple had moved on and on in a steadily decreasing scale of prosperity until they had reached Temperance, where they had settled down and invited fate to do its worst —an invitation which was promptly accepted. The maiden sisters at home wrote to Aurelia two or three times a year, and sent modest but serviceable presents to the children at Christmas, but refused to assist L. D. M. with the regular expenses of his rapidly growing family. His last investment—made shortly before the birth of Miranda (named in a lively hope of favours which never came)—was a small farm two miles from Temperance. Aurelia managed this herself; and so it proved a home at least, and a place for the unsuccessful Lorenzo to die and to be buried from—a duty somewhat too long deferred, many thought, which he performed on the day of Mira's birth.

It was in this happy-go-lucky household that Rebecca had grown up. It was just an ordinary family—two or three of the children were handsome and the rest plain, three of them rather clever, two industrious, and two commonplace and dull. Rebecca had her father's facility, and had been his aptest pupil. She " carried " the alto by ear, danced without being taught, played the melodeon without knowing the notes. Her love of books she inherited chiefly from her mother, who found it hard to sweep, or cook, or sew when there was a novel in the house. Fortunately, books were scarce, or the children might sometimes have gone ragged and hungry.

But other forces had been at work in Rebecca, and the traits of unknown forbears had been wrought into her fibre. Lorenzo de Medici was flabby and boneless, Rebecca was a thing of fire and spirit; he lacked energy and courage, Rebecca was plucky at two and dauntless at five. Mrs. Randall and Hannah had no sense of humour; Rebecca possessed and showed it as soon as she could walk and talk.

She had not been able, however, to borrow her parents' virtues and those of other generous ancestors, and escape all the weaknesses in the calendar. She had not her sister Hannah's patience, or her brother John's sturdy staying-power. Her will was sometimes wilfulness, and the ease with which she did most things led her to be impatient of hard tasks or long ones. But whatever else there was or was not, there was freedom at Randall's farm. The children grew, worked, fought, ate what and slept where they could; loved one another and their parents pretty well, but with no tropical passion; and educated themselves for nine months of the year, each one in his own way.

As a result of this method, Hannah, who could only have been developed by forces applied from without, was painstaking, humdrum, and limited; while Rebecca, who apparently needed nothing but space to develop in and a knowledge of terms in which to express herself, grew and grew and grew, always from within outward. Her forces of one sort and another had seemingly been set in motion when she was born; they needed no daily spur, but moved of their own accord—towards what no one knew, least of all Rebecca herself. The field for the exhibition of her creative instinct was painfully small, and the only use she had made of it as yet was to leave eggs out of the corn bread one day and milk another to see how it would turn out; to part Fanny's hair sometimes in the middle, sometimes on the right, and sometimes on the left side; and to play all sorts of fantastic pranks with the children, occasionally bringing them to the table as fictitious or historical characters found in her favourite books. Rebecca amused her mother and her family generally, but she never was counted of serious importance; and though considered "smart" and old for her age, she was never thought superior in any way. Aurelia's experience of genius, as exemplified in the deceased Lorenzo de Medici, led her into a greater admiration of plain, everyday common sense —a quality in which Rebecca, it must be confessed, seemed sometimes painfully deficient.

Hannah was her mother's favourite, so far as Aurelia could indulge herself in such recreations as partiality. The parent who is obliged to feed and clothe seven children on an income of fifteen dollars a month seldom has time to discriminate carefully between the various members of her brood; but Hannah at fourteen was at once companion and partner in all her mother's problems. She it was who kept the house while Aurelia busied herself in barn and field. Rebecca was capable of certain set tasks, such as keeping the small children from killing themselves and one another, feeding the poultry, picking up chips, hulling strawberries, wiping dishes; but she was thought irresponsible, and Aurelia, needing somebody to lean on (having never enjoyed that luxury with the gifted Lorenzo), leaned on Hannah. Hannah

showed the result of this attitude somewhat, being
a trifle careworn in face and sharp in manner. But she
was a self-contained, well-behaved, dependable child,
and that is the reason her aunts had invited her to
Riverboro to be a member of their family and partici-
pate in all the advantages of their loftier position in
the world. It was several years since Miranda and
Jane had seen the children, but they remembered with
pleasure that Hannah had not spoken a word during
the interview, and it was for this reason that they had
asked for the pleasure of her company. Rebecca, on
the other hand, had dressed up the dog in John's
clothes; and, being requested to get the three younger
children ready for dinner, she had held them under
the pump, and then proceeded to "smack" their hair
flat to their heads by vigorous brushing, bringing
them to the table in such a moist and hideous state
of shininess that their mother was ashamed of their
appearance. Rebecca's own black locks were commonly pushed smoothly off her forehead, but on this
occasion she formed what I must perforce call by its
only name—a spit-curl—directly in the centre of her
brow; an ornament which she was allowed to wear
a short time—only, in fact, till Hannah was able to
call her mother's attention to it, when she was sent
into the next room to remove it, and to come back
looking something like a Christian. This command
she interpreted somewhat too literally, perhaps, because she contrived in the space of two minutes an
extremely pious style of hair-dressing, fully as effective, if not as startling, as the first. These antics were
solely the result of nervous irritation, a mood born
of Miss Miranda Sawyer's stiff, grim, and martial

attitude. The remembrance of Rebecca was so vivid that their sister Aurelia's letter was something of a shock to the quiet, elderly spinsters of the brick house; for it said that Hannah could not possibly be spared for a few years yet, but that Rebecca would come as soon as she could be made ready: that the offer was most thankfully appreciated, and that the regular schooling and church privileges, as well as the influence of the Sawyer home, would doubtless be "the making of Rebecca."

III

A DIFFERENCE IN HEARTS

"I DON' know as I cal'lated to be the makin' of any child," Miranda had said as she folded Aurelia's letter and laid it in the light-stand drawer. "I s'posed, of course, Aurelia would send us the one we asked for, but it's just like her to palm off that wild young one on somebody else."

"You remember we said that Rebecca or even Jenny might come, in case Hannah couldn't," interposed Jane.

"I know we did, but we hadn't any notion it would turn out that way," grumbled Miranda.

"She was a mite of a thing when we saw her three years ago," ventured Jane; "she's had time to improve."

"And time to grow worse!"

"Won't it be kind of a privilege to put her on the right track?" asked Jane timidly.

"I don' know about the privilege part; it'll be considerable of a chore, I guess. If her mother hain't got her on the right track by now, she won't take to it herself all of a sudden."

This depressed and depressing frame of mind had lasted until the eventful day dawned on which Rebecca was to arrive.

"If she makes as much work after she comes as she has before, we might as well give up hope of ever gettin' any rest," sighed Miranda as she hung the dish-towels on the barberry bushes at the side-door.

"But we should have had to clean house, Rebecca or no Rebecca," urged Jane; "and I can't see why you've scrubbed and washed and baked as you have for that one child, nor why you've about bought out Watson's stock of dry goods."

"I know Aurelia, if you don't," responded Miranda. "I've seen her house, and I've seen that batch o' children, wearin' one another's clothes, and never carin' whether they had 'em on right sid' out or not; I know what they've had to live and dress on, and so do you. That child will like as not come here with a passel o' things borrowed from the rest o' the family. She'll have Hannah's shoes and John's undershirts and Mark's socks most likely. I suppose she never had a thimble on her finger in her life, but she'll know the feelin' o' one before she's be'n here many days. I've bought a piece of unbleached muslin and a piece o' brown gingham for her to make up; that'll keep her busy. Of course she won't pick up anything after her-

self; she probably never see a duster, and she'll be as
hard to train into our ways as if she was a heathen."

"She'll make a diff'rence," acknowledged Jane,
"but she may turn out more biddable 'n we think."

"She'll mind when she's spoken to, biddable or
not," remarked Miranda with a shake of the last
towel.

Miranda Sawyer had a heart, of course, but she had
never used it for any other purpose than the pumping
and circulating of blood. She was just, conscientious,
economical, industrious, a regular attendant at church
and Sunday-school, and a member of the State Missionary and Bible societies; but in the presence of all
these chilly virtues you longed for one warm little
fault, or lacking that, one likable failing, something
to make you sure she was thoroughly alive. She had
never had any education other than that of the neighbourhood district school, for her desires and ambitions
had all pointed to the management of the house, the
farm, and the dairy. Jane, on the other hand, had gone
to an academy, and also to a boarding-school for
young ladies; so had Aurelia; and after all the years
that had elapsed there was still a slight difference in
language and in manner between the elder and the
two younger sisters.

Jane, too, had had the inestimable advantage of a
sorrow; not the natural grief at the loss of her aged
father and mother, for she had been content to let
them go, but something far deeper. She was engaged
to marry young Tom Carter, who had nothing to
marry on, it is true, but who was sure to have some
time or other. Then the war broke out. Tom enlisted
at the first call. Up to that time Jane had loved him

with a quiet, friendly sort of affection, and had given her country a mild emotion of the same sort. But the strife, the danger, the anxiety of the time, set new currents of feeling in motion. Life became something other than the three meals a day, the round of cooking, washing, sewing, and church-going. Personal gossip vanished from the village conversation. Big things took the place of trifling ones—sacred sorrows of wives and mothers, pangs of fathers and husbands, self-denials, sympathies, new desire to bear one another's burdens. Men and women grew fast in those days of the nation's trouble and danger, and Jane awoke from the vague dull dream she had hitherto called life to new hopes, new fears, new purposes. Then, after a year's anxiety, a year when one never looked in the newspaper without dread and sickness of suspense, came the telegram saying that Tom was wounded; and without so much as asking Miranda's leave, she packed her trunk and started for the South. She was in time to hold Tom's hand through hours of pain; to show him for once the heart of a prim New England girl when it is ablaze with love and grief; to put her arms about him so that he could have a home to die in, and that was all—all; but it served.

It carried her through weary months of nursing—nursing of other soldiers for Tom's dear sake; it sent her home a better woman; and though she had never left Riverboro in all the years that lay between, and had grown into the counterfeit presentment of her sister and of all other thin, spare, New England spinsters, it was something of a counterfeit, and underneath was still the faint echo of that wild heart-

beat of her girlhood. Having learned the trick of
beating and loving and suffering, the poor faithful
heart persisted, although it lived on memories, and
carried on its sentimental operations mostly in secret.

"You're soft, Jane," said Miranda once; "you
allers was soft, and you allers will be. If 't wa'n't for
me keeping you stiffened up, I b'lieve you'd leak out
o' the house into the dooryard."

It was already past the appointed hour for Mr.
Cobb and his coach to be lumbering down the
street.

"The stage ought to be here," said Miranda,
glancing nervously at the tall clock for the twentieth
time. "I guess everything's done. I've tacked up
two thick towels back of her washstand, and put a
mat under her slop-jar; but children are awful hard
on furniture. I expect we shan't know this house a
year from now."

Jane's frame of mind was naturally depressed and
timorous, having been affected by Miranda's gloomy
presages of evil to come. The only difference between
the sisters in this matter was that while Miranda only
wondered how they could endure Rebecca, Jane had
flashes of inspiration in which she wondered how
Rebecca would endure them. It was in one of these
flashes that she ran up the back-stairs to put a vase
of apple-blossoms and a red tomato-pincushion on
Rebecca's bureau.

The stage rumbled to the side-door of the brick
house, and Mr. Cobb handed Rebecca out like a real
lady passenger. She alighted with great circumspec-
tion, put the bunch of faded flowers in he. Aunt

Miranda's hand, and received her salute; it could hardly be called a kiss without injuring the fair name of that commodity.

"You needn't 'a' bothered to bring flowers," remarked that gracious and tactful lady; "the garden's always full of 'em here when it comes time."

Jane then kissed Rebecca, giving a somewhat better imitation of the real thing than her sister.

"Put the trunk in the entry, Jeremiah, and we'll get it carried upstairs this afternoon," she said.

"I'll take it up for ye now, if ye say the word, girls."

"No, no; don't leave the horses; somebody 'll be comin' past, and we can call 'em in."

"Well, good-bye, Rebecca; good-day, Mirandy 'n' Jane. You've got a lively little girl there. I guess she'll be a first-rate company-keeper."

Miss Sawyer shuddered openly at the adjective "lively" as applied to a child, her belief being that though children might be seen, if absolutely necessary, they certainly should never be heard if she could help it. "We're not much used to noise, Jane and me," she remarked acidly.

Mr. Cobb saw that he had taken the wrong tack, but he was too unused to argument to explain himself readily, so he drove away, trying to think by what safer word than "lively" he might have described his interesting little passenger.

"I'll take you up and show you your room, Rebecca," Miss Miranda said. "Shut the mosquito-nettin' door tight behind you, so's to keep the flies out; it ain't fly-time yet, but I want you to start right. Take your passel along with ye, and then you won't

have to come down for it: always make your head
save your heels. Rub your feet on that braided rug;
hang your hat and cape in the entry there as you go
past."

"It's my best hat," said Rebecca.

"Take it upstairs, then, and put it in the clothes-
press; but I shouldn't 'a' thought you'd 'a' worn your
best hat on the stage."

"It's my only hat," explained Rebecca. "My
everyday hat wasn't good enough to bring. Fanny's
going to finish it."

"Lay your parasol in the entry closet."

"Do you mind if I keep it in my room, please?
It always seems safer."

"There ain't any thieves hereabouts, and if there
was, I guess they wouldn't make for your sunshade;
but come along. Remember to always go up the back
way; we don't use the front-stairs on account o' the
carpet; take care o' the turn, and don't ketch your
foot; look to your right and go in. When you've
washed your face and hands and brushed your hair
you can come down, and by-and-by we'll unpack your
trunk and get you settled before supper. Ain't you
got your dress on hind sid' foremost?"

Rebecca drew her chin down and looked at the row
of smoked pearl buttons running up and down the
middle of her flat little chest.

"Hind side foremost? Oh, I see! No, that's all
right. If you have seven children you can't keep
buttonin' and unbuttonin' 'em all the time—they
have to do themselves. We're always buttoned up
in front at our house. Mira's only three, but she's
buttoned up in front, too."

Miranda said nothing as she closed the door, but her looks were at once equivalent to and more eloquent than words.

Rebecca stood perfectly still in the centre of the floor and looked about her. There was a square of oilcloth in front of each article of furniture and a drawn-in rug beside the single four-poster, which was covered with a fringed white dimity counterpane.

Everything was as neat as wax, but the ceilings were much higher than Rebecca was accustomed to. It was a north room, and the window, which was long and narrow, looked out on the back buildings and the barn.

It was not the room, which was far more comfortable than Rebecca's own at the farm, nor the lack of view, nor yet the long journey, for she was not conscious of weariness; it was not the fear of a strange place, for she loved new places and courted new sensations; it was because of some curious blending of uncomprehended emotions that Rebecca stood her sunshade in the corner, tore off her best hat, flung it on the bureau with the porcupine quills on the underside, and stripping down the dimity spread, precipitated herself into the middle of the bed, and pulled the counterpane over her head.

In a moment the door opened quietly. Knocking was a refinement quite unknown in Riverboro, and if it had been heard of would never have been wasted on a child.

Miss Miranda entered, and as her eye wandered about the vacant room, it fell upon a white and tempestuous ocean of counterpane, an ocean breaking into strange movements of wave and crest and billow.

"*Rebecca!*"

The tone in which the word was voiced gave it all the effect of having been shouted from the housetops.

A dark ruffled head and two frightened eyes appeared above the dimity spread.

"What are you layin' on your good bed in the daytime for, messin' up the feathers, and dirtyin' the pillers with your dusty boots?"

Rebecca rose guiltily. There seemed no excuse to make. Her offence was beyond explanation or apology.

"I'm sorry, Aunt Mirandy. Something came over me; I don't know what."

"Well, if it comes over you very soon again we'll have to find out what 'tis. Spread your bed up smooth this minute, for 'Bijah Flagg's bringin' your trunk upstairs, and I wouldn't let him see such a cluttered-up room for anything; he'd tell it all over town."

When Mr. Cobb had put up his horses that night he carried a kitchen chair to the side of his wife, who was sitting on the back porch.

"I brought a little Randall girl down on the stage from Maplewood to-day, mother. She's kin to the Sawyer girls, an' is goin' to live with 'em," he said, as he sat down and began to whittle. "She's that Aurelia's child, the one that ran away with Susan Randall's son just before we come here to live."

"How old a child?"

"'Bout ten, or somewhere along there, an' small for her age. But, land! she might be a hundred to hear her talk! She kep' me jumpin' tryin' to answer her. Of all the queer children I ever come across, she's the queerest. She ain't no beauty—her face is all eyes; but if she ever grows up to them eyes an' fills out a little, she'll make folks stare. Land, mother! I wish't you could 'a' heard her talk."

"I don't see what she had to talk about, a child like that, to a stranger," replied Mrs. Cobb.

"Stranger or no stranger, 'twouldn't make no difference to her. She'd talk to a pump or a grind-stun; she'd talk to herself ruther 'n keep still."

"What did she talk about?"

"Blamed if I can repeat any of it! She kep' me so surprised, I didn't have my wits about me. She had a little pink sunshade—it kind o' looked like a doll's amberill—'n' she clung to it like a burr to a woollen stockin'. I advised her to open it up, the sun was so hot; but she said no, 'twould fade, an' she tucked it under her dress. 'It's the dearest thing in life to me,' says she; 'but it's a dreadful care.' Them's the very words, an' it's all the words I remember. 'It's the dearest thing in life to me; but it's an awful care!'" Here Mr. Cobb laughed aloud as he tipped his chair back against the side of the house. "There was another thing, but I can't get it right exactly. She was talkin' 'bout the circus parade an' the snake-charmer in a gold chariot, an' says she, 'She was so beautiful beyond compare, Mr. Cobb, that it made you have lumps in your throat to look at her.' She'll be comin' over to see you, mother, an' you can size her up for yourself. I don't know how she'll git on with Miranda Sawyer—poor little soul!"

This doubt was more or less openly expressed in Riverboro, which, however, had two opinions on the subject—one that it was a most generous thing in the Sawyer girls to take one of Aurelia's children to educate; the other that the education would be bought at a price wholly out of proportion to its intrinsic value.

Rebecca's first letters to her mother would seem to indicate that she cordially coincided with the latter view of the situation.

IV

REBECCA'S POINT OF VIEW

DEAR MOTHER,

I am safely here. My dress was not much tumbled and Aunt Jane helped me press it out. I like Mr. Cobb very much. He chews but throws newspapers straight up to the doors. I rode outside a little while, but got inside before I got to Aunt Miranda's house. I did not want to, but thought you would like it better. Miranda is such a long word that I think I will say Aunt M. and Aunt J. in my Sunday letters. Aunt J. has given me a dictionary to look up all the hard words in. It takes a good deal of time and I am glad people can talk without stoping to spell. It is much eesier to talk than write and much more fun. The brick house looks just the same as you have told us. The parler is splendid and gives you creeps and chills when you look in the door. The furnature is ellergant too, and all the rooms but there are no good sitting-down places exsept in the kitchen. The same cat is here but they do not save kittens when she has them, and the cat is too old to play with. Hannah told me once you ran away with father and I can see it would be nice. If Aunt M. would run away I think I should like to live with Aunt J. She does not hate me as bad as Aunt M. does. Tell Mark he can have my paint box, but I should like him to keep the red cake in case I come home again. I hope Hannah and John do not get tired doing my chores.

Your afectionate friend
REBECCA.

P.S.—Please give the piece of poetry to John because he likes my poetry even when it is not very good. This piece is not very good but it is true but I hope you won't mind what is in it as you ran away.

> This house is dark and dull and dreer
> No light doth shine from far or near
> Its like the tomb.
>
> And those of us who live herein
> Are most as dead as serrafim
> Though not as good.
>
> My gardian angel is asleep
> At leest he doth no vigil keep
> Ah! woe is me!
>
> Then give me back my lonely farm
> Where none alive did wish me harm
> Dear home of youth!

P.S. again.—I made the poetry like a piece in a book but could not get it right at first. You see "tomb" and "good" do not sound well together but I wanted to say "tomb" dreadfully and as serrafim are always "good" I couldn't take that out. I have made it over now. It does not say my thoughts as well but think it is more right. Give the best one to John as he keeps them in a box with his birds' eggs. This is the best one.

SUNDAY THOUGHTS

By Rebecca Rowena Randall

This house is dark and dull and drear
No light doth shine from far or near
    Nor ever could.

And those of us who live herein
Are most as dead as seraphim
    Though not as good.

My guardian angel is asleep
At least he doth no vigil keep
    But far doth roam.

Then give me back my lonely farm
Where none alive did wish me harm
    Dear childhood home!

Dear Mother,

    I am thrilling with unhappiness this morning. I got that out of Cora The Doctor's Wife whose husband's mother was very cross and unfealing to her like Aunt M. to me. I wish Hannah had come instead of me for it was Hannah that was wanted and she is better than I am and does not answer back so quick. Are there any peaces of my buff calico. Aunt M. wants enough to make a new waste button behind so I wont look so outlandish. The stiles are quite pretty in Riverboro and those at Meeting quite ellergant more so than in Temperance.

> This town is stilish, gay and fair,
> And full of wellthy riches rare,
> But I would pillow on my arm
> The thought of my sweet Brookside Farm.

School is pretty good. The Teacher can answer more questions than the Temperance one but not so many as I can ask. I am smarter than all the girls but one but not so smart as two boys. Emma Jane can add and subtract in her head like a streek of lightning and knows the speling book right through but has no thoughts of any kind. She is in the Third Reader but does not like stories in books. I am in the Sixth Reader but just because I cannot say the seventh multiplication Table Miss Dearborn threttens to put me in the baby primer class with Elijah and Elisha Simpson little twins.

> Sore is my heart and bent my stubborn pride,
> With Lijah and with Lisha am I tied,
> My soul recoyles like Cora Doctor's Wife,
> Like her I feer I cannot bare this life.

I am going to try for the speling prize but fear I cannot get it. I would not care but wrong speling looks dreadful in poetry. Last Sunday when I found seraphim in the dictionary I was ashamed I had made it serrafim but seraphim is not a word you can guess at like another long one outlandish in this letter which spells itself. Miss Dearborn says use the words you *can* spell and if you cant spell seraphim make angel do but angels are not just the same as seraphims. Seraphims are brighter whiter and have bigger wings and I think are older and longer dead than angels which are just freshly dead and after a long time in heaven around the great white throne grow to be seraphims.

I sew on brown gingham dresses every afternoon when Emma Jane and the Simpsons are playing house or running on the Logs when their mothers do not know it. Their mothers are afraid they will drown and Aunt M. is afraid I will wet my clothes so will not let me either. I can play from half-past four to supper and after supper a little bit and Saturday afternoons. I am glad our cow has a calf and it is spotted. It is going to be a good year for apples and hay and so you and John will be glad and we can pay a little more morgage. Miss Dearborn asked us what is the object of education and I said the object of mine was to help pay off the morgage. She told Aunt M. and I had to sew extra for punishment because she says a morgage is disgrace like stealing or smallpox and it will be all over town that we have one on our farm. Emma Jane is not morgaged nor Richard Carter nor Dr. Winship but the Simpsons are.

> Rise my soul, strain every nerve,
> Thy morgage to remove,
> Gain thy mother's heartfelt thanks
> Thy family's grateful love.

Pronounce family *quick* or it won't sound right.
                    Your loving little friend
                                    REBECCA.

DEAR JOHN,

You remember when we tide the new dog in the barn how he bit the rope and howled. I am just like him only the brick house is the barn and I cannot bite Aunt M. because I must be grateful and edducation is going to be the making of me and help you pay off the morgage when we grow up.

Your loving
BECKY.

V

WISDOM'S WAYS

THE day of Rebecca's arrival had been Friday, and on the Monday following she began her education at the school which was in Riverboro Centre, about a mile distant. Miss Sawyer borrowed a neighbour's horse and waggon and drove her to the schoolhouse, interviewing the teacher, Miss Dearborn, arranging for books, and generally starting the child on the path that was to lead to boundless knowledge. Miss Dearborn, it may be said in passing, had had no special preparation in the art of teaching. It came to her naturally, so her family said; and perhaps for this reason she, like Tom Tulliver's clergyman tutor, " set about it with that uniformity of method and independence of circumstances which distinguish the actions of animals understood to be under the immediate teaching of Nature." You remember the beaver which a naturalist tells us " busied himself as earnestly in constructing a dam in a room up three pair of stairs in London as if he had been laying his foundation in a lake in Upper Canada. It was his function to build; the absence of water or of possible progeny was an accident for which he was not accountable." In the same manner did Miss Dearborn lay what she fondly imagined to be foundations in the infant mind.

Rebecca walked to school after the first morning. She loved this part of the day's programme. When the dew was not too heavy and the weather was fair, there was a short-cut through the woods. She turned off the main road, crept through Uncle Josh Woodman's bars, waved away Mrs. Carter's cows, trod the short grass of the pasture, with its well-worn path running through gardens of buttercups and white-weed, and groves of ivory leaves and sweet fern. She descended a little hill, jumped from stone to stone across a woodland brook, startling the drowsy frogs, who were always winking and blinking in the morning sun. Then came the "woodsy bit," with her feet pressing the slippery carpet of brown pine-needles; the "woodsy bit" so full of dewy morning surprises —fungous growths of brilliant orange and crimson springing up round the stumps of dead trees, beautiful things born in a single night; and now and then the miracle of a little clump of waxen Indian pipes, seen just quickly enough to be saved from her careless tread. Then she climbed a stile, went through a grassy meadow, slid under another pair of bars, and came out into the road again, having gained nearly half a mile.

How delicious it all was! Rebecca clasped her Quackenbos's Grammar and Greenleaf's Arithmetic with a joyful sense of knowing her lessons. Her dinner-pail swung from her right hand, and she had a blissful consciousness of the two soda-biscuits spread with butter and syrup, the baked cup-custard, the doughnut, and the square of hard gingerbread. Sometimes she said whatever " piece " she was going to speak on the next Friday afternoon.

" A soldier of the Legion lay dying in Algiers;
    There was lack of woman's nursing, there was dearth of
        woman's tears."

How she loved the swing and the sentiment of it! How her young voice quivered whenever she came to the refrain :

" But we'll meet no more at Bingen, dear Bingen on the Rhine."

It always sounded beautiful in her ears, as she sent her tearful little treble into the clear morning air. Another early favourite (for we must remember that Rebecca's only knowledge of the great world of poetry consisted of the selections in vogue in school readers) was :

" Woodman, spare that tree,
    Touch not a single bough;
 In youth it sheltered me,
    And I'll protect it now."

When Emma Jane Perkins walked through the " short-cut " with her, the two children used to render this with appropriate dramatic action. Emma Jane always chose to be the woodman, because she had nothing to do but raise on high an imaginary axe. On the one occasion when she essayed the part of the tree's romantic protector, she represented herself as feeling " so awful foolish " that she refused to undertake it again, much to the secret delight of Rebecca, who found the woodman's rôle much too tame for her vaulting ambition. She revelled in the

impassioned appeal of the poet, and implored the
ruthless woodman to be as brutal as possible with
the axe, so that she might properly put greater spirit
into her lines. One morning, feeling more frisky than
usual, she fell upon her knees and wept in the woodman's petticoat. Curiously enough, her sense of proportion rejected this as soon as it was done.

"That wasn't right; it was silly, Emma Jane; but
I'll tell you where it might come in—in 'Give me
Three Grains of Corn.' You be the mother, and I'll
be the famishing Irish child. For pity's sake, put
the axe down! You are not the woodman any
longer!"

"What'll I do with my hands, then?" asked Emma
Jane.

"Whatever you like," Rebecca would answer
wearily. "You're just a mother—that's all. What
does *your* mother do with her hands? Now, here
goes:

> "'Give me three grains of corn, mother,
>   Only three grains of corn;
> 'Twill keep the little life I have
>   Till the coming of the morn.'"

This sort of thing made Emma Jane nervous and
fidgety; but she was Rebecca's slave, and hugged her
chains, no matter how uncomfortable they made her.

At the last pair of bars the two girls were sometimes met by a detachment of the Simpson children,
who lived in a black house with a red door and a red
barn behind on the Blueberry Plains road. Rebecca
felt an interest in the Simpsons from the first, because
there were so many of them, and they were so patched
and darned, just like her own brood at the home farm.

The little schoolhouse, with its flag-pole on top
and its two doors in front, one for boys and the other
for girls, stood on the crest of a hill, with rolling fields
and meadows on one side, a stretch of pine-woods on
the other, and the river glinting and sparkling in the
distance. It boasted no attractions within. All was
as bare and ugly and uncomfortable as it well could
be, for the villages along the river expended so much
money in repairing and rebuilding bridges that they
were obliged to be very economical in school privileges. The teacher's desk and chair stood on a platform in one corner; there was an uncouth stove, never
blackened oftener than once a year, a map of the
United States, two blackboards, a ten-quart tin pail
of water and long-handled dipper on a corner shelf,
and wooden desks and benches for the scholars, who
only numbered twenty in Rebecca's time. The seats
were higher in the back of the room, and the more
advanced and longer-legged pupils sat there, the position being greatly to be envied, as they were at once
nearer to the windows and farther from the teacher.

There were classes of a sort, although nobody,
broadly speaking, studied the same book with anybody else, or had arrived at the same degree of pro-
ficiency in any one branch of learning. Rebecca in
particular was so difficult to classify that Miss Dearborn at the end of a fortnight gave up the attempt
altogether. She read with Dick Carter and Living
Perkins, who were fitting for the academy; recited
arithmetic with lisping little "Thuthan Thimpthon,"
geography with Emma Jane Perkins, and grammar
after school hours to Miss Dearborn alone. Full to
the brim as she was of clever thoughts and quaint

D

fancies, she made at first but a poor hand at composition. The labour of writing and spelling, with the added difficulties of punctuation and capitals, interfered sadly with the free expression of ideas. She took history with Alice Robinson's class, which was attacking the subject of the Revolution, while Rebecca was bidden to begin with the discovery of America. In a week she had mastered the course of events up to the Revolution, and in ten days had arrived at Yorktown, where the class had apparently established summer quarters. Then, finding that extra effort would only result in her reciting with the oldest Simpson boy, she deliberately held herself back, for wisdom's ways were not those of pleasantness, nor her paths those of peace, if one were compelled to tread them in the company of Seesaw Simpson. Samuel Simpson was generally called Seesaw because of his difficulty in making up his mind. Whether it were a question of fact, of spelling, or of date, of going swimming or fishing, of choosing a book in the Sunday-school library or a stick of candy at the village store, he had no sooner determined on one plan of action than his wish fondly reverted to the opposite one. Seesaw was pale, flaxen-haired, blue-eyed, round-shouldered, and given to stammering when nervous. Perhaps because of his very weakness, Rebecca's decision of character had a fascination for him, and although she snubbed him to the verge of madness, he could never keep his eyes away from her. The force with which she tied her shoe when the lacing came undone, the flirt over shoulder she gave her black braid when she was excited or warm, her manner of studying—book on desk, arms folded, eyes fixed on the opposite wall—all had an abiding charm for Seesaw Simpson. When, having obtained permission, she walked to the water-pail in the corner and drank from the dipper, unseen forces dragged Seesaw from his seat to go and drink after her. It was not only that there was something akin to association and intimacy in drinking next, but there was the fearful joy of meeting her in transit, and receiving a cold and disdainful look from her wonderful eyes.

On a certain warm day in summer Rebecca's thirst exceeded the bounds of propriety. When she asked a third time for permission to quench it at the common fountain Miss Dearborn nodded yes, but lifted her eyebrows unpleasantly as Rebecca neared the desk. As she replaced the dipper Seesaw promptly raised his hand, and Miss Dearborn indicated a weary affirmative.

"What is the matter with you, Rebecca?" she asked.

"I had salt mackerel for breakfast," answered Rebecca.

There seemed nothing humorous about this reply, which was merely the statement of a fact, but an irrepressible titter ran through the school. Miss Dearborn did not enjoy jokes neither made nor understood by herself, and her face flushed.

"I think you had better stand by the pail for five minutes, Rebecca; it may help you to control your thirst.

Rebecca's heart fluttered. She to stand in the corner by the water-pail and be stared at by all the scholars. She unconsciously made a gesture of angry dissent and moved a step nearer her seat, but was arrested by Miss Dearborn's command in a still firmer voice.

"Stand by the pail, Rebecca! Samuel, how many times have you asked for water to-day?"

"This is the f-f-fourth."

"Don't touch the dipper, please. The school has done nothing but drink this afternoon; it has had no time whatever to study. I suppose you had something salt for breakfast, Samuel?" queried Miss Dearborn with sarcasm.

"I had m-m-mackerel, j-just like Reb-b-becca." (Irrepressible giggles by the school.)

"I judged so. Stand by the other side of the pail, Samuel."

Rebecca's head was bowed with shame and wrath. Life looked too black a thing to be endured. The punishment was bad enough, but to be coupled in correction with Seesaw Simpson was beyond human endurance.

Singing was the last exercise in the afternoon, and Minnie Smellie chose "Shall we Gather at the River?" It was a baleful choice and seemed to hold some secret and subtle association with the situation and general progress of events; or at any rate there was apparently some obscure reason for the energy and vim with which the scholars shouted the choral invitation again and again:

> "Shall we gather at the river—
> The beautiful, the beautiful river?"

Miss Dearborn stole a look at Rebecca's bent head and was frightened. The child's face was pale save for two red spots glowing on her cheeks. Tears hung on her lashes; her breath came and went quickly, and the hand that held her pocket-handkerchief trembled like a leaf.

"You may go to your seat, Rebecca," said Miss Dearborn at the end of the first song. "Samuel, stay where you are till the close of school. And let me tell you, scholars, that I asked Rebecca to stand by the pail only to break up this habit of incessant drinking, which is nothing but empty-mindedness and desire to walk to and fro over the floor. Every time Rebecca has asked for a drink to-day the whole school has gone to the pail one after another. She is really thirsty, and I dare say I ought to have punished you for following her example, not her for setting it. What shall we sing now, Alice?"

"'The Old Oaken Bucket,' please."

"Think of something dry, Alice, and change the subject. Yes, 'The Star-spangled Banner,' if you like, or anything else."

Rebecca sank into her seat and pulled the singing-book from her desk. Miss Dearborn's public explanation had shifted some of the weight from her heart, and she felt a trifle raised in her self-esteem.

Under cover of the general relaxation of singing, votive offerings of respectful sympathy began to make their appearance at her shrine. Living Perkins, who could not sing, dropped a piece of maple sugar in her lap as he passed her on his way to the blackboard to draw the map of Maine. Alice Robinson rolled a perfectly new slate pencil over the floor with her foot until it reached Rebecca's place, while her seat-mate, Emma Jane, had made up a little mound of paper balls and labelled them "Bullets for you know who."

Altogether existence grew brighter, and when she was left alone with the teacher for her grammar lesson she had nearly recovered her equanimity, which was more than Miss Dearborn had. The last clattering foot had echoed through the hall, Seesaw's backward glance of penitence had been met and answered defiantly by one of cold disdain.

"Rebecca, I am afraid I punished you more than I meant," said Miss Dearborn, who was only eighteen herself, and in her year of teaching country schools had never encountered a child like Rebecca.

"I hadn't missed a question this whole day, nor whispered either," quavered the culprit; "and I don't think I ought to be shamed just for drinking."

"You started all the others, or it seemed as if you did. Whatever you do they all do, whether you laugh, or miss, or write notes, or ask to leave the room, or drink; and it must be stopped."

"Sam Simpson is a copycoat!" stormed Rebecca. "I wouldn't have minded standing in the corner alone—that is, not so very much; but I couldn't bear standing with him."

"I saw that you couldn't, and that's the reason I told you to take your seat, and left him in the corner. Remember that you are a stranger in the place, and they take more notice of what you do, so you must be careful. Now let's have our conjugations. Give me the verb 'to be,' potential mood, past perfect tense."

"I might have been.   "We might have been.
 Thou mightst have been.   You might have been.
 He might have been.   They might have been."

"Give me an example, please."

"I might have been glad.
Thou mightst have been glad.
He, she, or it might have been glad."

"'He' or 'she' might have been glad because they are masculine and feminine, but could '*it*' have been glad?" asked Miss Dearborn, who was very fond of splitting hairs.

"Why not?" asked Rebecca.

"Because 'it' is neuter gender."

"Couldn't we say, 'The kitten might have been glad if it had known it was not going to be drowned'?"

"Ye—es," Miss Dearborn answered hesitatingly, never very sure of herself under Rebecca's fire; "but though we often speak of a baby, a chicken, or a kitten as 'it,' they are really masculine or feminine gender, not neuter."

Rebecca reflected a long moment and then asked, "Is a hollyhock neuter?"

"Oh yes, of course it is, Rebecca."

"Well, couldn't we say, 'The hollyhock might have been glad to see the rain, but there was a weak little hollyhock bud growing out of its stalk, and it was afraid that that might be hurt by the storm; so the big hollyhock was kind of afraid, instead of being real glad'?"

Miss Dearborn looked puzzled as she answered, "Of course, Rebecca, hollyhocks could not be sorry, or glad, or afraid, really."

"We can't tell, I s'pose," replied the child; "but *I* think they are, anyway. Now what shall I say?"

"The subjunctive mood, past perfect tense of the verb 'to know.'"

"If I had known.	"If we had known.
If thou hadst known.	If you had known.
If he had known.	If they had known.

"Oh, it is the saddest tense!" sighed Rebecca, with a little break in her voice; "nothing but *ifs, ifs, ifs!* And it makes you feel that if they only *had* known, things might have been better!"

Miss Dearborn had not thought of it before, but on reflection she believed the subjunctive mood was a "sad" one, and "if" rather a sorry "part of speech."

"Give me some more examples of the subjunctive, Rebecca, and that will do for this afternoon," she said.

"If I had not loved mackerel, I should not have been thirsty," said Rebecca with an April smile, as she closed her grammar. "If thou hadst loved me truly, thou wouldst not have stood me up in the corner. If Samuel had not loved wickedness, he would not have followed me to the water-pail."

"And if Rebecca had loved the rules of the school, she would have controlled her thirst," finished Miss Dearborn with a kiss, and the two parted friends.

VI

SUNSHINE IN A SHADY PLACE

THE little schoolhouse on the hill had its moments of triumph as well as its scenes of tribulation, but it was fortunate that Rebecca had her books and her new acquaintances to keep her interested and occupied, or life would have gone heavily with her that first summer in Riverboro. She tried to like her aunt Miranda (the idea of loving her had been given up at the moment of meeting), but failed ignominiously in the attempt. She was a very faulty and passionately human child, with no aspirations towards being an angel of the house, but she had a sense of duty and a desire to be good—respectably, decently good. Whenever she fell below this self-imposed standard she was miserable. She did not like to be under her aunt's roof, eating bread, wearing clothes, and studying books provided by her, and dislike her so heartily all the time. She felt instinctively that this was wrong and mean, and whenever the feeling of remorse was strong within her she made a desperate effort to please her grim and difficult relative. But how could she succeed when she was never herself in her aunt Miranda's presence? The searching look of the eyes, the sharp voice, the hard knotty fingers, the thin straight lips, the long silences, the " front-piece " that didn't match her hair, the very obvious " parting " that seemed sewed in with linen thread on black net— there was not a single item that appealed to Rebecca, There are certain narrow, unimaginative, and autocratic old people who seem to call out the most mischievous, and sometimes the worst traits in children. Miss Miranda, had she lived in a populous neighbourhood, would have had her doorbell pulled, her gate tied up, or " dirt traps " set in her garden paths. The Simpson twins stood in such awe of her that they could not be persuaded to come to the side-door even when Miss Jane held gingerbread cookies in her outstretched hands.

It is needless to say that Rebecca irritated her aunt

with every breath she drew. She continually forgot and started up the front-stairs because it was the shortest route to her bedroom; she left the dipper on the kitchen shelf instead of hanging it up over the pail; she sat in the chair the cat liked best; she was willing to go on errands, but often forgot what she was sent for; she left the screen-doors ajar, so that flies came in; her tongue was ever in motion; she sang or whistled when she was picking up chips; she was always messing with flowers—putting them in vases, pinning them on her dress, and sticking them in her hat; finally, she was an everlasting reminder of her foolish, worthless father, whose handsome face and engaging manner had so deceived Aurelia, and perhaps, if the facts were known, others besides Aurelia. The Randalls were aliens. They had not been born in Riverboro nor even in York County. Miranda would have allowed, on compulsion, that in the nature of things a large number of persons must necessarily be born outside this sacred precinct; but she had her opinion of them, and it was not a flattering one. Now, if Hannah had come—Hannah took after the other side of the house; she was "all Sawyer." (Poor Hannah! that was true.) Hannah spoke only when spoken to, instead of first, last, and all the time; Hannah at fourteen was a member of the Church; Hannah liked to knit; Hannah was, probably, or would have been, a pattern of all the smaller virtues; instead of which here was this black-haired gipsy, with eyes as big as cartwheels, installed as a member of the household.

What sunshine in a shady place was Aunt Jane to Rebecca! Aunt Jane, with her quiet voice, her understanding eyes, her ready excuses, in these first difficult weeks, when the impulsive little stranger was trying to settle down into the "brick house ways." She did learn them in part, and by degrees, and the constant fitting of herself to these new and difficult standards of conduct seemed to make her older than ever for her years.

The child took her sewing and sat beside Aunt Jane in the kitchen, while Aunt Miranda had the post of observation at the sitting-room window. Sometimes they would work on the side-porch, where the clematis and woodbine shaded them from the hot sun. To Rebecca the lengths of brown gingham were interminable. She made hard work of sewing, broke the thread, dropped her thimble into the syringa bushes, pricked her finger, wiped the perspiration from her forehead, could not match the checks, puckered the seams. She polished her needles to nothing, pushing them in and out of the emery strawberry, but they always squeaked. Still, Aunt Jane's patience held good, and some small measure of skill was creeping into Rebecca's fingers, fingers that held pencil, paint-brush, and pen so cleverly, and were so clumsy with the dainty little needle.

When the first brown gingham frock was completed, the child seized what she thought an opportune moment, and asked her aunt Miranda if she might have another colour for the next one.

"I bought a whole piece of the brown," said Miranda laconically. "That'll give you two more dresses, with plenty for new sleeves, and to patch and let down with, an' be more economical."

"I know. But Mr. Watson says he'll take back

part of it, and let us have pink and blue for the same price."

"Did you ask him?"

"Yes'm."

"It was none o' your business."

"I was helping Emma Jane choose aprons, and didn't think you'd mind which colour I had. Pink keeps clean just as nice as brown, and Mr. Watson says it'll boil without fading."

"Mr. Watson's a splendid judge of washing, I guess. I don't approve of children being rigged out in fancy colours, but I'll see what your Aunt Jane thinks."

"I think it would be all right to let Rebecca have one pink and one blue gingham," said Jane. "A child gets tired of sewing on one colour. It's only natural she should long for a change; besides, she'd look like a charity child always wearing the same brown with a white apron. And it's dreadful unbecoming to her!"

"'Handsome is as handsome does,' say I. Rebecca never 'll come to grief along of her beauty, that's certain, and there's no use in humouring her to think about her looks. I believe she's vain as a peacock now, without anything to be vain of."

"She's young, and attracted to bright things—that's all. I remember well enough how I felt at her age."

"You was considerable of a fool at her age, Jane."

"Yes, I was, thank the Lord! I only wish I'd known how to take a little of my foolishness along with me, as some folks do, to brighten my declining years."

There finally was a pink gingham, and when it was nicely finished, Aunt Jane gave Rebecca a delightful surprise. She showed her how to make a pretty trimming of narrow white linen tape, by folding it in pointed shapes, and sewing it down very flat with neat little stitches.

"It'll be good fancy work for you, Rebecca; for your aunt Miranda won't like to see you always reading in the long winter evenings. Now, if you think you can baste two rows of white tape round the bottom of your pink skirt, and keep it straight by the checks, I'll stitch them on for you, and trim the waist and sleeves with pointed tape-trimming, so the dress 'll be real pretty for second best."

Rebecca's joy knew no bounds. "I'll baste like a house afire!" she exclaimed. "It's a thousand yards round that skirt, as well I know, having hemmed it; but I could sew pretty trimming on if it was from here to Milltown. Oh, do you think Aunt Mirandy 'll ever let me go to Milltown with Mr. Cobb? He's asked me again, you know; but one Saturday I had to pick strawberries, and another it rained, and I don't think she really approves of my going. It's *twenty-nine* minutes past four, Aunt Jane, and Alice Robinson has been sitting under the currant-bushes for a long time waiting for me. Can I go and play?"

"Yes, you may go; and you'd better run as far as you can out behind the barn, so 't your noise won't distract your Aunt Mirandy. I see Susan Simpson and the twins and Emma Jane Perkins hiding behind the fence."

Rebecca leaped off the porch, snatched Alice Robinson from under the currant-bushes, and, what was much more difficult, succeeded by means of a complicated system of signals in getting Emma Jane away from the Simpson party, and giving them the slip altogether. They were much too small for certain pleasurable activities planned for that afternoon, but they were not to be despised, for they had the most fascinating dooryard in the village. In it, in bewildering confusion, were old sleighs, pungs, horse-rakes, hogsheads, settees without backs, bedsteads without heads, in all stages of disability, and never the same on two consecutive days. Mrs. Simpson was seldom at home, and even when she was had little concern as to what happened on the premises. A favourite diversion was to make the house into a fort, gallantly held by a handful of American soldiers against a besieging force of the British army. Great care was used in apportioning the parts, for there was no disposition to let anybody win but the Americans. Seesaw Simpson was usually made commander-in-chief of the British army—and a limp and uncertain one he was, capable, with his contradictory orders and his fondness for the extreme rear, of leading any regiment to an inglorious death. Sometimes the long-suffering house was a log hut, and the brave settlers defeated a band of hostile Indians, or occasionally were massacred by them; but in either case the Simpson house looked, to quote a Riverboro expression, " as if the devil had been having an auction in it."

Next to this uncommonly interesting playground as a field of action came, in the children's opinion, the " secret spot." There was a velvety stretch of ground in the Sawyer pasture which was full of fascinating hollows and hillocks, as well as verdant levels, on which to build houses. A group of trees concealed it somewhat from view, and flung a grateful shade over the dwellings erected there. It had been hard, though sweet, labour to take armfuls of "stickins" and "cutrounds" from the mill to this secluded spot; and that it had been done mostly after supper in the dusk of the evenings gave it a still greater flavour. Here in soap-boxes, hidden among the trees, were stored all their treasures—wee baskets and plates and cups made of burdock balls, bits of broken china for parties, dolls—soon to be outgrown, but serving well as characters in all sorts of romances enacted there—deaths, funerals, weddings, christenings. A tall, square house of stickins was to be built round Rebecca this afternoon, and she was to be Charlotte Corday leaning against the bars of her prison.

It was a wonderful experience standing inside the building with Emma Jane's apron wound about her hair—wonderful to feel that when she leaned her head against the bars they seemed to turn to cold iron; that her eyes were no longer Rebecca Randall's, but mirrored something of Charlotte Corday's hapless woe.

" Ain't it lovely?" sighed the humble twain, who had done most of the labour, but who generously admired the result.

" I hate to have to take it down," said Alice; " it's been such a sight of work."

" If you think you could move up some stones and just take off the top rows, I could step out over," suggested Charlotte Corday. " Then leave the stones, and you two can step down into the prison to-morrow and be the two little Princes in the Tower, and I can murder you."

" What Princes? What Tower?" asked Alice and Emma Jane in one hreath. " Tell us about them."

"Not now; it's my supper-time." (Rebecca was a somewhat firm disciplinarian.)

" It would be elergant being murdered by you," said Emma Jane loyally, " though you are awful real when you murder; or we could have Elijah and Elisha for the Princes."

" They'd yell when they was murdered," objected Alice. " You know how silly they are at plays, all except Clara Belle. Besides, if we once show them this secret place, they'll play in it all the time; and perhaps they'd steal things, like their father."

" They needn't steal just because their father does," argued Rebecca; " and don't you ever talk about it before them if you want to be my secret, partic'lar friends. My mother tells me never to say hard things about people's own folks to their face. She says nobody can bear it, and it's wicked to shame them for what isn't their fault. Remember Minnie Smellie!"

Well, they had no difficulty in recalling that dramatic episode, for it had occurred only a few days before; and a version of it, that would have melted the stoniest heart, had been presented to every girl in the village by Minnie Smellie herself, who, though it was Rebecca and not she who came off victorious in the bloody battle of words, nursed her resentment, and intended to have revenge.

VII

Mr. Simpson spent little time with his family, owing to certain awkward methods of horse-trading, or the " swapping " of farm implements and vehicles of various kinds—operations in which his customers were never long suited. After every successful trade he generally passed a longer or shorter term in gaol; for when a poor man without goods or chattels has the inveterate habit of swapping, it follows naturally that he must have something to swap, and having nothing of his own, it follows still more naturally that he must swap something belonging to his neighbours.

Mr. Simpson was absent from the home circle for the moment because he had exchanged the Widow Rideout's sleigh for Joseph Goodwin's plough. Goodwin had lately moved to North Edgewood, and had never before met the urbane and persuasive Mr. Simpson. The Goodwin plough Mr. Simpson speedily bartered with a man " over Wareham way," and got in exchange for it an old horse which his owner did not need, as he was leaving town to visit his daughter for a year. Simpson fattened the aged animal, keeping him for several weeks (at early morning or after nightfall) in one neighbour's pasture after another, and then exchanged him with a Milltown man for a top buggy. It was at this juncture that the Widow Rideout missed her sleigh from the old carriage-house. She had not used it for fifteen years, and might not sit in it for another fifteen, but it was property, and she did not intend to part with it without a struggle. Such is the suspicious nature of the village mind that the moment she discovered her loss her thought at once reverted to Abner Simpson. So complicated, however, was the nature of this particular business transaction, and so tortuous the paths of its progress (partly owing to the complete disappearance of the owner of the horse, who had gone to the West and left no address), that it took the sheriff many weeks to prove Mr. Simpson's guilt to the town's and to the Widow Rideout's satisfaction. Abner himself avowed his complete innocence, and told the neighbours how a red-haired man with a hare-lip and a pepper-and-salt suit of clothes had called him up one morning about daylight, and offered to swap him a good sleigh for an old cider-press he had layin' out in the dooryard. The bargain was struck, and he, Abner, had paid the hare-lipped stranger four dollars and seventy-five cents to boot; whereupon the mysterious one set down the sleigh, took the press on his cart, and vanished up the road, never to be seen or heard from afterwards.

"If I could once ketch that consarned old thief," exclaimed Abner righteously, "I'd make him dance— workin' off a stolen sleigh on me an' takin' away my good money an' cider-press, to say nothin' o' my character!"

"You'll never ketch him, Ab," responded the sheriff. "He's cut off the same piece o' goods as that there cider-press and that there character and that there four-seventy-five o' yourn; nobody ever see any of 'em but you, and you'll never see 'em again!"

Mrs. Simpson, who was decidedly Abner's better half, took in washing and went out to do days' cleaning, and the town helped in the feeding and clothing of the children. George, a lanky boy of fourteen, did chores on neighbouring farms, and the others, Samuel, Clara Belle, Susan, Elijah, and Elisha, went to school when sufficiently clothed and not otherwise more pleasantly engaged.

There were no secrets in the villages that lay along the banks of Pleasant River. There were many hard-working people among the inhabitants, but life wore away so quietly and slowly that there was a good deal of spare time for conversation—under the trees at noon in the hayfield; hanging over the bridge at night-fall; seated about the stove in the village store of an evening. These meeting-places furnished ample ground for the discussion of current events as viewed by the masculine eye, while choir rehearsals, sewing societies, reading circles, church picnics, and the like, gave opportunity for the expression of feminine opinion. All this was taken very much for granted, as a rule, but now and then some supersensitive person made violent objections to it, as a theory of life.

Delia Weeks, for example, was a maiden lady who did dressmaking in a small way; she fell ill, and although attended by all the physicians in the neighbourhood, was sinking slowly into a decline, when her cousin Cyrus asked her to come and keep house for him in Lewiston. She went, and in a year grew into a robust, hearty, cheerful woman. Returning to Riverboro on a brief visit, she was asked if she meant to end her days away from home.

"I do most certainly, if I can get any other place to stay," she responded candidly. "I was bein' worn to a shadder here, tryin' to keep my little secrets to myself, an' never succeedin'. First they had it I wanted to marry the minister, and when he took a wife in Standish I was known to be disappointed. Then for five or six years they suspicioned I was tryin' for a place to teach school, and when I gave up hope, an' took to dressmakin', they pitied me and sympathized with me for that. When father died I was bound I'd never let anybody know how I was left, for that spites 'em worse than anything else; but there's ways o' findin' out, an' they found out, hard as I fought 'em! Then there was my brother James that went to Arizona when he was sixteen. I gave good news of him for thirty years runnin', but Aunt Achsy Tarbox had a ferretin' cousin that went out to Tombstone for her health, and she wrote to a post-master, or to some kind of a town authority, and found Jim, and wrote back Aunt Achsy all about him, and just how unfortunate he'd been. They knew when I had my teeth out and a new set made; they knew when I put on a false front-piece; they knew when the fruit-pedlar asked me to be his third wife. I never told 'em, an' you can be sure *he* never did, but they don't *need* to be told in this village; they have nothin' to do but guess, an' they'll guess right every time. I was all tuckered out tryin' to mislead 'em and deceive 'em and side-track 'em, but the minute I got where I wa'n't put under a microscope by day an' a telescope by night, and had myself *to* myself, without sayin' 'By your leave,' I begun to pick up. Cousin Cyrus is an old man an' consid'able trouble, but he thinks my teeth are handsome, an' says I've got a splendid suit of hair. There ain't a person in Lewiston that knows about the minister, or father's will, or Jim's doin's, or the fruit-pedlar; an' if they should find out, they wouldn't care, an' they couldn't remember; for Lewiston's a busy place, thanks be!"

Miss Delia Weeks may have exaggerated matters somewhat, but it is easy to imagine that Rebecca, as well as all the other Riverboro children, had heard the particulars of the Widow Rideout's missing sleigh, and Abner Simpson's supposed connection with it.

There is not an excess of delicacy or chivalry in the ordinary country school, and several choice conundrums and bits of verse dealing with the Simpson affair were bandied about among the scholars, uttered always, be it said to their credit, in undertones, and when the Simpson children were not in the group.

Rebecca Randall was of precisely the same stock, and had had much the same associations as her schoolmates, so one can hardly say why she so hated mean gossip, and so instinctively held herself aloof from it.

Among the Riverboro girls of her own age was a certain excellently named Minnie Smellie, who was anything but a general favourite. She was a ferret-eyed, blonde-haired, spindle-legged little creature, whose mind was a cross between that of a parrot and a sheep. She was suspected of copying answers from other girls' slates, although she had never been caught in the act. Rebecca and Emma Jane always knew when she had brought a tart or a triangle of layer cake with her school luncheon, because on those days she forsook the cheerful society of her mates, and sought a safe

solitude in the woods, returning after a time with
a jocund smile on her smug face.

After one of these private luncheons Rebecca had
been tempted beyond her strength, and when Minnie
took her seat among them, asked: " Is your headache
better, Minnie? Let me wipe off that strawberry-jam
over your mouth."

There was no jam there, as a matter of fact, but the
guilty Minnie's handkerchief went to her crimson face
in a flash.

Rebecca confessed to Emma Jane that same afternoon that she felt ashamed of her prank. " I do hate
her ways," she exclaimed; " but I'm sorry I let her
know we 'spected her, and so, to make up, I gave her
that little piece of broken coral I keep in my bead
purse—you know the one?"

" It don't hardly seem as if she deserved that, and
her so greedy," remarked Emma Jane.

" I know it, but it makes me feel better," said
Rebecca largely. " And, then, I've had it two years,
and it's broken, so it wouldn't ever be any real good,
beautiful as it is to look at."

The coral had partly served its purpose as a recon-
ciling bond, when one afternoon Rebecca, who had
stayed after school for her grammar lesson as usual,
was returning home by way of the short-cut. Far
ahead beyond the bars she espied the Simpson
children just entering the woodsy bit. Seesaw was
not with them, so she hastened her steps in order to
secure company on her homeward walk. They were
speedily lost to view, but when she had almost over-
taken them she heard in the trees beyond Minnie
Smellie's voice lifted high in song and the sound of

a child's sobbing. Clara Belle, Susan, and the twins were running along the path, and Minnie was dancing up and down, shrieking:

> " ' What made the sleigh love Simpson so?'
>   The eager children cried;
> ' Why, Simpson loved the sleigh, you know,'
>   The teacher quick replied."

The last glimpse of the routed Simpson tribe and the last flutter of their tattered garments disappeared in the dim distance. The fall of one small stone cast by the valiant Elijah, known as "the fighting twin," did break the stillness of the woods for a moment; but it did not come within a hundred yards of Minnie, who shouted "Gaol-birds!" at the top of her lungs, and then turned, with an agreeable feeling of excitement, to meet Rebecca, standing perfectly still in the path, with a day of reckoning plainly set forth in her blazing eyes.

Minnie's face was not pleasant to see, for a coward detected at the moment of wrongdoing is not an object of delight.

"Minnie Smellie, if ever—I—catch—you—singing—that—to the Simpsons again—do you know what I'll do?" asked Rebecca in a tone of concentrated rage.

"I don't know, and I don't care," said Minnie jauntily, though her looks belied her.

"I'll take that piece of coral away from you, and I *think* I shall slap you besides!"

"You wouldn't darst!" retorted Minnie. "If you do, I'll tell my mother and the teacher, so there!"

"I don't care if you tell your mother, my mother, and all your relations, and the President," said

Rebecca, gaining courage as the noble words fell from her lips. "I don't care if you tell the town, the whole of York County, the State of Maine, and—and the nation!" she finished grandiloquently. "Now, you run home, and remember what I say. If you do it again, and especially if you say 'Gaol-birds!' if I think its right, and my duty, I shall punish you somehow."

The next morning at recess Rebecca observed Minnie telling the tale with variations to Huldah Meserve. "She *threatened* me," whispered Minnie; "but I never believe a word she says."

The latter remark was spoken with the direct intention of being overheard, for Minnie had spasms of bravery when well surrounded by the machinery of law and order.

As Rebecca went back to her seat, she asked Miss Dearborn if she might pass a note to Minnie Smellie, and received permission. This was the note:

> " Of all the girls that are so mean,
>   There's none like Minnie Smellie.
> I'll take away the gift I gave,
>   And pound her into jelly.

" *P.S.—Now do you believe me?*

"R. RANDALL."

The effect of this piece of doggerel was entirely convincing, and for days afterwards, whenever Minnie met the Simpsons, even a mile from the brick house, she shuddered and held her peace.

VIII

On the very next Friday after this " dreadfullest fight that ever was seen," as Bunyan says in " Pilgrim's Progress," there were great doings in the little school-house on the hill. Friday afternoon was always the time chosen for dialogues, songs, and recitations; but it cannot be stated that it was a gala day in any true sense of the word. Most of the children hated "speak-ing pieces "—hated the burden of learning them, dreaded the danger of breaking down in them. Miss Dearborn commonly went home with a headache, and never left her bed during the rest of the afternoon or evening; and the casual female parent who attended the exercises sat on a front bench, with beads of cold sweat on her forehead, listening to the all-too-familiar halts and stammers. Sometimes a bellowing infant, who had clean forgotten his verse, would cast himself bodily on the maternal bosom, and be borne out into the open air, where he was sometimes kissed and occasionally spanked; but, in any case, the failure added an extra dash of gloom and dread to the occa-sion. The advent of Rebecca had somehow infused a new spirit into these hitherto terrible afternoons. She had taught Elijah and Elisha Simpson, so that they recited three verses of something with such comical effect that they delighted themselves, the teacher, and the school; while Susan, who lisped, had been provided with a humorous poem, in which she impersonated a lisping child. Emma Jane and Rebecca had a dialogue, and the sense of companionship buoyed up Emma Jane and gave her self-reliance. In fact, Miss Dearborn announced on this particular Friday morning that the exercises promised to be so interesting that she had invited the doctor's wife, the minister's wife, two members of the school committee, and a few mothers. Living Perkins was asked to decorate one of the blackboards and Rebecca the other. Living, who was the star artist of the school, chose the map of North America. Rebecca liked better to draw things less realistic; and speedily, before the eyes of the enchanted multitude, there grew under her skilful fingers an American flag, done in red, white, and blue chalk, every star in its right place, every stripe fluttering in the breeze. Beside this appeared a figure of Columbia, copied from the top of the cigar-box that held the crayons.

Miss Dearborn was delighted. "I propose we give Rebecca a good hand-clapping for such a beautiful picture—one that the whole school may well be proud of."

The scholars clapped heartily, and Dick Carter, waving his hand, gave a rousing cheer.

Rebecca's heart leaped for joy, and to her confusion she felt the tears rising in her eyes. She could hardly see the way back to her seat, for in her ignorant, lonely little life she had never been singled out for applause, never lauded, nor crowned, as in this wonderful, dazzling moment. If "nobleness enkindleth nobleness," so does enthusiasm beget enthusiasm, and so do wit and talent enkindle wit and talent. Alice Robinson proposed that the school should sing "Three Cheers for the Red, White, and Blue," and when they came to the chorus all point to Rebecca's flag. Dick Carter suggested that Living Perkins and Rebecca Randall should sign their names to their pictures, so that the visitors would know who drew them. Huldah Meserve asked permission to cover the largest holes in the plastered walls with boughs and fill the water-pail with wild-flowers. Rebecca's mood was above and beyond all practical details. She sat silent, her heart so full of grateful joy that she could hardly remember the words of her dialogue. At recess she bore herself modestly, notwithstanding her great triumph; while in the general atmosphere of goodwill the Smellie-Randall hatchet was buried, and Minnie gathered maple-boughs and covered the ugly stove with them under Rebecca's direction.

Miss Dearborn dismissed the morning session at quarter to twelve, so that those who lived near enough could go home for a change of dress. Emma Jane and Rebecca ran nearly every step of the way from sheer excitement, only stopping to breathe at the stiles.

"Will your Aunt Mirandy let you wear your best, or only your buff calico?" asked Emma Jane.

"I think I'll ask Aunt Jane," Rebecca replied. "Oh, if my pink was only finished! I left Aunt Jane making the buttonholes."

"I'm going to ask my mother to let me wear her garnet ring," said Emma Jane. "It would look perfectly elergant flashing in the sun when I point to the flag. Good-bye! Don't wait for me going back; I may get a ride."

Rebecca found the side-door locked, but she knew that the key was under the step, and so, of course, did everybody else in Riverboro, for they all did about

the same thing with it. She unlocked the door and
went into the dining-room, to find her lunch laid on
the table and a note from Aunt Jane, saying that they
had gone to Moderation with Mrs. Robinson in her
carryall. Rebecca swallowed a piece of bread-and-
butter, and flew up the front-stairs to her bedroom.
On the bed lay the pink gingham dress finished by
Aunt Jane's kind hands. Could she, dare she, wear
it without asking? Did the occasion justify a new
costume, or would her aunts think she ought to keep
it for the concert?

"I'll wear it," thought Rebecca. "They're not
here to ask, and maybe they wouldn't mind a bit. It's
only gingham, after all, and wouldn't be so grand if
it wasn't new, and hadn't tape-trimming on it, and
wasn't pink."

She unbraided her two pigtails, combed out the
waves of her hair and tied them back with a ribbon,
changed her shoes, and then slipped on the pretty
frock, managing to fasten all but the three middle
buttons, which she reserved for Emma Jane.

Then her eye fell on her cherished pink sunshade,
the exact match, and the girls had never seen it. It
wasn't quite appropriate for school, but she needn't
take it into the room; she would wrap it in a piece
of paper, just show it, and carry it coming home. She
glanced in the parlour looking-glass downstairs, and
was electrified at the vision. It seemed almost as if
beauty of apparel could go no further than that
heavenly pink gingham dress! The sparkle of her
eyes, glow of her cheeks, sheen of her falling hair,
passed unnoticed in the all-conquering charm of the
rose-coloured garment. Goodness! it was twenty

minutes to one, and she would be late. She danced out the side-door, pulled a pink rose from a bush at the gate, and covered the mile between the brick house and the seat of learning in an incredibly short time, meeting Emma Jane, also breathless and resplendent, at the entrance.

"Rebecca Randall!" exclaimed Emma Jane, "you're handsome as a picture!"

"I?" laughed Rebecca. "Nonsense! it's only the pink gingham."

"You're not good-looking every day," insisted Emma Jane; "but you're different somehow. See my garnet ring; mother scrubbed it in soap and water. How on earth did your Aunt Mirandy let you put on your bran' new dress?"

"They were both away, and I didn't ask," Rebecca responded anxiously. "Why? Do you think they'd have said no?"

"Miss Mirandy always says no, doesn't she?" asked Emma Jane.

"Ye—es; but this afternoon is very special—almost like a Sunday-school concert."

"Yes," assented Emma Jane, "it is, of course; with your name on the board, and our pointing to your flag, and our elergant dialogue, and all that."

The afternoon was one succession of solid triumphs for everybody concerned. There were no real failures at all, no tears, no parents ashamed of their offspring. Miss Dearborn heard many admiring remarks passed upon her ability, and wondered whether they belonged to her or partly, at least, to Rebecca. The child had no more to do than several others, but she was somehow in the foreground. It transpired afterwards at various village entertainments that Rebecca couldn't be kept in the background; it positively refused to hold her. Her worst enemy could not have called her pushing. She was ready and willing, and never shy; but she sought for no chances of display, and was, indeed, remarkably lacking in self-consciousness, as well as eager to bring others into whatever fun or entertainment there was. If wherever the MacGregor sat was the head of the table, so in the same way wherever Rebecca stood was the centre of the stage. Her clear high treble soared above all the rest in the choruses, and somehow everybody watched her, took note of her gestures, her whole-souled singing, her irrepressible enthusiasm.

Finally it was all over, and it seemed to Rebecca as if she should never be cool and calm again, as she loitered on the homeward path. There would be no lessons to learn to-night, and the vision of helping with the preserves on the morrow had no terrors for her—fears could not draw breath in the radiance that flooded her soul. There were thick gathering clouds in the sky, but she took no note of them save to be glad that she could raise her sunshade. She did not tread the solid ground at all, or have any sense of belonging to the common human family, until she entered the side-yard of the brick house and saw Aunt Miranda standing in the open doorway. Then with a rush she came back to earth.

IX

"There she is, over an hour late. A little more, an' she'd 'a' been caught in a thunder-shower; but she'd never look ahead," said Miranda to Jane. "And, added to all her other iniquities, if she ain't rigged out in that new dress, steppin' along with her father's dancin'-school steps, and swingin' her parasol for all the world as if she was play-actin'! Now, I'm the oldest, Jane, an' I intend to have my say out. If you don't like it, you can go into the kitchen till it's over. Step right in here, Rebecca; I want to talk to you. What did you put on that good new dress for on a school-day without permission?"

"I had intended to ask you at noontime; but you weren't at home, so I couldn't," began Rebecca.

"You did no such thing. You put it on because you was left alone, though you knew well enough I wouldn't have let you."

"If I'd been *certain* you wouldn't have let me, I'd never have done it," said Rebecca, trying to be truthful. "But I wasn't *certain*, and it was worth risking. I thought perhaps you might, if you knew it was almost a real exhibition at school."

"Exhibition!" exclaimed Miranda scornfully. "You are exhibition enough by yourself, I should say. Was you exhibitin' your parasol?"

"The parasol *was* silly," confessed Rebecca, hanging her head. "But it's the only time in my whole life when I had anything to match it, and it looked so

79

beautiful with the pink dress! Emma Jane and I spoke a dialogue about a city girl and a country girl, and it came to me just the minute before I started how nice it would come in for the city girl; and it did. I haven't hurt my dress a mite, Aunt Mirandy."

"It's the craftiness and underhandedness of your actions that's the worst," said Miranda coldly. "And look at the other things you've done! It seems as if Satan possessed you! You went up the front-stairs to your room, but you didn't hide your tracks, for you dropped your handkerchief on the way up. You left the screen out of your bedroom window for the flies to come in all over the house. You never cleared away your lunch nor set away a dish, *and you left the side-door unlocked* from half-past twelve to three o'clock, so 't anybody could 'a' come in and stolen what they liked!"

Rebecca sat down heavily in her chair as she heard the list of her transgressions. How could she have been so careless? The tears began to flow now as she attempted to explain sins that never could be explained or justified.

"Oh, I'm so sorry!" she faltered. "I was trimming the schoolroom and got belated, and ran all the way home. It was hard getting into my dress alone, and I hadn't time to eat but a mouthful, and just at the last minute, when I honestly—*honestly* would have thought about clearing away and locking up, I looked at the clock, and knew I could hardly get back to school in time to form in the line; and I thought how dreadful it would be to go in late, and get my first black mark on a Friday afternoon, with

the minister's wife and the doctor's wife and the
school committee all there."

"Don't wail and carry on now; it's no good cryin'
over spilt milk," answered Miranda. "An ounce of
good behaviour is worth a pound of repentance.
Instead of tryin' to see how little trouble you can
make in a house that ain't your own home, it seems
as if you tried to see how much you could put us out.
Take that rose out o' your dress, and let me see the
spot it's made on your yoke, an' the rusty holes where
the wet pin went in. No, it ain't; but it's more by
luck than forethought. I ain't got any patience with
your flowers, and frizzled-out hair, and furbelows,
an' airs an' graces, for all the world like your Miss-
Nancy father.

Rebecca lifted her head in a flash. "Look here,
Aunt Mirandy: I'll be as good as I know how to be.
I'll mind quick when I'm spoken to, and never leave
the door unlocked again; but I won't have my father
called names. He was a p-perfectly l-lovely father,
that's what he was; and it's *mean* to call him Miss
Nancy!"

"Don't you dare answer me back that imperdent
way, Rebecca, tellin' me I'm mean. Your father was
a vain, foolish, shiftless man, an' you might as well
hear it from me as anybody else. He spent your
mother's money, and left her with seven children to
provide for."

"It's s-something to leave s-seven nice children,"
sobbed Rebecca.

"Not when other folks have to help feed, clothe,
and educate 'em," responded Miranda. "Now you
step upstairs, put on your nightgown, go to bed, and

F

stay there till to-morrow mornin'. You'll find a
bowl o' crackers an' milk on your bureau, an' I don't
want to hear a sound from you till breakfast-time.
Jane, run an' take the dish-towels off the line, and
shut the shed doors; we're goin' to have a turrible
shower."

"We've had it, I should think," said Jane quietly,
as she went to do her sister's bidding. "I don't often
speak my mind, Mirandy; but you ought not to have
said what you did about Lorenzo. He was what he
was, and can't be made any different; but he was
Rebecca's father, and Aurelia always says he was a
good husband."

Miranda had never heard the proverbial phrase
about the only "good Indian"; but her mind worked
in the conventional manner when she said grimly:
"Yes; I've noticed that dead husbands are usually
good ones. But the truth needs an airin' now and
then; and that child will never amount to a hill o'
beans till she gets some of her father trounced out of
her. I'm glad I said just what I did."

"I dare say you are," remarked Jane, with what
might be described as one of her annual bursts of
courage. "But all the same, Mirandy, it wasn't good
manners, and it wasn't good religion."

The clap of thunder that shook the house just at
that moment made no such peal in Miranda Sawyer's
ears as Jane's remark made when it fell with a deafen-
ing roar on her conscience.

Perhaps, after all, it is just as well to speak only
once a year, and then speak to the purpose.

Rebecca mounted the back-stairs wearily, closed the
door of her bedroom, and took off the beloved pink

gingham with trembling fingers. Her cotton hand-kerchief was rolled into a hard ball; and in the intervals of reaching the more difficult buttons that lay between her shoulder-blades and her belt she dabbed her wet eyes carefully, so that they should not rain salt-water on the finery that had been worn at such a price. She smoothed it out carefully, pinched up the white ruffle at the neck, and laid it away in a drawer, with an extra little sob at the roughness of life. The withered pink rose fell on the floor. Rebecca looked at it, and thought to herself, "Just like my happy day!" Nothing could show more clearly the kind of child she was than the fact that she instantly perceived the symbolism of the rose, and laid it in the drawer with the dress, as if she were burying the whole episode with all its sad memories. It was a child's poetic instinct, with a dawning hint of woman's sentiment in it.

She braided her hair in the two accustomed pig-tails, took off her best shoes (which had happily escaped notice), with all the while a fixed resolve growing in her mind, that of leaving the brick house and going back to the farm. She would not be received there with open arms—there was no hope of that—but she would help her mother about the house, and send Hannah to Riverboro in her place. "I hope she'll like it!" she thought in a momentary burst of vindictiveness. She sat by the window trying to make some sort of plan, watching the lightning play over the hilltop and the streams of rain chasing each other down the lightning-rod. And this was the day that had dawned so joyfully! It had been a red sunrise, and she had leaned on the window-sill studying her

lesson and thinking what a lovely world it was. And
what a golden morning! The changing of the bare,
ugly little schoolroom into a bower of beauty; Miss
Dearborn's pleasure at her success with the Simpson
twins' recitation; the privilege of decorating the
blackboard; the happy thought of drawing Columbia
from the cigar-box; the intoxicating moment when
the school clapped her. And what an afternoon! How
it went on from glory to glory, beginning with Emma
Jane's telling her, Rebecca Randall, that she was as
" handsome as a picture."

She lived through the exercises again in memory,
especially her dialogue with Emma Jane, and her
inspiration of using the bough-covered stove as a
mossy bank where the country girl could sit and
watch her flocks. This gave Emma Jane a feeling of
such ease that she never recited better; and how
generous it was of her to lend the garnet ring to the
city girl, fancying truly how it would flash as she
furled her parasol and approached the awe-stricken
shepherdess! She had thought Aunt Miranda might
be pleased that the niece invited down from the farm
had succeeded so well at school; but no, there was
no hope of pleasing her in that or in any other way.
She would go to Maplewood on the stage next
day with Mr. Cobb and get home somehow from
Cousin Ann's. On second thoughts, her aunts might
not allow it. Very well, she would slip away now, and
see if she could stay all night with the Cobbs and be
off next morning before breakfast.

Rebecca never stopped long to think, more's the
pity, so she put on her oldest dress and hat and
jacket, then wrapped her nightdress, comb, and tooth-

brush in a bundle and dropped it softly out of the window. Her room was in the L, and her window at no very dangerous distance from the ground, though had it been, nothing could have stopped her at that moment. Somebody who had gone on the roof to clean out the gutters had left a cleat nailed to the side of the house about half-way between the window and the top of the back porch. Rebecca heard the sound of the sewing-machine in the dining-room, and the chopping of meat in the kitchen; so knowing the whereabouts of both her aunts, she scrambled out of the window, caught hold of the lightning-rod, slid down to the helpful cleat, jumped to the porch, used the woodbine trellis for a ladder, and was flying up the road in the storm before she had time to arrange any details of her future movements.

Jeremiah Cobb sat at his lonely supper at the table by the kitchen-window. "Mother," as he, with his old-fashioned habits, was in the habit of calling his wife, was nursing a sick neighbour. Mrs. Cobb was mother only to a little headstone in the churchyard, where reposed "Sarah Ann, beloved daughter of Jeremiah and Sarah Cobb, aged seventeen months"; but the name of mother was better than nothing, and served at any rate as a reminder of her woman's crown of blessedness.

The rain still fell, and the heavens were dark, though it was scarcely five o'clock. Looking up from his "dish of tea," the old man saw at the open door a very figure of woe. Rebecca's face was so swollen with tears and so sharp with misery that for a moment he scarcely recognised her. Then, when he heard her voice asking, "Please may I come in, Mr. Cobb?" he cried, "Well I vow! it's my little lady passenger! Come to call on old Uncle Jerry and pass the time o' day, hev ye? Why, you're wet as sops. Draw up to the stove. I made a fire, hot as it was, thinkin' I wanted somethin' warm for my supper, bein' kind o' lonesome without mother. She's settin' up with Seth Strout to-night. There, we'll hang your soppy hat on the nail, put your jacket over the chair-rail, an' then you turn your back to the stove an' dry yourself good."

Uncle Jerry had never before said so many words at a time, but he had caught sight of the child's red eyes and tear-stained cheeks, and his big heart went out to her in her trouble, quite regardless of any circumstances that might have caused it.

Rebecca stood still for a moment, until Uncle Jerry took his seat again at the table, and then, unable to contain herself longer, cried: "Oh, Mr. Cobb, I've run away from the brick house, and I want to go back to the farm. Will you keep me to-night and take me up to Maplewood in the stage? I haven't got any money for my fare, but I'll earn it somehow afterwards."

"Well, I guess we won't quarrel 'bout money, you and me," said the old man; "and we've never had our ride together, anyway, though we allers meant to go down river, not up."

"I shall never see Milltown now!" sobbed Rebecca.

"Come over here side o' me an' tell me all about it," coaxed Uncle Jerry. "Jest set down on that there wooden cricket an' out with the whole story."

Rebecca leaned her aching head against Mr. Cobb's homespun knee and recounted the history of her trouble. Tragic as that history seemed to her passionate and undisciplined mind, she told it truthfully and without exaggeration.

X

RAINBOW BRIDGES

UNCLE JERRY coughed and stirred in his chair a good deal during Rebecca's recital, but he carefully concealed any undue feeling of sympathy, just muttering, "Poor little soul! We'll see what we can do for her!"

"You will take me to Maplewood, won't you, Mr. Cobb?" begged Rebecca piteously.

"Don't you fret a mite," he answered, with a crafty little notion at the back of his mind; "I'll see the lady passenger through somehow. Now take a bite o' somethin' to eat, child. Spread some o' that tomato preserve on your bread; draw up to the table. How'd you like to set in mother's place an' pour me out another cup o' hot tea?"

Mr. Jeremiah Cobb's mental machinery was simple, and did not move very smoothly save when propelled by his affection or sympathy. In the present case these were both employed to his advantage, and mourning his stupidity and praying for some flash of inspiration to light his path, he blundered along, trusting to Providence.

Rebecca, comforted by the old man's tone, and

timidly enjoying the dignity of sitting in Mrs. Cobb's seat and lifting the blue china teapot, smiled faintly, smoothed her hair, and dried her eyes.

"I suppose your mother'll be turrible glad to see you back again?" queried Mr. Cobb.

A tiny fear—just a baby thing—in the bottom of Rebecca's heart stirred and grew larger the moment it was touched with a question.

"She won't like it that I ran away, I s'pose, and she'll be sorry that I couldn't please Aunt Mirandy; but I'll make her understand, just as I did you."

"I s'pose she was thinkin' o' your schoolin', lettin' you come down here; but land! you can go to school in Temperance, I s'pose?"

"There's only two months' school now in Temperance, and the farm's too far from all the other schools."

"Oh well, there's other things in the world beside edjercation," responded Uncle Jerry, attacking a piece of apple-pie.

"Ye—es; though mother thought that was going to be the making of me," returned Rebecca sadly, giving a dry little sob as she tried to drink her tea.

"It'll be nice for you to be all together again at the farm—such a houseful o' children!" remarked the dear old deceiver, who longed for nothing so much as to cuddle and comfort the poor little creature.

"It's too full, that's the trouble. But I'll make Hannah come to Riverboro in my place."

"S'pose Mirandy 'n' Jane'll have her? I should be 'most afraid they wouldn't. They'll be kind o' mad at your goin' home, you know, and you can't hardly blame 'em."

This was quite a new thought—that the brick house

might be closed to Hannah, since she, Rebecca, had turned her back upon its cold hospitality.

"How is this school down here in Riverboro—pretty good?" inquired Uncle Jerry, whose brain was working with an altogether unaccustomed rapidity, so much so that it almost terrified him.

"Oh, it's a splendid school! And Miss Dearborn is a splendid teacher!"

"You like her, do you? Well, you'd better believe she returns the compliment. Mother was down to the store this afternoon buyin' liniment for Seth Strout, an' she met Miss Dearborn on the bridge. They got to talkin' 'bout school, for mother has summer-boarded a lot o' the school-marms, an' likes 'em. 'How does the little Temperance girl git along?' asks mother. 'Oh, she's the best scholar I have!' says Miss Dearborn. 'I could teach school from sun-up to sundown if scholars was all like Rebecca Randall,' says she."

"Oh, Mr. Cobb, *did* she say that?" glowed Rebecca, her face sparkling and dimpling in an instant. "I've tried hard all the time, but I'll study the covers right off the books now."

"You mean you would if you'd ben goin' to stay here," interposed Uncle Jerry. "Now, ain't it too bad you've jest got to give it all up on account o' your Aunt Mirandy? Well, I can't hardly blame ye. She's cranky an' she's sour; I should think she'd ben nussed on bonny clabber an' green apples. She needs bearin' with; an' I guess you ain't much on patience, be ye?"

"Not very much," replied Rebecca dolefully.

"If I'd had this talk with ye yesterday," pursued

Mr. Cobb, "I believe I'd have advised ye different. It's too late now, an' I don't feel to say you've ben all in the wrong; but if 'twas to do over again, I'd say, well, your Aunt Mirandy gives you clothes and board and schoolin', and is goin' to send you to Wareham at a big expense. She's turrible hard to get along with, an' kind o' heaves benefits at your head same 's she would bricks. But they're benefits jest the same, an' mebbe it's your job to kind o' pay for 'em in good behaviour. Jane's a leetle bit more easy-goin' than Mirandy, ain't she? or is she jest as hard to please?"

"Oh, Aunt Jane and I get along splendidly," exclaimed Rebecca. "She's just as good and kind as she can be, and I like her better all the time. I think she kind of likes me, too. She smoothed my hair once. I'd let her scold me all day long, for she understands. But she can't stand up for me against Aunt Mirandy; she's about as afraid of her as I am."

"Jane 'll be real sorry to-morrow to find you've gone away, I guess. But never mind, it can't be helped. If she has a kind of a dull time with Mirandy, on account o' her bein' so sharp, why, of course she'd set great store by your comp'ny. Mother was talkin' with her after prayer-meetin' the other night. 'You wouldn't know the brick house, Sarah,' says Jane. 'I'm keepin' a sewin' school, an' my scholar has made three dresses. What do you think o' that,' says she, 'for an old maid's child? I've taken a class in Sunday-school,' says Jane, 'an' think o' renewin' my youth an' goin' to the picnic with Rebecca,' says she. An' mother declares she never see her look so young 'n' happy."

There was a silence that could be felt in the little

kitchen, a silence only broken by the ticking of the
tall clock and the beating of Rebecca's heart, which,
it seemed to her, almost drowned the voice of the
clock. The rain ceased, a sudden rosy light filled the
room, and through the window a rainbow arch could
be seen spanning the heavens like a radiant bridge.
Bridges took one across difficult places, thought
Rebecca, and Uncle Jerry seemed to have built
one over her troubles and given her strength to
walk.

"The shower's over," said the old man, filling his
pipe; "it's cleared the air, washed the face o' the
airth nice an' clean, an' everything to-morrer will
shine like a new pin—when you an' I are drivin' up
river."

Rebecca pushed her cup away, rose from the table,
and put on her hat and jacket quietly. "I'm not going
to drive up river, Mr. Cobb," she said. "I'm going
to stay here and—catch bricks; catch 'em without
throwing 'em back, too. I don't know as Aunt
Mirandy will take me in after I've run away; but I'm
going back now while I have the courage. You
wouldn't be so good as to go with me, would you,
Mr. Cobb?"

"You'd better b'lieve your Uncle Jerry don't propose to leave till he gits this thing fixed up," cried the
old man delightedly. "Now you've had all you can
stand to-night, poor little soul, without gettin' a fit
o' sickness; an' Mirandy 'll be sore an' cross, an' in
no condition for argyment; so my plan is jest this:
to drive you over to the brick house in my top buggy;
to have you set back in the corner, an' I git out
an' go to the side-door; an' when I git your Aunt

Mirandy 'n' Aunt Jane out int' the shed to plan for
a load o' wood I'm goin' to have hauled there this
week, you'll slip out o' the buggy and go upstairs
to bed. The front-door won't be locked, will it?"

"Not this time of night," Rebecca answered; "not
till Aunt Mirandy goes to bed. But oh! what if it
should be?"

"Well, it won't; an', if 't is, why, we'll have to face
it out; though, in my opinion, there's things that
won't bear facin' out, an' had better be settled comfortable an' quiet. You see, you ain't run away yet;
you've only come over here to consult me 'bout runnin' away, an' we've concluded it ain't wuth the
trouble. The only real sin you've committed, as I
figger it out, was in comin' here by the winder when
you'd ben sent to bed. That ain't so very black, an'
you can tell your Aunt Jane 'bout it come Sunday,
when she's chock-full o' religion, an' she can advise
you when you'd better tell your Aunt Mirandy. I
don't believe in deceivin' folks, but if you've hed
hard thoughts, you ain't obleeged to own 'em up.
Take 'em to the Lord in prayer, as the hymn says,
and then don't go on hevin' 'em. Now, come on.
I'm all hitched up to go over to the post-office. Don't
forget your bundle. 'It's always a journey, mother,
when you carry a nightgown'—them's the first words
your Uncle Jerry ever heard you say. He didn't think
you'd be bringin' your nightgown over to his house.
Step in an' curl up in the corner. We ain't goin' to
let folks see little runaway gals, 'cause they're goin'
back to begin all over ag'in!"

When Rebecca crept upstairs, and, undressing in

the dark, finally found herself in her bed that night, though she was aching and throbbing in every nerve, she felt a kind of peace stealing over her. She had been saved from foolishness and error, kept from troubling her poor mother, prevented from angering and mortifying her aunts.

Her heart was melted now, and she determined to win Aunt Miranda's approval by some desperate means, and to try and forget the one thing that rankled worst—the scornful mention of her father, of whom she thought with the greatest admiration, and whom she had not yet heard criticised, for such sorrows and disappointments as Aurelia Randall had suffered had never been communicated to her children.

It would have been some comfort to the bruised, unhappy little spirit to know that Miranda Sawyer was passing an uncomfortable night, and that she tacitly regretted her harshness, partly because Jane had taken such a lofty and virtuous position in the matter. She could not endure Jane's disapproval, although she would never have confessed to such a weakness.

As Uncle Jerry drove homeward under the stars, well content with his attempts at keeping the peace, he thought wistfully of the touch of Rebecca's head on his knee and the rain of her tears on his hand; of the sweet reasonableness of her mind when she had the matter put rightly before her; of her quick decision when she had once seen the path of duty; of the touching hunger for love and understanding that were so characteristic in her. "Lord A'mighty!" he ejaculated under his breath—"Lord A'mighty! to hector and abuse a child like that one! 'Tain't *abuse* exactly, I know, or 'twouldn't be to some o' your elephant-hided young ones; but to that little tender Will-o'-the-wisp a hard word's like a lash. Miranda Sawyer would be a heap better woman if she had a little gravestun to remember, same 's mother 'n' I have."

"I never see a child improve in her work as Rebecca has to-day," remarked Miranda Sawyer to Jane on Saturday evening. "That settin' down I gave her was probably just what she needed, and I dare say it'll last for a month."

"I'm glad you're pleased," returned Jane. "A cringing worm is what you want, not a bright, smiling child. Rebecca looks to me as if she'd been through the Seven Years' War. When she came downstairs this morning, it seemed to me she'd grown old in the night. If you follow my advice, which you seldom do, you'll let me take her and Emma Jane down beside the river to-morrow afternoon, and bring Emma Jane home to a good Sunday supper. Then, if you'll let her go to Milltown with the Cobbs on Wednesday, that'll hearten her up a little and coax back her appetite. Wednesday's a holiday on account of Miss Dearborn's going home to her sister's wedding, and the Cobbs and Perkinses want to go down to the agricultural fair."

XI

"THE STIRRING OF THE POWERS"

REBECCA'S visit to Milltown was all that her glowing fancy had painted it, except that recent readings about Rome and Venice disposed her to believe that those cities might have an advantage over Milltown in the matter of mere pictorial beauty. So soon does the soul outgrow its mansions, that after once seeing Milltown her fancy ran out to the future sight of Portland, for that, having islands and a harbour and two public monuments, must be far more beautiful than Milltown, which would, she felt, take its proud place among the cities of the earth, by reason of its tremendous business activity rather than by any irresistible appeal to the imagination.

It would be impossible for two children to see more, do more, walk more, talk more, eat more, or ask more questions, than Rebecca and Emma Jane did on that eventful Wednesday.

"She's the best company I ever see in all my life," said Mrs. Cobb to her husband that evening. "We ain't had a dull minute this day. She's well-mannered, too; she didn't ask for anything, and was thankful for whatever she got. Did you watch her face when we went into that tent where they was actin' out 'Uncle Tom's Cabin'? And did you take notice of the way she told us about the book when we sat down to have our ice-cream? I tell you, Harriet Beecher Stowe herself couldn't 'a' done it better justice."

"I took it all in," responded Mr. Cobb, who was pleased that "mother" agreed with him about

Rebecca. "I ain't sure but she's goin' to turn out somethin' remarkable—a singer, or a writer, or a lady doctor, like that Miss Parks up to Cornish."

"Lady doctors are always home'paths, ain't they?" asked Mrs. Cobb, who, it is needless to say, was distinctly of the old school in medicine.

"Land no, mother! there ain't no home'path 'bout Miss Parks. She drives all over the country."

"I can't see Rebecca as a lady doctor, somehow," mused Mrs. Cobb. "Her gift o' gab is what's goin' to be the makin' o' her. Mebbe she'll lecture, or recite pieces, like that Portland elocutionist that come out here to the harvest supper."

"I guess she'll be able to write down her own pieces," said Mr. Cobb confidently. "She could make 'em up faster 'n she could read 'em out of a book."

"It's a pity she's so plain-looking," remarked Mrs. Cobb, blowing out the candle.

"*Plain-looking*, mother!" exclaimed her husband in astonishment. "Look at the eyes of her; look at the hair of her, an' the smile, an' that there dimple! Look at Alice Robinson, that's called the prettiest child on the river, an' see how Rebecca shines her ri' down out o' sight! I hope Mirandy 'll favour her comin' over to see us real often, for she'll let off some of her steam here, an' the brick house 'll be consid'able safer for everybody concerned. We've known what it was to hev children, even if 'twas more 'n thirty years ago, an' we can make allowances."

Notwithstanding the encomiums of Mr. and Mrs. Cobb, Rebecca made a poor hand at composition writing at this time. Miss Dearborn gave her every sort of subject that she had ever been given herself:

"Cloud Pictures," "Abraham Lincoln," "Nature," "Philanthropy," "Slavery," "Intemperance," "Joy and Duty," "Solitude," but with none of them did Rebecca seem to grapple satisfactorily.

"Write as you talk, Rebecca," insisted poor Miss Dearborn, who secretly knew that she could never manage a good composition herself.

"But gracious me, Miss Dearborn! I don't talk about nature and slavery. I can't write unless I have something to say, can I?"

"That is what compositions are for," returned Miss Dearborn doubtfully: "to make you have things to say. Now, in your last one, on solitude, you haven't said anything very interesting, and you've made it too common and every-day to sound well. There are too many 'yous' and 'yours' in it; you ought to say 'one' now and then, to make it seem more like good writing. 'One opens a favourite book'; 'One's thoughts are a great comfort in solitude,' and so on."

"I don't know any more about solitude this week than I did about joy and duty last week," grumbled Rebecca.

"You tried to be funny about joy and duty," said Miss Dearborn reprovingly, "so of course you didn't succeed."

"I didn't know you were going to make us read the things out loud," said Rebecca, with an embarrassed smile of recollection.

"Joy and Duty" had been the inspiring subject given to the older children for a theme to be written in five minutes.

Rebecca had wrestled, struggled, perspired in vain.

When her turn came to read she was obliged to confess she had written nothing.

"You have at least two lines, Rebecca," insisted the teacher, "for I see them on your slate."

"I'd rather not read them, please; they are not good," pleaded Rebecca.

"Read what you have, good or bad, little or much; I am excusing nobody."

Rebecca rose, overcome with secret laughter, dread, and mortification; then in a low voice she read the couplet :

"When Joy and Duty clash
Let Duty go to smash."

Dick Carter's head disappeared under the desk, while Living Perkins choked with laughter.

Miss Dearborn laughed too; she was little more than a girl, and the training of the young idea seldom appealed to the sense of humour.

"You must stay after school and try again, Rebecca," she said, but she said it smilingly. "Your poetry hasn't a very nice idea in it for a good little girl who ought to love duty."

"It wasn't *my* idea," said Rebecca apologetically. "I had only made the first line when I saw you were going to ring the bell and say the time was up. I had 'clash' written, and I couldn't think of anything then but 'hash' or 'rash' or 'smash.' I'll change it to this :

"When Joy and Duty clash,
'Tis Joy must go to smash."

"That is better," Miss Dearborn answered, "though I cannot think 'going to smash' is a pretty expression for poetry."

Having been instructed in the use of the indefinite pronoun " one " as giving a refined and elegant touch to literary efforts, Rebecca painstakingly rewrote her composition on solitude, giving it all the benefit of Miss Dearborn's suggestion. It then appeared in the following form, which hardly satisfied either teacher or pupil:

" SOLITUDE "

" It would be false to say that one could ever be alone when one has one's lovely thoughts to comfort one. One sits by one's self, it is true, but one thinks; one opens one's favourite book and reads one's favourite story; one speaks to one's aunt or one's brother, fondles one's cat, or looks at one's photograph album. There is one's work also: what a joy it is to one, if one happens to like work. All one's little household tasks keep one from being lonely. Does one ever feel bereft when one picks up one's chips to light one's fire for one's evening meal? Or when one washes one's milk-pail before milking one's cow? One would fancy not.

"R. R. R."

" It is perfectly dreadful," sighed Rebecca when she read it aloud after school. " Putting in ' one ' all the time doesn't make it sound any more like a book, and it looks silly besides."

" You say such queer things," objected Miss Dearborn. " I don't see what makes you do it. Why did you put in anything so common as picking up chips?"

" Because I was talking about ' household tasks ' in the sentence before, and it *is* one of my household tasks. Don't you think calling supper 'one's evening meal' is pretty? and isn't 'bereft' a nice word?"

"Yes, that part of it does very well. It is the cat, the chips, and the milk-pail that I don't like."

"All right!" sighed Rebecca. "Out they go! Does the cow go too?"

"Yes, I don't like a cow in a composition," said the difficult Miss Dearborn.

The Milltown trip had not been without its tragic consequences of a small sort; for the next week Minnie Smellie's mother told Miranda Sawyer that she'd better look after Rebecca, for she was given to "swearing and profane language"; that she had been heard saying something dreadful that very afternoon, saying it before Emma Jane and Living Perkins, who only laughed and got down on all fours and chased her.

Rebecca, on being confronted and charged with the crime, denied it indignantly, and Aunt Jane believed her.

"Search your memory, Rebecca, and try to think what Minnie overheard you say," she pleaded. "Don't be ugly and obstinate, but think real hard. When did they chase you up the road, and what were you doing?"

A sudden light broke upon Rebecca's darkness.

"Oh! I see it now," she exclaimed. "It had rained hard all the morning, you know, and the road was full of puddles. Emma Jane, Living, and I were walking along, and I was ahead. I saw the water streaming over the road towards the ditch, and it reminded me of 'Uncle Tom's Cabin' at Milltown, when Eliza took her baby and ran across the Mississippi on the ice blocks, pursued by the bloodhounds. We couldn't keep from laughing after we came out of the tent because they were acting on such a small platform that Eliza had to run round and round, and part of the time the one dog they had pursued her, and part of the time she had to pursue the dog. I knew Living would remember, too, so I took off my waterproof and wrapped it round my books for a baby; then I shouted, '*My God! the river!*' just like that—the same as Eliza did in the play; then I leaped from puddle to puddle, and Living and Emma Jane pursued me like the bloodhounds. It's just like that stupid Minnie Smellie who doesn't know a game when she sees one. And Eliza wasn't swearing when she said, 'My God! the river!' It was more like praying."

"Well, you've got no call to be prayin', any more than swearin', in the middle of the road," said Miranda; "but I'm thankful it's no worse. You're born to trouble as the sparks fly upward, an' I'm afraid you allers will be till you learn to bridle your unruly tongue."

"I wish sometimes that I could bridle Minnie's," murmured Rebecca, as she went to set the table for supper.

"I declare she *is* the beatin'est child!" said Miranda, taking off her spectacles and laying down her mending. "You don't think she's a leetle mite crazy, do you, Jane?"

"I don't think she's like the rest of us," responded Jane thoughtfully and with some anxiety in her pleasant face; "but whether it's for the better or the worse I can't hardly tell till she grows up. She's got the making of 'most anything in her, Rebecca has; but I feel sometimes as if we were not fitted to cope with her."

"Stuff an' nonsense!" said Miranda. "Speak for yourself. I feel fitted to cope with any child that ever was born int' the world!"

"I know you do, Mirandy; but that don't *make* you so," returned Jane with a smile.

The habit of speaking her mind freely was certainly growing on Jane to an altogether terrifying extent.

XII

"SEE THE PALE MARTYR"

IT was about this time that Rebecca, who had been reading about the Spartan boy, conceived the idea of some mild form of self-punishment, to be applied on occasions when she was fully convinced in her own mind that it would be salutary. The immediate cause of the decision was a somewhat sadder accident than was common, even in a career prolific in such things.

Clad in her best, Rebecca had gone to take tea with the Cobbs; but while crossing the bridge she was suddenly overcome by the beauty of the river, and leaned over the newly painted rail to feast her eyes on the dashing torrent of the fall. Resting her elbows on the topmost board, and inclining her little figure forward in delicious ease, she stood there dreaming.

The river above the dam was a glassy lake, with all the loveliness of blue heaven and green shore reflected in its surface. The fall was a swirling wonder of water, ever pouring itself over and over inexhaustibly in luminous golden gushes, that lost themselves in snowy depths of foam. Sparkling in the sunshine, gleaming under the summer moon, cold and grey beneath a November sky, trickling over the dam in some burning July drought, swollen with turbulent power in some April freshet—how many young eyes gazed into the mystery and majesty of the falls along that river, and how many young hearts dreamed out their futures leaning over the bridge-rail, seeing " the vision splendid " reflected there, and often, too, watching it fade into " the light of common day."

Rebecca never went across the bridge without bending over the rail to wonder and to ponder, and at this special moment she was putting the finishing touches on a poem :

> Two maidens by a river strayed
>   Down in the state of Maine.
> The one was called Rebecca,
>   The other Emma Jane.
> " I would my life were like the stream,"
>   Said her named Emma Jane,
> " So quiet and so very smooth,
>   So free from every pain."
>
> " I'd rather be a little drop
>   In the great rushing fall !
> I would not choose the glassy lake
>   'Twould not suit me at all !"

> (It was the darker maiden spoke
>   The words I just have stated;
> The maidens twain were simply friends,
>   And not at all related.)

> But O! alas! we may not have
>   The things we hope to gain;
> The quiet life may come to me
>   The rush to Emma Jane!

"I don't like 'the rush to Emma Jane,' and I can't think of anything else. Oh, what a smell of paint! Oh, it is *on* me! Oh, it's all over my best dress! Oh, what *will* Aunt Miranda say?"

With tears of self-reproach streaming from her eyes, Rebecca flew up the hill, sure of sympathy, and hoping against hope for help of some sort.

Mrs. Cobb took in the situation at a glance, and professed herself able to remove almost any stain from almost any fabric; and in this she was corroborated by Uncle Jerry, who vowed that mother could get anything out. Sometimes she took the cloth right along with the spot, but she had a sure hand, mother had.

The damaged garment was removed and partially immersed in turpentine, while Rebecca graced the festal board clad in a blue calico wrapper of Mrs. Cobb's.

"Don't let it take your appetite away," crooned Mrs. Cobb. "I've got cream biscuit and honey for you. If the turpentine don't work, I'll try French chalk, magneshy, and warm suds. If they fail, father shall run over to Strout's, and borry some of the stuff Marthy got in Milltown to take the currant-pie out of her weddin' dress."

"I ain't got to understandin' this paintin' accident yet," said Uncle Jerry jocosely, as he handed Rebecca the honey. "Bein' as how there's 'Fresh Paint' signs hung all over the breedge, so 't a blind asylum couldn't miss 'em, I can't hardly account for your gettin' int' the pesky stuff."

"I didn't notice the signs," Rebecca said dolefully. "I suppose I was looking at the falls."

"The falls has been there sence the beginnin' o' time, an' I cal'late they'll be there till the end on't; so you needn't 'a' been in sech a brash to git a sight of 'em. Children comes turrible high, mother; but I s'pose we must have 'em," he said, winking at Mrs. Cobb.

When supper was cleared away, Rebecca insisted on washing and wiping the dishes, while Mrs. Cobb worked on the dress with an energy that plainly showed the gravity of the task. Rebecca kept leaving her post at the sink to bend anxiously over the basin and watch her progress, while Uncle Jerry offered advice from time to time.

"You must 'a' laid all over the breedge, deary," said Mrs. Cobb, "for the paint's not only on your elbows and yoke and waist, but it about covers your front breadth."

As the garment began to look a little better Rebecca's spirits took an upward turn, and at length she left it to dry in the fresh air, and went into the sitting-room.

"Have you a piece of paper, please?" asked Rebecca. "I'll copy out the poetry I was making while I was lying in the paint."

Mrs. Cobb sat by her mending basket, and Uncle

Jerry took down a gingham bag of strings, and occupied himself in taking the snarls out of them— a favourite evening amusement with him.

Rebecca soon had the lines copied in her round schoolgirl hand, making such improvements as occurred to her on sober second thought.

THE TWO WISHES

By Rebecca Randall

Two maidens by a river strayed;
  'Twas in the state of Maine.
Rebecca was the darker one,
  The fairer, Emma Jane.
The fairer maiden said " I would
  My life were as the stream;
So peaceful, and so smooth and still,
  So pleasant and serene."

" I'd rather be a little drop
  In the great rushing fall!
I'd never choose the quiet lake;
  'Twould not please me at all."
(It was the darker maiden spoke
  The words we just have stated;
The maidens twain were simply friends,
  Not sisters, or related.)

But O! alas! we may not have
  The things we hope to gain.
The quiet life may come to me
  The rush to Emma Jane!

She read it aloud, and the Cobbs thought it not only surpassingly beautiful, but a marvellous production.

" I guess if that writer that lived on Congress

Street in Portland could 'a' heard your poetry he'd 'a' been astonished," said Mrs. Cobb. "If you ask me, I say this piece is as good as that one o' his, 'Tell me not in mournful numbers,' and consid'able clearer."

"I never could fairly make out what 'mournful numbers' was," remarked Mr. Cobb critically.

"Then I guess you never studied fractions!" flashed Rebecca. "See here, Uncle Jerry, and Aunt Sarah: would you write another verse, especially for a last one, as they usually do—one with 'thoughts' in it—to make a better ending?"

"If you can grind 'em out jest by turnin' the crank, why, I should say the more the merrier; but I don't hardly see how you could have a better endin'," observed Mr. Cobb.

"It is horrid!" grumbled Rebecca. "I ought not to have put that 'me' in. I'm writing the poetry. Nobody ought to know it *is* me standing by the river; it ought to be 'Rebecca,' or 'the darker maiden'; and 'the rush to Emma Jane' is simply dreadful. Sometimes I think I never will try poetry, it's so hard to make it come right; and other times it just says itself. I wonder if this would be better:

> But oh! alas! we may not gain
> The good for which we pray.
> The quiet life may come to one
> Who likes it rather gay.

I don't know whether that is worse or not. Now for a new last verse!"

In a few minutes the poetess looked up, flushed and triumphant. "It was as easy as nothing. Just hear!" And she read slowly, with her pretty, pathetic voice:

> " Then if our lot be bright or sad,
>   Be full of smiles or tears,
>   The thought that God has planned it so
>   Should help us bear the years. '

Mr. and Mrs. Cobb exchanged dumb glances of admiration; indeed, Uncle Jerry was obliged to turn his face to the window and wipe his eyes furtively with the string-bag.

"How in the world did you do it?" Mrs. Cobb exclaimed.

"Oh, it's easy," answered Rebecca; "the hymns at meeting are all like that. You see, there's a school newspaper printed at Wareham Academy once a month. Dick Carter says the editor is always a boy, of course; but he allows girls to try and write for it, and then chooses the best. Dick thinks I can be in it."

"*In* it!" exclaimed Uncle Jerry. "I shouldn't be a bit surprised if you had to write the whole paper; an' as for any boy editor, you could lick him writin', I bate ye, with one hand tied behind ye."

"Can we have a copy of the poetry to keep in the family Bible?" inquired Mrs. Cobb respectfully.

"Oh! would you like it?" asked Rebecca. "Yes indeed! I'll do a clean, nice one with violet ink and a fine pen. But I must go and look at my poor dress."

The old couple followed Rebecca into the kitchen. The frock was quite dry, and in truth it had been helped a little by Aunt Sarah's ministrations; but the colours had run in the rubbing, the pattern was blurred, and there were muddy streaks here and there. As a last resort it was carefully smoothed with a warm iron, and Rebecca was urged to attire herself, that they might see if the spots showed as much when it was on.

They did most uncompromisingly, and to the dullest eye. Rebecca gave one searching look, and then said, as she took her hat from a nail in the entry: "I think I'll be going. Good-night. If I've got to have a scolding, I want it quick and get it over."

"Poor little onlucky misfortunate thing!" sighed Uncle Jerry, as his eyes followed her down the hill. "I wish she could pay some attention to the ground under her feet; but I vow, if she was ourn I'd let her slop paint all over the house before I could scold her. Here's her poetry she's left behind. Read it out ag'in, mother. Land!" he continued, chuckling, as he lighted his cob pipe; "I can just see the last flap o' that boy-editor's shirt-tail as he legs it for the woods, while Rebecky settles down in his revolvin' cheer! I'm puzzled as to what kind of a job editin' is, exactly; but she'll find out, Rebecky will. An' she'll just edit for all she's worth!

> "'The thought that God has planned it so
> Should help us bear the years.'

Land, mother! that takes right hold, kind o' like the Gospel. How do you suppose she thought that out?"

"She couldn't have thought it out at her age," said Mrs. Cobb; "she must have just guessed it was that way. We know some things without bein' told, Jeremiah."

Rebecca took her scolding (which she richly deserved) like a soldier. There was considerable of it, and Miss Miranda remarked, among other things, that so absent-minded a child was sure to grow up into a drivelling idiot. She was bidden to stay away from Alice Robinson's birthday party, and doomed to wear her dress, stained and streaked as it was, until it was worn out. Aunt Jane six months later mitigated this martyrdom by making her a ruffled dimity pinafore, artfully shaped to conceal all the spots. She was blessedly ready with these mediations between the poor little sinner and the full consequences of her sin.

When Rebecca had heard her sentence and gone to the north chamber she began to think. If there was anything she did not wish to grow into, it was an idiot of any sort, particularly a drivelling one; and she resolved to punish herself every time she incurred what she considered to be the righteous displeasure of her virtuous relative. She didn't mind staying away from Alice Robinson's. She had told Emma Jane it would be like a picnic in a graveyard, the Robinson house being as near an approach to a tomb as a house can manage to be. Children were commonly brought in at the back-door, and requested to stand on newspapers while making their call, so that Alice was begged by her friends to "receive" in the shed or barn whenever possible. Mrs. Robinson was not only "turrible neat," but "turrible close," so that the refreshments were likely to be peppermint lozenges and glasses of well-water.

After considering the relative values, as penances, of a piece of hair-cloth worn next the skin, and a pebble in the shoe, she dismissed them both. The hair-cloth could not be found, and the pebble would attract the notice of the Argus-eyed aunt, besides being a foolish bar to the activity of a person who had to do housework and walk a mile and a half to school.

Her first experimental attempt at martyrdom had not been a distinguished success. She had stayed at home from the Sunday-school concert, a function of which, in ignorance of more alluring ones, she was extremely fond. As a result of her desertion, two infants who relied upon her to prompt them (she always knew everybody's recitations better than they did themselves) broke down ignominiously. The class to which she belonged had to read a difficult chapter of Scripture in rotation, and the various members spent an arduous Sabbath afternoon counting out verses according to their seats in the pew, and practising the ones that would inevitably fall to them. They were too ignorant to realize, when they were called upon, that Rebecca's absence would make everything come wrong, and the blow descended with crushing force when the Jebusites and Amorites, the Girgashites, Hivites, and Perizzites had to be pronounced by the persons of all others least capable of grappling with them.

Self-punishment, then, to be adequate and proper, must begin, like charity, at home, and, unlike charity, should end there too. Rebecca looked about the room vaguely as she sat by the window. She must give up something, and, truth to tell, she possessed little to give, hardly anything, but—yes, that would do, the beloved pink parasol. She could not hide it in the attic, for in some moment of weakness she would be sure to take it out again. She feared she had not the moral energy to break it into bits. Her eyes moved from the parasol to the apple-trees in the side-yard, and then fell to the well-kerb. That would do: she would fling her dearest possession into the depths of the water. Action followed quickly upon decision, as usual. She slipped down in the darkness, stole out the front-door, approached the place of sacrifice, lifted the cover of the well, gave one unresigned shudder, and flung the parasol downward with all her force. At the crucial instant of renunciation she was greatly helped by the reflection that she closely resembled the heathen mothers who cast their babes to the crocodiles in the Ganges.

She slept well and arose refreshed, as a consecrated spirit always should and sometimes does. But there was great difficulty in drawing water after breakfast. Rebecca, chastened and uplifted, had gone to school. Abijah Flagg was summoned, lifted the well-cover, explored, found the inciting cause of trouble, and with considerable difficulty succeeded in removing it. The fact was that the ivory hook of the parasol had caught in the chain gear, and when the first attempt at drawing water was made, the little offering of a contrite heart was jerked up, bent, its strong ribs jammed into the well side, and entangled with a twig root. It is needless to say that no sleight-of-hand performer, however expert, unless aided by the powers of darkness, could have accomplished this feat; but a luckless child in pursuit of virtue had done it with a turn of the wrist.

We will draw a veil over the scene that occurred after Rebecca's return from school. You who read may be well advanced in years, you may be gifted in rhetoric, ingenious in argument; but even you might quail at the thought of explaining the tortuous mental processes that led you into throwing your beloved pink parasol into Miranda Sawyer's well. Perhaps you feel equal to discussing the efficacy of spiritual self-chastisement with a person who closes her lips into a thin line and looks at you out of blank, uncomprehending eyes. Common sense, right, and logic were all arrayed on Miranda's side. When poor Rebecca, driven to the wall, had to avow the reasons lying behind the sacrifice of the sunshade, her aunt said, "Now, see here, Rebecca: you're too big to be whipped, and I shall never whip you; but when you think you ain't punished enough just tell me, and I'll make out to invent a little something more. I ain't so smart as some folks, but I can do that much; and whatever it is, it'll be something that won't punish the whole family, and make 'em drink ivory dust, wood chips, and pink silk rags with their water."

XIII

SNOW-WHITE; ROSE-RED

JUST before Thanksgiving the affairs of the Simpsons reached what might have been called a crisis even in their family, which had been born and reared in a state of adventurous poverty and perilous uncertainty.

Riverboro was doing its best to return the entire tribe of Simpsons to the land of its fathers, so to speak, thinking rightly that the town which had given

H

them birth, rather than the town of their adoption, should feed them, and keep a roof over their heads until the children were of an age for self-support. There was little to eat in the household and less to wear, though Mrs. Simpson did, as always, her poor best. The children managed to satisfy their appetites by sitting modestly outside their neighbours' kitchen-doors when meals were about to be served. They were not exactly popular favourites, but they did receive certain undesirable morsels from the more charitable housewives.

Life was rather dull and dreary, however; and in the chill and gloom of November weather, with the vision of other people's turkeys bursting with fat, and other people's golden pumpkins and squashes and corn being garnered into barns, the young Simpsons groped about for some inexpensive form of excitement, and settled upon the selling of soap for a premium. They had sold enough to their immediate neighbours during the earlier autumn to secure a child's handcart, which, though very weak on its pins, could be trundled over the country roads. With large business sagacity, and an executive capacity which must have been inherited from their father, they now proposed to extend their operations to a larger area, and distribute soap to contiguous villages, if these villages could be induced to buy. The Excelsior Soap Company paid a very small return of any kind to its infantile agents, who were scattered through the State, but it inflamed their imaginations by the issue of circulars with highly-coloured pictures of the premiums to be awarded for the sale of a certain number of cakes. It was at this juncture that Clara

Belle and Susan Simpson consulted Rebecca, who
threw herself solidly and wholeheartedly into the
enterprise, promising her help and that of Emma
Jane Perkins. The premiums within their possible
grasp were three—a bookcase, a plush reclining chair,
and a banquet lamp. Of course, the Simpsons had no
books, and casting aside without thought or pang the
plush chair, which might have been of some use in a
family of seven persons (not counting Mr. Simpson,
who ordinarily sat elsewhere at the town's expense),
they warmed themselves rapturously in the vision of
the banquet lamp, which speedily became to them
more desirable than food, drink, or clothing. Neither
Emma Jane nor Rebecca perceived anything incon-
gruous in the idea of the Simpsons striving for a
banquet lamp. They looked at the picture daily, and
knew that if they themselves were free agents, they
would toil, suffer, ay, sweat, for the happy privilege
of occupying the same room with that lamp through
the coming winter evenings. It looked to be about
eight feet tall in the catalogue, and Emma Jane
advised Clara Belle to measure the height of the
Simpson ceilings; but a note in the margin of the
circular informed them that it stood two and a half
feet high when set up in all its dignity and splendour
on a proper table, three dollars extra. It was only of
polished brass, continued the circular, though it was
invariably mistaken for solid gold; and the shade that
accompanied it (at least, it accompanied it if the agent
sold a hundred extra cakes) was of crinkled crêpe
paper, printed in a dozen delicious hues, from which
the joy-dazzled agent might take his choice.

Seesaw Simpson was not in the syndicate. Clara

Belle was rather a successful agent, but Susan, who could only say "thoap," never made large returns; and the twins, who were somewhat young to be thoroughly trustworthy, could be given only a half-dozen cakes at a time, and were obliged to carry with them on their business trips a brief document stating the price per cake, dozen, and box. Rebecca and Emma Jane offered to go two or three miles in some one direction, and see what they could do in the way of stirring up a popular demand for the Snow-White and Rose-Red brands, the former being devoted to laundry purposes, and the latter being intended for the toilet.

There was a great amount of hilarity in the preparation for this event, and a long council in Emma Jane's attic. They had the soap company's circular from which to arrange a proper speech, and they had, what was still better, the remembrance of a certain patent-medicine vendor's discourse at the Milltown Fair. His method, when once observed, could never be forgotten; nor his manner, nor his vocabulary. Emma Jane practised it on Rebecca, and Rebecca on Emma Jane.

"Can I sell you a little soap this afternoon? It is called the Snow-White and Rose-Red Soap—six cakes in an ornamental box; only twenty cents for the white, twenty-five cents for the red. It is made from the purest ingredients, and if desired could be eaten by an invalid with relish and profit."

"Oh, Rebecca, don't let's say that!" interposed Emma Jane hysterically. "It makes me feel like a fool."

"It takes so little to make you feel like a fool,

Emma Jane," rebuked Rebecca, "that sometimes I think that you must *be* one. I don't get to feeling like a fool so awfully easy; now leave out that eating part if you don't like it, and go on."

"The Snow-White is probably the most remarkable laundry soap ever manufactured. Immerse the garments in a tub, lightly rubbing the more soiled portions with the soap; leave them submerged in water from sunset to sunrise, and then the youngest baby can wash them without the slightest effort."

"*Babe*, not baby," corrected Rebecca from the circular.

"It's just the same thing," argued Emma Jane.

"Of course it's just the same *thing;* but a baby has got to be called babe or infant in a circular, the same as it is in poetry! Would you rather say infant?"

"No," grumbled Emma Jane; "infant is worse even than babe. Rebecca, do you think we'd better do as the circular says, and let Elijah or Elisha try the soap before we begin selling?"

"I can't imagine a babe doing a family wash with *any* soap," answered Rebecca; "but it must be true or they would never dare to print it, so don't let's bother. Oh, won't it be the greatest fun, Emma Jane? At some of the houses, where they can't possibly know me, I shan't be frightened, and I shall reel off the whole rigmarole, invalid, babe, and all. Perhaps I shall say even the last sentence, if I can remember it: 'We sound every chord in the great mac-ro-cosm of satisfaction.'"

This conversation took place on a Friday afternoon at Emma Jane's house, where Rebecca, to her unbounded joy was to stay over Sunday, her aunts having gone to Portland to the funeral of an old friend. Saturday being a holiday, they were going to have the old white horse, drive to North Riverboro three miles away, eat a twelve o'clock dinner with Emma Jane's cousins, and be back at four o'clock punctually.

When the children asked Mrs. Perkins if they could call at just a few houses coming and going, and sell a little soap for the Simpsons, she at first replied decidedly in the negative. She was an indulgent parent, however, and really had little objection to Emma Jane amusing herself in this unusual way; it was only for Rebecca, as the niece of the difficult Miranda Sawyer, that she raised scruples; but when fully persuaded that the enterprise was a charitable one she acquiesced.

The girls called at Mr. Watson's store, and arranged for several large boxes of soap to be charged to Clara Belle Simpson's account. These were lifted into the back of the waggon, and a happier couple never drove along the country road than Rebecca and her companion. It was a glorious Indian summer day, which suggested nothing of Thanksgiving, near at hand as it was. It was a rustly day, a scarlet and buff, yellow and carmine, bronze and crimson day. There were still many leaves on the oaks and maples, making a goodly show of red and brown and gold. The air was like sparkling cider, and every field had its heaps of yellow and russet good things to eat, all ready for the barns, the mills, and the markets. The horse forgot his twenty years, sniffed the sweet bright air, and trotted like a colt; Nokomis Mountain looked blue and clear in the distance; Rebecca stood in the waggon, and apostrophized the landscape with sudden joy of living:

> " Great, wide, beautiful, wonderful World,
> With the wonderful water round you curled,
> And the wonderful grass upon your breast :
> World, you are beautifully drest!"

Dull Emma Jane had never seemed to Rebecca so near, so dear, so tried and true; and Rebecca, to Emma Jane's faithful heart, had never been so brilliant, so bewildering, so fascinating, as in this visit together, with its intimacy, its freedom, and the added delights of an exciting business enterprise.

A gorgeous leaf blew into the waggon.

" Does colour make you sort of dizzy?" asked Rebecca.

" No," answered Emma Jane after a long pause— " no, it don't; not a mite."

" Perhaps dizzy isn't just the right word, but it's nearest. I'd like to eat colour, and drink it, and sleep in it. If you could be a tree, which one would you choose?"

Emma Jane had enjoyed considerable experience of this kind, and Rebecca had succeeded in unstopping her ears, ungluing her eyes, and loosening her tongue, so that she could " play the game " after a fashion.

" I'd rather be an apple-tree in blossom—that one that blooms pink by our pig-pen."

Rebecca laughed. There was always something unexpected in Emma Jane's replies. " I'd choose to be that scarlet maple just on the edge of the pond there "—and she pointed with the whip. "Then I could see so much more than your pink apple-tree by the pig-pen. I could look at all the rest of the woods, see my scarlet dress in my beautiful looking-glass, and watch all the yellow and brown trees growing upside down in the water. When I'm old enough to earn money, I'm going to have a dress like this leaf, all ruby colour—thin, you know, with a sweeping train and ruffly, curly edges; then I think I'll have a brown sash like the trunk of the tree, and where could I be green? Do they have green petticoats, I wonder? I'd like a green petticoat coming out now and then underneath to show what my leaves were like before I was a scarlet maple."

"I think it would be awful homely," said Emma Jane. "I'm going to have a white satin with a pink sash, pink stockings, bronze slippers, and a spangled fan."

XIV

MR. ALADDIN

A SINGLE hour's experience of the vicissitudes incident to a business career clouded the children's spirits just the least bit. They did not accompany each other to the doors of their chosen victims, feeling sure that together they could not approach the subject seriously; but they parted at the gate of each house, the one holding the horse while the other took the soap samples, and interviewed anyone who seemed of a coming-on disposition. Emma Jane had disposed of three single cakes, Rebecca of three small boxes. For a difference in their ability to persuade the public was clearly defined at the start, though neither of them ascribed either success or defeat to anything but the imperious force of circumstances. Housewives looked at Emma Jane and desired no soap; listened to her description of its merits, and still desired none. Other stars in their courses governed Rebecca's doings. The people whom she interviewed either remembered their present need of soap, or reminded themselves that they would need it in the future; the notable point in the case being that lucky Rebecca accomplished, with almost no effort, results that poor little Emma Jane failed to attain by hard and conscientious labour.

"It's your turn, Rebecca, and I'm glad, too," said Emma Jane, drawing up to a gateway and indicating a house that was set a considerable distance from the road. "I haven't got over trembling from the last place yet." (A lady had put her head out of an upstairs window and called: "Go away, little girl. Whatever you have in your box, we don't want any.") "I don't know who lives here, and the blinds are all shut in front. If there's nobody at home you mustn't count it, but take the next house as yours."

Rebecca walked up the lane and went to the side-door. There was a porch there, and seated in a rocking-chair husking corn was a good-looking young man—or was he middle-aged? Rebecca could not make up her mind. At all events, he had an air of the city about him—well-shaven face, well-trimmed moustache, well-fitting clothes. Rebecca was a trifle shy at this unexpected encounter, but there was nothing to be done but explain her presence, so she asked: "Is the lady of the house at home?"

"I am the lady of the house at present," said the stranger, with a whimsical smile. "What can I do for you?"

"Have you ever heard of the—would you like, or I mean—do you need any soap?" queried Rebecca.

"Do I look as if I did?" he responded unexpectedly.

Rebecca dimpled. "I didn't mean *that*. I have some soap to sell; I mean, I would like to introduce to you a very remarkable soap, the best now on the market. It is called the——"

"Oh, I must know that soap," said the gentleman genially. "Made out of pure vegetable fats, isn't it?"

"The very purest," corroborated Rebecca.

"No acid in it?"

"Not a trace."

"And yet a child could do the Monday washing with it and use no force?"

"A babe," corrected Rebecca.

"Oh, a babe, eh? That child grows younger every year, instead of older—wise child!"

This was great good fortune, to find a customer who knew all the virtues of the article in advance. Rebecca dimpled more and more, and at her new friend's invitation sat down on a stool at his side near the edge of the porch. The beauties of the ornamental box which held the Rose-Red were disclosed, and the prices of both that and the Snow-White were unfolded. Presently she forgot all about her silent partner at the gate, and was talking as if she had known this grand personage all her life.

"I'm keeping house to-day, but I don't live here," explained the delightful gentleman. "I'm just on a visit to my aunt, who has gone to Portland. I used to be here as a boy, and I am very fond of the spot."

"I don't think anything takes the place of the farm where one lived when one was a child," observed Rebecca, nearly bursting with pride at having at last successfully used the indefinite pronoun in general conversation.

The man darted a look at her, and put down his ear of corn. "So you consider your childhood a thing of the past, do you, young lady?"

"I can still remember it," answered Rebecca gravely, "though it seems a long time ago."

"I can remember mine well enough, and a particularly unpleasant one it was," said the stranger.

"So was mine," sighed Rebecca. "What was your worst trouble?"

"Lack of food and clothes principally."

"Oh!" exclaimed Rebecca sympathetically, "mine was no shoes, and too many babies, and not enough books. But you're all right and happy now, aren't you?" she asked doubtfully, for, though he looked handsome, well-fed, and prosperous, any child could see that his eyes were tired and his mouth was sad when he was not speaking.

"I'm doing pretty well, thank you," said the man, with a delightful smile. "Now tell me, how much soap ought I to buy to-day?"

"How much has your aunt on hand now?" suggested the very modest and inexperienced agent. "And how much would she need?"

"Oh, I don't know about that. Soap keeps, doesn't it?"

"I'm not certain," said Rebecca conscientiously; "but I'll look in the circular—it's sure to tell;" and she drew the document from her pocket.

"What are you going to do with the magnificent profits you get from this business?"

"We are not selling for our own benefit," said Rebecca confidentially. "My friend, who is holding the horse at the gate, is the daughter of a very rich blacksmith, and doesn't need any money. I am poor, but I live with my aunts in a brick house, and, of course, they wouldn't like me to be a pedlar. We are trying to get a premium for some friends of ours."

Rebecca had never thought of alluding to the circumstances with her previous customers, but unexpectedly she found herself describing Mr. Simpson, Mrs. Simpson, and the Simpson family, their poverty, their joyless life, and their abject need of a banquet lamp to brighten their existence.

"You needn't argue that point," laughed the man, as he stood up to get a glimpse of the "rich blacksmith's daughter" at the gate. "I can see that they ought to have it if they want it, and especially if you want them to have it. I've known what it was myself to do without a banquet lamp. Now give me the circular, and let's do some figuring. How much do the Simpsons lack at this moment?"

"If they sell two hundred more cakes this month and next they can have the lamp by Christmas," Rebecca answered; "and they can get a shade by summer-time. But I'm afraid I can't help very much after to-day, because my Aunt Miranda may not like to have me."

"I see. Well, that's all right. I'll take three hundred cakes, and that will give them shade and all."

Rebecca had been seated on a stool very near to the edge of the porch, and at this remark she made a sudden movement, tipped over, and disappeared into a clump of lilac bushes. It was a very short distance, fortunately, and the amused capitalist picked her up, set her on her feet, and brushed her off. "You should never seem surprised when you have taken a large order," said he; "you ought to have replied, 'Can't you make it three hundred and fifty?' instead of capsizing in that unbusinesslike way."

"Oh, I could never say anything like that!" exclaimed Rebecca, who was blushing crimson at her awkward fall. "But it doesn't seem right for you to buy so much. Are you sure you can afford it?"

"If I can't, I'll save on something else," returned the jocose philanthropist.

"What if your aunt shouldn't like the kind of soap?" queried Rebecca nervously.

"My aunt always likes what I like," he returned.

"Mine doesn't," exclaimed Rebecca.

"Then there's something wrong with your aunt."

"Or with me," laughed Rebecca.

"What is your name, young lady?"

"Rebecca Rowena Randall, sir."

"What?"—with an amused smile. "*Both?* Your mother was generous."

"She couldn't bear to give up either of the names, she says."

"Do you want to hear my name?"

"I think I know already," answered Rebecca, with a bright glance. "I'm sure you must be Mr. Aladdin in the 'Arabian Nights.' Oh, please, can I run down and tell Emma Jane? She must be so tired waiting, and she will be so glad."

At the man's nod of assent Rebecca sped down the lane, crying irrepressibly as she neared the waggon: "Oh, Emma Jane! Emma Jane! we are sold out!"

Mr. Aladdin followed smilingly to corroborate this astonishing, unbelievable statement, lifted all their boxes from the back of the waggon, and, taking the circular, promised to write to the Excelsior Company that night concerning the premium.

"If you could contrive to keep a secret—you two little girls—it would be rather a nice surprise to have the lamp arrive at the Simpsons' on Thanksgiving Day, wouldn't it?" he asked, as he tucked the old lap-robe cosily over their feet.

They gladly assented, and broke into a chorus of excited thanks, during which tears of joy stood in Rebecca's eyes.

"Oh, don't mention it!" laughed Mr. Aladdin, lifting his hat. "I was a sort of commercial traveller myself once—years ago—and I like to see the thing well done. Good-bye, Miss Rebecca Rowena! Just let me know whenever you have anything to sell, for I'm certain beforehand I shall want it."

"Good-bye, Mr. Aladdin; I surely will!" cried Rebecca, tossing back her dark braids delightedly and waving her hand.

"Oh, Rebecca!" said Emma Jane in an awe-struck

whisper. "He raised his hat to us, and we not thirteen! It'll be five years before we're ladies."

"Never mind," answered Rebecca; "we are the *beginnings* of ladies, even now."

"He tucked the lap-robe round us, too," continued Emma Jane in an ecstasy of reminiscence. "Oh! isn't he perfectly elergant? And wasn't it lovely of him to buy us out? And just think of having both the lamp and the shade for one day's work! Aren't you glad you wore your pink gingham now, even if mother did make you put on flannel underneath? You do look so pretty in pink and red, Rebecca, and so homely in drab and brown!"

"I know it," sighed Rebecca. "I wish I was like you—pretty in all colours!" and Rebecca looked longingly at Emma Jane's fat, rosy cheeks; at her blue eyes, which said nothing; at her neat nose, which had no character; at her red lips, from between which no word worth listening to had ever issued.

"Never mind," said Emma Jane comfortingly. "Everybody says you're awful bright and smart, and mother thinks you'll be better looking all the time as you grow older. You wouldn't believe it, but I was a dreadful homely baby, and homely right along till just a year or two ago, when my red hair began to grow dark. What was the nice man's name?"

"I never thought to ask!" ejaculated Rebecca. "Aunt Miranda would say that was just like me, and it is. But I called him Mr. Aladdin because he gave us a lamp. You know the story of Aladdin and the wonderful lamp?"

"Oh, Rebecca! how could you call him a nick-name the very first time you ever saw him?"

"Aladdin isn't a nickname exactly; anyway, he laughed and seemed to like it."

By dint of superhuman effort, and putting such a seal upon their lips as never mortals put before, the two girls succeeded in keeping their wonderful news to themselves, although it was obvious to all beholders that they were in an extraordinary and abnormal state of mind.

On Thanksgiving Day the lamp arrived in a large packing-box, and was taken out and set up by Seesaw Simpson, who suddenly began to admire and respect the business ability of his sisters. Rebecca had heard the news of its arrival, but waited until nearly dark before asking permission to go to the Simpsons', so that she might see the gorgeous trophy lighted and sending a blaze of crimson glory through its red crêpe paper shade.

XV

THE BANQUET LAMP

THERE had been company at the brick house to the bountiful Thanksgiving dinner which had been provided at one o'clock—the Burnham sisters, who lived between North Riverboro and Shaker Village, and who for more than a quarter of a century had come to pass the holiday with the Sawyers every year. Rebecca sat silent with a book after the dinner dishes were washed, and when it was nearly five asked if she might go to the Simpsons'.

"What do you want to run after those Simpson children for on a Thanksgiving Day?" queried Miss Miranda. "Can't you set still for once and listen to the improvin' conversation of your elders? You never can let well enough alone, but want to be for ever on the move."

"The Simpsons have a new lamp, and Emma Jane and I promised to go up and see it lighted, and make it a kind of a party."

"What under the canopy did they want of a lamp, and where did they get the money to pay for it? If Abner was at home, I should think he'd been swappin' again," said Miss Miranda.

"The children got it as a prize for selling soap," replied Rebecca; "they've been working for a year, and you know I told you that Emma Jane and I helped them the Saturday afternoon you were in Portland."

"I didn't take notice, I s'pose, for it's the first time I ever heard the lamp mentioned. Well, you can go for an hour, and no more. Remember, it's as dark at six as it is at midnight. Would you like to take along some Baldwin apples? What have you got in the pocket of that new dress that makes it sag down so?"

"It's my nuts and raisins from dinner," replied Rebecca, who never succeeded in keeping the most innocent action a secret from her Aunt Miranda. "They're just what you gave me on my plate."

"Why didn't you eat them?"

"Because I'd had enough dinner, and I thought if I saved these it would make the Simpsons' party

I

better," stammered Rebecca, who hated to be scolded and examined before company.

"They were your own, Rebecca," interposed Aunt Jane; "and if you chose to save them to give away, it's all right. We ought never to let this day pass without giving our neighbours something to be thankful for, instead of taking all the time to think of our own mercies."

The Burnham sisters nodded approvingly as Rebecca went out, and remarked that they had never seen a child grow and improve so fast in so short a time.

"There's plenty of room left for more improvement, as you'd know if she lived in the same house with you," answered Miranda. "She's into every namable thing in the neighbourhood, an' not only into it, but generally at the head an' front of it, especially when it's mischief. Of all the foolishness I ever heard of, that lamp beats everything; it's just like those Simpsons, but I didn't suppose the children had brains enough to sell anything."

"One of them must have," said Miss Ellen Burnham, "for the girl that was selling soap at the Ladds' in North Riverboro was described by Adam Ladd as the most remarkable and winning child he ever saw."

"It must have been Clara Belle, and I should never call her remarkable," answered Miss Miranda. "Has Adam been home again?"

"Yes; he's been staying a few days with his aunt. There's no limit to the money he's making, they say; and he always brings presents for all the neighbours. This time it was a full set of furs for

Mrs. Ladd; and to think we can remember the time he was a barefoot boy without two shirts to his back! It is strange he hasn't married, with all his money, and him so fond of children that he always has a pack of them at his heels."

"There's hope for him still, though," said Miss Jane smilingly; "for I don't s'pose he's more than thirty."

"He could get a wife in Riverboro if he was a hundred and thirty," remarked Miss Miranda.

"Adam's aunt says he was so taken with the little girl that sold the soap—Clara Belle, did you say her name was?—that he declared he was going to bring her a Christmas present," continued Miss Ellen.

"Well, there's no accountin' for tastes," exclaimed Miss Miranda. "Clara Belle's got cross-eyes and red hair, but I'd be the last one to grudge her a Christmas present; the more Adam Ladd gives to her the less the town 'll have to."

"Isn't there another Simpson girl?" asked Miss Lydia Burnham. "For this one couldn't have been cross-eyed; I remember Mrs. Ladd saying Adam remarked about this child's handsome eyes. He said it was her eyes that made him buy the three hundred cakes. Mrs. Ladd has it stacked up in the shed chamber."

"Three hundred cakes!" ejaculated Miranda. "Well, there's one crop that never fails in River-boro!"

"What's that?" asked Miss Lydia politely.

"The fool crop!" responded Miranda tersely, and changed the subject, much to Jane's gratitude, for she had been nervous and ill at ease for the last fifteen minutes. What child in Riverboro could be described as remarkable and winning, save Rebecca? What child had wonderful eyes, except the same Rebecca? And, finally, was there ever a child in the world who could make a man buy soap by the hundred cakes, save Rebecca?

Meantime the "remarkable" child had flown up the road in the deepening dusk, but she had not gone far before she heard the sound of hurrying footsteps, and saw a well-known figure coming in her direction. In a moment she and Emma Jane met and exchanged a breathless embrace.

"Something awful has happened!" panted Emma Jane.

"Don't tell me it's broken!" exclaimed Rebecca.

"No, oh no, not that! It was packed in straw, and every piece came out all right. And I was there, and I never said a single thing about your selling the three hundred cakes that got the lamp, so that we could be together when you told."

"*Our* selling the three hundred cakes," corrected Rebecca. "You did as much as I."

"No, I didn't, Rebecca Randall. I just sat at the gate and held the horse."

"Yes, but *whose* horse was it that took us to North Riverboro? And besides, it just happened to be my turn. If you had gone in and found Mr. Aladdin, you would have had the wonderful lamp given to you. But what's the trouble?"

"The Simpsons have no kerosene and no wicks. I guess they thought a banquet lamp was something that lighted itself, and burned without any help. See-saw has gone to the doctor's to try if he can borrow a wick, and mother let me have a pint of oil; but she says she won't give me any more. We never thought of the expense of keeping up the lamp, Rebecca."

"No, we didn't; but let's not worry about that till after the party. I have a handful of nuts and raisins and some apples."

"I have peppermints and maple sugar," said Emma Jane. "They had a real Thanksgiving dinner: the doctor gave them sweet potatoes and cranberries and turnips; father sent a spare-rib, and Mrs. Cobb a chicken and a jar of mince-meat."

At half-past five one might have looked in at the Simpsons' windows and seen the party at its height. Mrs. Simpson had let the kitchen fire die out, and had brought the baby to grace the festal scene. The lamp seemed to be having the party and receiving the guests. The children had taken the one small table in the house, and it was placed in the far corner of the room to serve as a pedestal. On it stood the sacred, the adored, the long-desired object, almost as beautiful and nearly half as large as the advertisement. The brass glistened like gold, and the crimson paper shade glowed like a giant ruby. In the wide splash of light that it flung upon the floor sat the Simpsons in reverent and solemn silence, Emma Jane standing behind them hand in hand with Rebecca. There seemed to be no desire for conversation; the occasion was too thrilling and serious for that. The lamp, it was tacitly felt by everybody, was dignifying the party, and providing sufficient entertainment simply by its presence, being fully as satisfactory in its way as a pianola or a string band.

"I wish father could see it," said Clara Belle loyally.

"If he onth thaw it he'd want to thwap it," murmured Susan sagaciously.

At the appointed hour Rebecca dragged herself reluctantly away from the enchanting scene.

"I'll turn the lamp out the minute I think you and Emma Jane are home," said Clara Belle. "And oh, I'm so glad you both live where you can see it shine from our windows! I wonder how long it will burn without bein' filled if I only keep it lit one hour every night."

"You needn't put it out for want o' karosene," said Seesaw, coming in from the shed, "for there's a great kag of it settin' out there. Mr. Tubbs brought it over from North Riverboro, and said somebody sent an order by mail for it."

Rebecca squeezed Emma Jane's arm, and Emma Jane gave a rapturous return squeeze. "It was Mr. Aladdin," whispered Rebecca, as they ran down the path to the gate. Seesaw followed them, and handsomely offered to see them "a piece" down the road; but Rebecca declined his escort with such decision that he did not press the matter, and went to bed to dream of her instead. In his dreams flashes of lightning proceeded from both her eyes, and she held a flaming sword in either hand.

Rebecca entered the home dining-room joyously. The Burnham sisters had gone, and the two aunts were knitting.

"It was a heavenly party!" she cried, taking off her hat and cape.

"Go back and see if you have shut the door tight, and then lock it," said Miss Miranda in her usual austere manner.

"It was a heavenly party!" reiterated Rebecca, coming in again, much too excited to be easily crushed. "And oh, Aunt Jane, Aunt Miranda, if you'll only come into the kitchen and look out of the sink window you can see the banquet lamp shining all red, just as if the Simpsons' house was on fire."

"And probably it will be before long," observed Miranda. "I've got no patience with such foolish goin's-on."

Jane accompanied Rebecca into the kitchen. Although the feeble glimmer which she was able to see from that distance did not seem to her a dazzling exhibition, she tried to be as enthusiastic as possible.

"Rebecca, who was it that sold the three hundred cakes of soap to Mr. Ladd in North Riverboro?"

"Mr. *who?*" exclaimed Rebecca.

"Mr. Ladd, in North Riverboro."

"Is that his real name?" queried Rebecca in astonishment. "I didn't make a bad guess;" and she laughed softly to herself.

"I asked you who sold the soap to Adam Ladd?" resumed Miss Jane.

"Adam Ladd! Then he's A. Ladd, too. What fun!"

"Answer me, Rebecca!"

"Oh, excuse me, Aunt Jane; I was so busy thinking. Emma Jane and I sold the soap to Mr. Ladd."

"Did you tease him or make him buy it?"

"Now, Aunt Jane, how could I make a big grown-up man buy anything if he didn't want to? He needed the soap dreadfully as a present for his aunt."

Miss Jane still looked a little unconvinced, though she only said: "I hope your Aunt Miranda won't mind; but you know how particular she is, Rebecca, and I really wish you wouldn't do anything out of the ordinary without asking her first, for your actions are very queer."

"There can't be anything wrong this time," Rebecca answered confidently. "Emma Jane sold her cakes to her own relations and to Uncle Jerry Cobb, and I went first to those new tenements near the lumber-mill, and then to the Ladds'. Mr. Ladd bought all we had, and made us promise to keep the secret until the premium came; and I've been going about ever since as if the banquet lamp was inside of me all lighted up and burning for everybody to see."

Rebecca's hair was loosened and falling over her forehead in ruffled waves; her eyes were brilliant, her cheeks crimson; there was a hint of everything in the girl's face—of sensitiveness and delicacy as well as of ardour; there was the sweetness of the mayflower and the strength of the young oak, but one could easily divine that she was one of

> "The soul's by nature pitched too high,
> By suffering plunged too low."

"That's just the way you look, for all the world as if you did have a lamp burning inside of you," sighed Aunt Jane. "Rebecca! Rebecca! I wish you could take things easier, child; I am fearful for you sometimes."

XVI

SEASONS OF GROWTH

THE days flew by; as summer had melted into autumn, so autumn had given place to winter. Life in the brick house had gone on more placidly of late, for Rebecca was honestly trying to be more careful in the performance of her tasks and duties, as well as more quiet in her plays, and she was slowly learning the power of the soft answer in turning away wrath.

Miranda had not, perhaps, quite as many opportunities in which to lose her temper, but it is only just to say that she had not fully availed herself of all that had offered themselves.

There had been one outburst of righteous wrath occasioned by Rebecca's overhospitable habits, which were later shown in a still more dramatic and unexpected fashion.

On a certain Friday afternoon she asked her Aunt Miranda if she might take half her bread and milk upstairs to a friend.

"What friend have you got up there, for pity's sake?" demanded Aunt Miranda.

"The Simpson baby, come to stay over Sunday—that is, if you're willing; Mrs. Simpson says she is. Shall I bring her down and show her? She's dressed in an old dress of Emma Jane's, and she looks sweet."

"You can bring her down, but you can't show her to me! You can smuggle her out the way you smuggled her in, and take her back to her mother. Where on earth do you get your notions, borrowing a baby for Sunday?"

"You're so used to a house without a baby, you don't know how dull it is," sighed Rebecca resignedly, as she moved towards the door; "but at the farm there was always a nice fresh one to play with and cuddle. There were too many, but that's not half as bad as none at all. Well, I'll take her back. She'll be dreadfully disappointed, and so will Mrs. Simpson. She was planning to go to Milltown."

"She can un-plan then," observed Miss Miranda.

"Perhaps I can go up there and take care of the baby?" suggested Rebecca. "I brought her home so 't I could do my Saturday work just the same."

"You've got enough to do right here, without any borrowed babies to make more steps. Now, no answering back; just give the child some supper, and carry it home where it belongs."

"You don't want me to go down the front way; hadn't I better just come through this room and let you look at her? She has yellow hair and big blue eyes! Mrs. Simpson says she takes after her father."

Miss Miranda smiled acidly as she said she couldn't take after her father, for he'd take anything there was before she got there!

Aunt Jane was in the linen-chest upstairs sorting out the clean sheets and pillow-cases for Saturday, and Rebecca sought comfort from her.

"I brought the Simpson baby home, Aunt Jane, thinking it would help us over a dull Sunday, but Aunt Miranda won't let her stay. Emma Jane has the promise of her next Sunday, and Alice Robinson the next. Mrs. Simpson wanted I should have her first because I've had so much experience in babies. Come in and look at her sitting up in my bed, Aunt

Jane! Isn't she lovely! She's the fat, gurgly kind, not thin and fussy like some babies, and I thought I was going to have her to undress and dress twice each day. Oh dear! I wish I could have a printed book with everything set down in it that I *could* do, and then I wouldn't get disappointed so often."

"No book could be printed that would fit you, Rebecca," answered Aunt Jane, "for nobody could imagine beforehand the things you'd want to do. Are you going to carry that heavy child home in your arms?"

"No, I'm going to drag her in the little soap-waggon. Come, baby! Take your thumb out of your mouth, and come to ride with Becky in your go-cart." She stretched out her strong young arms to the crowing baby, sat down in a chair with the child, turned her upside down unceremoniously, took from her waistband and scornfully flung away a crooked pin, walked with her (still in a highly reversed position) to the bureau, selected a large safety-pin, and proceeded to attach her brief red flannel petticoat to a sort of shirt that she wore. Whether flat on her stomach, or head down, heels in the air, the Simpson baby knew she was in the hands of an expert, and continued gurgling placidly, while Aunt Jane regarded the pantomime with a kind of dazed awe.

"Bless my soul, Rebecca!" she ejaculated; "it beats all how handy you are with babies!"

"I ought to be; I've brought up three and a half of 'em," Rebecca responded cheerfully, pulling up the infant Simpson's stockings.

"I should think you'd be fonder of dolls than you are," said Jane.

"I do like them, but there's never any change in a doll; it's always the same everlasting old doll, and you have to make believe it's cross or sick, or it loves you, or can't bear you. Babies are more trouble, but nicer."

Miss Jane stretched out a thin hand with a slender, worn band of gold on the finger, and the baby curled her dimpled fingers round it and held it fast.

"You wear a ring on your engagement finger, don't you, Aunt Jane? Did you ever think about getting married?"

"Yes, dear, long ago."

"What happened, Aunt Jane?"

"He died—just before."

"Oh!" And Rebecca's eyes grew misty.

"He was a soldier, and he died of a gunshot wound in a hospital down South."

"Oh, Aunt Jane!"—softly. "Away from you?"

"No, I was with him."

"Was he young?"

"Yes, young and brave and handsome, Rebecca; he was Mr. Carter's brother Tom."

"Oh! I'm so glad you were with him! Wasn't he glad, Aunt Jane?"

Jane looked back across the half-forgotten years, and the vision of Tom's gladness flashed upon her: his haggard smile, the tears in his tired eyes, his out-stretched arms, his weak voice saying, "Oh, Jenny! dear Jenny! I've wanted you so, Jenny!" It was too much! She had never breathed a word of it before to a human creature, for there was no one who would have understood. Now, in a shamefaced way, to hide her brimming eyes, she put her head down on the young shoulder beside her, saying, "It was hard, Rebecca!"

The Simpson baby had cuddled down sleepily in Rebecca's lap, leaning her head back and sucking her thumb contentedly. Rebecca put her cheek down until it touched her aunt's grey hair and softly patted her, as she said, "I'm sorry, Aunt Jane!"

The girl's eyes were soft and tender, and the heart within her stretched a little and grew—grew in sweetness and intuition and depth of feeling. It had looked into another heart, felt it beat, and heard it sigh; and that is how all hearts grow.

Episodes like these enlivened the quiet course of everyday existence, made more quiet by the departure of Dick Carter, Living Perkins, and Huldah Meserve for Wareham, and the small attendance at the winter school, from which the younger children of the place stayed away during the cold weather.

Life, however, could never be thoroughly dull or lacking in adventure to a child of Rebecca's temperament. Her nature was full of adaptability, fluidity, receptivity. She made friends everywhere she went, and snatched up acquaintances in every corner.

It was she who ran to the shed door to take the dish to the "meat-man" or "fish-man"; she who knew the family histories of the itinerant fruit vendors and tin pedlars; she who was asked to take supper or pass the night with children in neighbouring villages—children of whose parents her aunts had never so much as heard. As to the nature of these friendships, which seemed so many to the eye of the superficial observer, they were of various kinds, and while the girl pursued them with enthusiasm and ardour, they left her unsatisfied and heart-hungry; they were never intimacies such as are so readily made by shallow natures. She loved Emma Jane, but it was a friendship born of propinquity and circumstance, not of true affinity. It was her neighbour's amiability, constancy, and devotion that she loved, and although she rated these qualities at their true value, she was always searching beyond them for intellectual treasures —searching and never finding, for although Emma Jane had the advantage in years, she was still immature. Huldah Meserve had an instinctive love of fun which appealed to Rebecca; she also had a fascinating knowledge of the world, from having visited her married sisters in Milltown and Portland; but on the other hand there was a certain sharpness and lack of sympathy in Huldah which repelled rather than attracted. With Dick Carter she could at least talk intelligently about lessons. He was a very ambitious boy, full of plans for his future, which he discussed quite freely with Rebecca, but when she broached the subject of her future his interest sensibly lessened. Into the world of the ideal Emma Jane, Huldah and Dick alike never seemed to have peeped, and the consciousness of this was always a fixed gulf between them and Rebecca.

"Uncle Jerry" and "Aunt Sarah" Cobb were dear friends of quite another sort, a very satisfying and perhaps a somewhat dangerous one. A visit from Rebecca always sent them into a twitter of delight. Her merry conversation and quaint comments on life in general fairly dazzled the old couple, who hung on her lightest word as if it had been a prophet's utterance; and Rebecca, though she had had no previous experience, owned to herself a perilous pleasure in being dazzling, even to a couple of dear, humdrum old people like Mr. and Mrs. Cobb. Aunt Sarah flew to the pantry or cellar whenever Rebecca's slim little shape first appeared on the crest of the hill, and a jelly tart or a frosted cake was sure to be forthcoming. The sight of old Uncle Jerry's spare figure in its clean white shirt-sleeves, whatever the weather, always made Rebecca's heart warm when she saw him peer longingly from the kitchen window. Before the snow came many was the time he had to come out to sit on a pile of boards at the gate, to see if by any chance she was mounting the hill that led to their house. In the autumn Rebecca was often the old man's companion while he was digging potatoes or shelling beans, and now in the winter, when a younger man was driving the stage, she sometimes stayed with him while he did his evening milking. It is safe to say that he was the only creature in Riverboro who possessed Rebecca's entire confidence; the only being to whom she poured out her whole heart, with its wealth of hopes and dreams and vague ambitions. At the brick house she practised scales and exercises, but at the Cobbs' cabinet organ she sang like a bird, improvising simple accompaniments that seemed to her ignorant auditors nothing short of marvellous. Here she was happy, here she was loved, here she was drawn out of herself and admired and made much of. But, she thought, if there were somebody who not only loved, but understood; who spoke her language, comprehended her desires, and responded to her mysterious longings! Perhaps in the big world of Wareham there would be people who thought and dreamed and wondered as she did.

In reality Jane did not understand her niece very much better than Miranda. The difference between the sisters was, that while Jane was puzzled, she was also attracted, and when she was quite in the dark for an explanation of some quaint or unusual action she was sympathetic as to its possible motive, and believed the best. A greater change had come over Jane than over any other person in the brick house; but it had been wrought so secretly and concealed so religiously that it scarcely appeared to the ordinary observer. Life had now a motive utterly lacking before. Breakfast was not eaten in the kitchen, because it seemed worth while, now that there were three persons, to lay the cloth in the dining-room. It was also a more bountiful meal than of yore, when there was no child to consider. The morning was made cheerful by Rebecca's start for school, the packing of the luncheon-basket, the final word about umbrella, waterproof, or rubbers; the parting admonition and the unconscious waiting at the window for the last wave of the hand. She found herself taking pride in Rebecca's improved appearance, her rounder throat and cheeks, and her better colour. She was wont to mention the length of Rebecca's hair, and add a word as to its remarkable evenness and lustre, at times when Mrs. Perkins grew too diffuse about Emma Jane's complexion. She threw herself whole-heartedly on her niece's side when it became a question between a crimson or a brown linsey-woolsey dress, and went through a memorable struggle with her sister concerning the purchase of a red bird for

Rebecca's black felt hat. No one guessed the quiet pleasure that lay hidden in her heart when she watched the girl's dark head bent over her lessons at night, nor dreamed of her joy in certain quiet evenings when Miranda went to prayer-meeting; evenings when Rebecca would read aloud " Hiawatha," or " Barbara Frietchie," " The Bugle Song," or " The Brook." Her narrow, humdrum existence bloomed under the dews that fell from this fresh spirit; her dulness brightened under the kindling touch of the younger mind, took fire from the " vital spark of heavenly flame " that seemed always to radiate from Rebecca's presence.

Rebecca's idea of being a painter like her friend Miss Ross was gradually receding, owing to the apparently insuperable difficulties in securing any instruction. Her Aunt Miranda saw no wisdom in cultivating such a talent, and could not conceive that any money could ever be earned by its exercise. " Hand-painted pictures " were held in little esteem in Riverboro, where the cheerful chromo or the dignified steel engraving were respected and valued. There was a slight, a very slight hope, that Rebecca might be allowed a few music-lessons from Miss Morton, who played the church cabinet organ; but this depended entirely upon whether Mrs. Morton would decide to accept a hayrack in return for a year's instruction from her daughter. She had the matter under advisement; but a doubt as to whether or not she would sell or rent her hayfields kept her from coming to a conclusion. Music, in common with all other accomplishments, was viewed by Miss Miranda as a trivial, useless, and foolish amusement; but

K

she allowed Rebecca an hour a day for practice on the old piano, and a little extra time for lessons if Jane could secure them without payment of actual cash.

The news from Sunnybrook Farm was hopeful rather than otherwise. Cousin Ann's husband had died, and John, Rebecca's favourite brother, had gone to be the man of the house to the widowed cousin. He was to have good schooling in return for his care of the horse and cow and barn, and, what was still more dazzling, the use of the old doctor's medical library of two or three dozen volumes. John's whole heart was set on becoming a country doctor, with Rebecca to keep house for him, and the vision seemed now so true, so near, that he could almost imagine his horse ploughing through snowdrifts on errands of mercy, or, less dramatic, but none the less attractive, could see a physician's neat turnout trundling along the shady country roads, a medicine case between his, Dr. Randall's, feet, and Miss Rebecca Randall sitting in a black silk dress by his side.

Hannah now wore her hair in a coil and her dresses a trifle below her ankles, these concessions being due to her extreme height. Mark had broken his collarbone, but it was healing well. Little Mira was growing very pretty. There was even a rumour that the projected railroad from Temperance to Plumville might go near the Randall Farm, in which case land would rise in value from nothing-at-all an acre to something at least resembling a price. Mrs. Randall refused to consider any improvement in their financial condition as a possibility. Content to work from sunrise to sunset to gain a mere subsistence for her

children, she lived in their future, not in her own
present, as a mother is wont to do when her own lot
seems hard and cheerless.

XVII

GREY DAYS AND GOLD

WHEN Rebecca looked back upon the year or two
that followed the Simpsons' Thanksgiving party, she
could only see certain milestones rising in the quiet
pathway of the months.

The first milestone was Christmas Day. It was
a fresh, crystal morning, with icicles hanging like
dazzling pendants from the trees and a glaze of pale
blue on the surface of the snow. The Simpsons' red
barn stood out, a glowing mass of colour in the white
landscape. Rebecca had been busy for weeks before,
trying to make a present for each of the seven persons
at Sunnybrook Farm, a somewhat difficult proceeding
on an expenditure of fifty cents, hoarded by incredible
exertion. Success had been achieved, however, and
the precious packet had been sent by post two days
previous. Miss Sawyer had bought her niece a nice
grey squirrel muff and tippet, which was even more
unbecoming, if possible, than Rebecca's other articles
of wearing apparel; but Aunt Jane had made her the
loveliest dress of green cashmere, a soft, soft green like
that of a young leaf. It was very simply made, but
the colour delighted the eye. Then there was a beautiful "tatting" collar from her mother, some scarlet

mittens from Mrs. Cobb, and a handkerchief from
Emma Jane.

Rebecca herself had fashioned an elaborate tea-cosy
with a letter "M" in outline stitch, and a pretty
frilled pincushion marked with a "J," for her two
aunts, so that taken all together the day would have
been an unequivocal success had nothing else
happened; but something else did.

There was a knock at the door at breakfast-time,
and Rebecca, answering it, was asked by a boy if
Miss Rebecca Randall lived there. On being told
that she did, he handed her a parcel bearing her
name, a parcel which she took like one in a dream
and bore into the dining-room.

"It's a present; it must be," she said, looking at
it in a dazed sort of way; "but I can't think who it
could be from."

"A good way to find out would be to open it,"
remarked Miss Miranda.

The parcel being untied proved to have two
smaller packages within, and Rebecca opened with
trembling fingers the one addressed to her. Anybody's fingers would have trembled. There was a
case which, when the cover was lifted, disclosed a
long chain of delicate pink coral beads—a chain
ending in a cross made of coral rosebuds. A card
with "Merry Christmas from Mr. Aladdin" lay
under the cross.

"Of all things!" exclaimed the two old ladies,
rising in their seats. "Who sent it?"

"Mr. Ladd," said Rebecca under her breath.

"Adam Ladd! Well I never! Don't you remember Ellen Burnham said he was going to send

Rebecca a Christmas present? But I never supposed he'd think of it again," said Jane. "What's the other package?"

It proved to be a silver chain with a blue enamel locket on it, marked for Emma Jane. That added the last touch—to have him remember them both! There was a letter also, which ran:

"DEAR MISS REBECCA ROWENA,

"My idea of a Christmas present is something entirely unnecessary and useless. I have always noticed when I give this sort of thing that people love it, so I hope I have not chosen wrong for you and your friend. You must wear your chain this afternoon, please, and let me see it on your neck, for I am coming over in my new sleigh to take you both to drive. My aunt is delighted with the soap.

"Sincerely your friend,
"ADAM LADD."

"Well, well!" cried Miss Jane, "isn't that kind of him? He's very fond of children, Lyddy Burnham says. Now eat your breakfast, Rebecca, and after we've done the dishes you can run over to Emma's and give her her chain. What's the matter, child?"

Rebecca's emotions seemed always to be stored, as it were, in adjoining compartments, and to be continually getting mixed. At this moment, though her joy was too deep for words, her bread-and-butter almost choked her, and at intervals a tear stole furtively down her cheek.

Mr. Ladd called as he promised, and made the acquaintance of the aunts, understanding them both in five minutes as well as if he had known them for years. On a footstool near the open fire sat Rebecca silent and shy, so conscious of her fine apparel and the presence of Aunt Miranda that she could not utter a word. It was one of her "beauty days." Happiness, excitement, the colour of the green dress, and the touch of lovely pink in the coral necklace, had transformed the little brown wren for the time into a bird of plumage, and Adam Ladd watched her with evident satisfaction. Then there was the sleigh ride, during which she found her tongue, and chattered like any magpie; and so ended that glorious Christmas Day. And many and many a night thereafter did Rebecca go to sleep with the precious coral chain under her pillow, one hand always upon it to be certain that it was safe.

Another milestone was the departure of the Simpsons from Riverboro bag and baggage, the banquet lamp being their most conspicuous possession. It was delightful to be rid of Seesaw's hateful presence; but otherwise the loss of several playmates at one fell swoop made rather a gap in Riverboro's "younger set," and Rebecca was obliged to make friends with the Robinson baby, he being the only long-clothes child in the village that winter. The faithful Seesaw had called at the side-door of the brick house on the evening before his departure, and, when Rebecca answered his knock, stammered solemnly: "Can I k-keep comp'ny with you when you g-g-grow up?"

"Certainly *not*," replied Rebecca, closing the door somewhat too speedily upon her precocious swain.

Mr. Simpson had come home in time to move his

wife and children back to the town that had given them birth—a town by no means waiting with open arms to receive them. The Simpsons' moving was presided over by the village authorities, and somewhat anxiously watched by the entire neighbourhood; but, in spite of all precautions, a pulpit chair, several kerosene lamps, and a small stove disappeared from the church, and were successfully swapped in the course of Mr. Simpson's driving tour from the old home to the new. It gave Rebecca and Emma Jane some hours of sorrow to learn that a certain village in the wake of Abner Simpson's line of progress had acquired, through the medium of an ambitious young minister, a magnificent lamp for its new church parlours. No money changed hands in the operation, for the minister succeeded in getting the lamp in return for an old bicycle. The only pleasant feature of the whole affair was that Mr. Simpson, wholly unable to console his offspring for the loss of the beloved object, mounted the bicycle and rode away on it, not to be seen or heard of again for many a long day.

The year was notable also as being the one in which Rebecca shot up like a young tree. She had seemingly never grown an inch since she was ten years old, but, once started, she attended to growing precisely as she did other things—with such energy that Miss Jane did nothing for months but lengthen skirts, sleeves, and waists. In spite of all the arts known to a thrifty New England woman, the limit of letting down and piecing down was reached at last, and the dresses were sent to Sunnybrook Farm to be made over for Jenny.

There was another milestone—a sad one—marking a little grave under a willow-tree at Sunnybrook Farm. Mira, the baby of the Randall family, died, and Rebecca went home for a fortnight's visit. The sight of the small still shape that had been Mira—the baby who had been her special charge ever since her birth—woke into being a host of new thoughts and wonderments, for it is sometimes the mystery of death that brings one to a consciousness of the still greater mystery of life.

It was a sorrowful home-coming for Rebecca. The death of Mira, the absence of John—who had been her special comrade—the sadness of her mother, the isolation of the little house, and the pinching economies that went on within it, all conspired to depress a child who was so sensitive to beauty and harmony as Rebecca.

Hannah seemed to have grown into a woman during Rebecca's absence. There had always been a strange, unchildlike air about Hannah, but in certain ways she now appeared older than Aunt Jane—soberer and more settled. She was pretty, though in a colourless fashion—pretty and capable.

Rebecca walked through all the old playgrounds and favourite haunts of her early childhood—all her familiar, her secret places, some of them known to John, some to herself alone. There was the spot where the Indian pipes grew; the particular bit of marshy ground where the fringed gentians used to be largest and bluest; the rock maple where she found the oriole's nest; the hedge where the field-mice lived; the moss-covered stump where the white toadstools were wont to spring up as if by magic;

the hole at the root of the old pine where an ancient
and honourable toad made his home—these were the
landmarks of her childhood, and she looked at them
as across an immeasurable distance. The dear little
sunny brook—her chief companion after John—was
sorry company at this season. There was no laughing
water sparkling in the sunshine. In summer the
merry stream had danced over white pebbles on its
way to deep pools, where it could be still and think.
Now, like Mira, it was cold and quiet, wrapped in
its shroud of snow; but Rebecca knelt by the brink,
and, putting her ear to the glaze of ice, fancied where
it used to be deepest she could hear a faint tinkling
sound. It was all right. Sunnybrook would sing
again in the spring; perhaps Mira, too, would have
her singing time somewhere—she wondered where
and how. In the course of these lonely rambles she
was ever thinking—thinking of one subject. Hannah
had never had a chance—never been freed from the
daily care and work of the farm. She (Rebecca) had
enjoyed all the privileges thus far. Life at the brick
house had not been by any means a path of roses, but
there had been comfort and the companionship of
other children, as well as chances for study and reading. Riverboro had not been the world itself, but
it had been a glimpse of it through a tiny peephole
that was infinitely better than nothing. Rebecca shed
more than one quiet tear before she could trust herself
to offer up as a sacrifice that which she so much
desired for herself. Then one morning, as her visit
neared its end, she plunged into the subject boldly,
and said : " Hannah, after this term I'm going to stay
at home and let you go away. Aunt Miranda has

always wanted you, and it's only fair you should have your turn."

Hannah was darning stockings, and she threaded her needle and snipped off the yarn before she answered: "No, thank you, Becky. Mother couldn't do without me, and I hate going to school. I can read and write and cipher as well as anybody now, and that's enough for me. I'd die rather than teach school for a living. The winter 'll go fast, for Will Melville is going to lend me his mother's sewing-machine, and I'm going to make white petticoats out of the piece of muslin Aunt Jane sent, and have 'em just solid with tucks. Then there's going to be a singing-school and a social circle in Temperance after New Year's; and I shall have a real good time now I'm grown up. I'm not one to be lonesome, Becky," Hannah ended with a blush. "I love this place."

Rebecca saw that she was speaking the truth, but she did not understand the blush till a year or two later.

XVIII

REBECCA REPRESENTS THE FAMILY

THERE was another milestone; it was more than that, it was an "event"—an event that made a deep impression in several quarters, and left a wake of smaller events in its train. This was the coming to Riverboro of the Reverend Amos Burch and wife, returned missionaries from Syria.

The Aid Society had called its meeting for a certain Wednesday in March of the year in which Rebecca ended her Riverboro school-days, and began her studies at Wareham. It was a raw, blustering day, snow on the ground and a look in the sky of more to follow. Both Miranda and Jane had taken cold, and decided that they could not leave the house in such weather, and this deflection from the path of duty worried Miranda, since she was an officer of the society. After making the breakfast-table sufficiently uncomfortable and wishing plaintively that Jane wouldn't always insist on being sick at the same time she was, she decided that Rebecca must go to the meeting in their stead. "You'll be better than no-body, Rebecca," she said flatteringly; "your Aunt Jane shall write an excuse from afternoon school for you; you can wear your rubber boots, and come home by the way of the meetin'-house. This Mr. Burch, if I remember right, used to know your grandfather Sawyer, and stayed here once when he was candidat-in'. He'll mebbe look for us there, and you must just go and represent the family, an' give him our respects. Be careful how you behave. Bow your head in prayer; sing all the hymns, but not too loud and bold; ask after Mis' Strout's boy; tell everybody what awful colds we've got; if you see a good chance, take your pocket-handkerchief and wipe the dust off the melodeon before the meetin' begins, and get twenty-five cents out of the sittin'-room match-box in case there should be a collection."

Rebecca willingly assented. Anything interested her, even a village missionary meeting, and the idea of representing the family was rather intoxicating.

The service was held in the Sunday-school room, and although the Rev. Mr. Burch was on the platform when Rebecca entered, there were only a dozen persons present. Feeling a little shy and considerably too young for this assemblage, Rebecca sought the shelter of a friendly face, and seeing Mrs. Robinson in one of the side-seats near the front, she walked up the aisle and sat beside her.

"Both my aunts had bad colds," she said softly, "and sent me to represent the family."

"That's Mrs. Burch on the platform with her husband," whispered Mrs. Robinson. "She's awful tanned up, ain't she? If you're going to save souls seems like to hev' to part with your complexion. Eudoxy Morton ain't come yet; I hope to the land she will, or Mis' Deacon Milliken 'll pitch the tunes where we can't reach 'em with a ladder. Can't you pitch, afore she gits her breath and clears her throat?"

Mrs. Burch was a slim, frail little woman with dark hair, a broad low forehead, and patient mouth. She was dressed in a well-worn black silk, and looked so tired that Rebecca's heart went out to her.

"They're as poor as Job's turkey," whispered Mrs. Robinson; "but if you give 'em anything they'd turn right round and give it to the heathen. His congregation up to Parsonsfield clubbed together and give him that gold watch he carries; I s'pose he'd 'a' handed that over too, only heathens always tell time by the sun 'n' don't need watches. Eudoxy ain't comin'; now, for massy's sake, Rebecca, do git ahead of Mis' Deacon Milliken, and pitch real low."

The meeting began with prayer, and then the Rev. Mr. Burch announced, to the tune of Mendon:

> " Church of our God! arise and shine,
>   Bright with the beams of truth Divine;
>   Then shall thy radiance stream afar,
>   Wide as the heathen nations are.

> " Gentiles and kings thy light shall view,
>   And shall admire and love thee too;
>   They come, like clouds across the sky,
>   As doves that to their windows fly."

" Is there anyone present who will assist us at the instrument?" he asked unexpectedly.

Everybody looked at everybody else, and nobody moved; then there came a voice out of a far corner saying informally, " Rebecca, why don't you?" It was Mrs. Cobb. Rebecca could have played Mendon in the dark, so she went to the melodeon and did so without any ado, no member of her family being present to give her self-consciousness.

The talk that ensued was much the usual sort of thing. Mr. Burch made impassioned appeals for the spreading of the Gospel, and added his entreaties that all who were prevented from visiting in person the peoples who sat in darkness should contribute liberally to the support of others who could. But he did more than this. He was a pleasant, earnest speaker, and he interwove his discourse with stories of life in a foreign land—of the manners, the customs, the speech, the point of view, even giving glimpses of the daily round, the common task, of his own household, the work of his devoted helpmate, and their little group of children, all born under Syrian skies.

Rebecca sat entranced, having been given the key of another world. Riverboro had faded; the Sunday-school room, with Mrs. Robinson's red plaid shawl, and Deacon Milliken's wig, on crooked, the bare benches and torn hymn-books, the hanging texts and maps, were no longer visible, and she saw blue skies and burning stars, white turbans and gay colours; Mr. Burch had not said so, but perhaps there were mosques and temples and minarets and date-palms. What stories they must know, those children born under Syrian skies! Then she was called upon to play "Jesus shall reign where'er the sun."

The contribution-box was passed and Mr. Burch prayed. As he opened his eyes and gave out the last hymn, he looked at the handful of people, at the scattered pennies and dimes in the contribution-box, and reflected that his mission was not only to gather funds for the building of his church, but to keep alive in all these remote and lonely neighbourhoods that love for the cause which was its only hope in the years to come.

"If any of the sisters will provide entertainment," he said, "Mrs. Burch and I will remain among you to-night and to-morrow. In that event we could hold a parlour meeting. My wife and one of my children would wear the native costume, we would display some specimens of Syrian handiwork, and give an account of our educational methods with the children. These informal parlour meetings, admitting of questions or conversation, are often the means of interesting those not commonly found at church services; so, I repeat, if any member of the congregation desires it, and offers her hospitality, we will gladly stay and tell you more of the Lord's work."

A pall of silence settled over the little assembly. There was some cogent reason why every "sister" there was disinclined for company. Some had no spare room, some had a larder less well stocked than usual, some had sickness in the family, some were "unequally yoked together with unbelievers," who disliked strange ministers. Mrs. Burch's thin hands fingered her black silk nervously. Would no one speak? thought Rebecca, her heart fluttering with sympathy. Mrs. Robinson leaned over and whispered significantly: "The missionaries always used to be entertained at the brick house. Your grandfather never would let 'em sleep anywheres else when he was alive." She meant this for a stab at Miss Miranda's parsimony, remembering the four spare chambers closed from January to December; but Rebecca thought it was intended as a suggestion. If it had been a former custom, perhaps her aunts would want her to do the right thing; for what else was she representing the family? So, delighted that duty lay in so pleasant a direction, she rose from her seat, and said in the pretty voice and with the quaint manner that so separated her from all the other young people in the village: "My aunts, Miss Miranda and Miss Jane Sawyer, would be very happy to have you visit them at the brick house, as the ministers always used to do when their father was alive. They sent their respects by me." The "respects" might have been the freedom of the city, or an equestrian statue, when presented in this way, and the aunts would have shuddered could they have foreseen the manner of delivery; but it was vastly impressive to the audience, who concluded that Mirandy Sawyer must be making her way uncommonly fast to mansions in the skies, else what meant this abrupt change of heart?

Mr. Burch bowed courteously, accepted the invitation " in the same spirit in which it was offered," and asked Brother Milliken to lead in prayer.

If the Eternal Ear could ever tire, it would have ceased long ere this to listen to Deacon Milliken, who had wafted to the Throne of Grace the same prayer, with very slight variations, for forty years. Mrs. Perkins followed. She had several petitions at her command, good sincere ones, too, but a little cut and dried, made of Scripture texts laboriously woven together. Rebecca wondered why she always ended, at the most peaceful seasons, with the form, " Do Thou be with us, God of Battles, while we strive onward, like Christian soldiers, marching as to war." But everything sounded real to her to-day. She was in a devout mood, and many things Mr. Burch had said had moved her strangely. As she lifted her head the minister looked directly at her, and said: " Will our young sister close the service by leading us in prayer?"

Every drop of blood in Rebecca's body seemed to stand still and her heart almost stopped beating. Mrs. Cobb's excited breathing could be heard distinctly in the silence. There was nothing extraordinary in Mr. Burch's request. In his journeyings among country congregations he was constantly in the habit of meeting young members who had " experienced religion," and joined the church when nine or ten years old. Rebecca was now thirteen. She had played the melodeon, led the singing, delivered her aunts' invitation with an air of great worldly wisdom, and he, concluding that she must be a youthful pillar of the church, called upon her with the utmost simplicity.

Rebecca's plight was pathetic. How could she refuse? How could she explain she was not a "member"? How could she pray before all those elderly women? John Rogers at the stake hardly suffered more than this poor child for the moment as she rose to her feet, forgetting that ladies prayed sitting, while deacons stood in prayer. Her mind was a maze of pictures that the Rev. Mr. Burch had flung on the screen. She knew the conventional phraseology, of course. What New England child accustomed to Wednesday evening meetings does not? But her own secret prayers were different. However, she began slowly and tremulously:

"Our Father who art in Heaven, . . . Thou art God in Syria just the same as in Maine; . . . over there to-day are blue skies and yellow stars and burning suns . . . the great trees are waving in the warm air, while here the snow lies thick under our feet, . . . but no distance is too far for God to travel, and so He is with us here as He is with them there, . . . and our thoughts rise to Him 'as doves that to their windows fly.' . . .

"We cannot all be missionaries, teaching people to be good: . . . some of us have not learned yet how to be good ourselves; but if Thy kingdom is to come and Thy will is to be done on earth as it is in heaven, everybody must try and everybody must help . . . those who are old and tired and those who are young and strong. . . . The little children of whom we have heard, those born under Syrian skies, have strange and interesting work to do for Thee, and some of us would like to travel in far lands and do wonderful brave things for the heathen, and gently take away their idols of wood and stone. But perhaps we have to stay at home and do what is given us to do . . . sometimes even things we dislike, . . . but that must be what it means in the hymn we sang, when it talked about the sweet perfume that rises with every morning sacrifice. . . . This is the way that God teaches us to be meek and patient, and the thought that He has willed it so should rob us of our fears and help us bear the years. Amen."

Poor little ignorant, fantastic child! Her petition was simply a succession of lines from the various hymns, and images the minister had used in his sermon, but she had her own way of recombining and applying these things, even of using them in a new connection, so that they had a curious effect of belonging to her. The words of some people might generally be written with a minus sign after them, the minus meaning that the personality of the speaker subtracted from, rather than added to, their weight; but Rebecca's words might always have borne the plus sign.

The "Amen" said, she sat down, or presumed she sat down, on what she believed to be a bench and there was a benediction. In a moment or two, when the room ceased spinning, she went up to Mrs. Burch, who kissed her affectionately and said, "My dear, how glad I am that we are going to stay with you! Will half-past five be too late for us to come? It is three now, and we have to go to the station for our valise and for our children. We left them there, being uncertain whether we should go back or stop here."

Rebecca said that half-past five was their supper hour, and then accepted an invitation to drive home with Mrs. Cobb. Her face was flushed and her lip quivered in a way that Aunt Sarah had learned to know, so the homeward drive was taken almost in silence. The bleak wind and Aunt Sarah's quieting presence brought her back to herself, however, and she entered the brick house cheerily. Being too full of news to wait in the side entry to take off her rubber boots, she carefully lifted a braided rug into the sitting-room and stood on that while she opened her budget.

"There are your shoes warming by the fire," said Aunt Jane. "Slip them right on while you talk."

XIX

DEACON ISRAEL'S SUCCESSOR

"It was a very small meeting, Aunt Miranda," began Rebecca, "and the missionary and his wife are lovely people, and they are coming here to stay all night and to-morrow with you. I hope you won't mind."

"Coming here!" exclaimed Miranda, letting her knitting fall in her lap and taking her spectacles off, as she always did in moments of extreme excitement. "Did they invite themselves?"

"No," Rebecca answered. "I had to invite them for you; but I thought you'd like to have such interesting company. It was this way——"

"Stop your explainin', and tell me first when they'll be here. Right away?"

"No, not for two hours—about half-past five."

"Then you can explain, if you can, who gave you any authority to invite a passel of strangers to stop here overnight, when you know we ain't had any company for twenty years, and don't intend to have any for another twenty, or, at any rate, while I'm the head of the house."

"Don't blame her, Miranda, till you've heard her story," said Jane. "It was in my mind right along, if we went to the meeting, some such thing might happen, on account of Mr. Burch knowing father."

"The meeting was a small one," began Rebecca. "I gave all your messages, and everybody was disappointed you couldn't come, for the president wasn't there, and Mrs. Matthews took the chair, which was a pity, for the seat wasn't nearly big enough for her, and she reminded me of a line in a hymn we sang, 'Wide as the heathen nations are,' and she wore that kind of a beaver garden-hat that always gets on one side. And Mr. Burch talked beautifully about the Syrian heathen, and the singing went real well, and there looked to be about forty cents in the basket that was passed on our side. And that wouldn't save even a heathen baby, would it? Then Mr. Burch said if any sister would offer entertainment they would pass the night, and have a parlour meeting in Riverboro to-morrow, with Mrs. Burch in Syrian costume, and lovely foreign things to show. Then he waited and waited, and nobody said a word. I was so mortified I didn't know what to do. And then he repeated what he said, and explained why he wanted to stay, and you could see he thought it was his duty. Just then Mrs. Robinson whispered to me and said the

missionaries always used to go to the brick house
when grandfather was alive, and that he never would
let them sleep anywhere else. I didn't know you had
stopped having them, because no travelling ministers
have been here, except just for a Sunday morning,
since I came to Riverboro. So I thought I ought to
invite them, as you weren't there to do it for yourself,
and you told me to represent the family."

"What did you do—go up and introduce yourself
as folks was goin' out?"

"No; I stood right up in meeting. I had to, for
Mr. Burch's feelings were getting hurt at nobody's
speaking. So I said, 'My aunts, Miss Miranda and
Miss Jane Sawyer, would be happy to have you visit
at the brick house, just as the missionaries always did
when their father was alive, and they sent their
respects by me.' Then I sat down, and Mr. Burch
prayed for grandfather, and called him a man of God,
and thanked our Heavenly Father that his spirit was
still alive in his descendants (that was you), and that
the good old house where so many of the brethren
had been cheered and helped, and from which so many
had gone out strengthened for the fight, was still
hospitably open for the stranger and wayfarer."

Sometimes, when the heavenly bodies are in just
the right conjunction, nature seems to be the most
perfect art. The word or the deed coming straight
from the heart, without any thought of effect, seems
inspired.

A certain gateway in Miranda Sawyer's soul had
been closed for years; not all at once had it been done,
but gradually, and without her full knowledge. If
Rebecca had plotted for days, and with the utmost

cunning, she could not have effected an entrance into that forbidden country, and now, unknown to both of them, the gate swung on its stiff and rusty hinges, and the favouring wind of opportunity opened it wider and wider as time went on. All things had worked together amazingly for good. The memory of old days had been evoked, and the daily life of a pious and venerated father called to mind; the Sawyer name had been publicly dignified and praised; Rebecca had comported herself as the granddaughter of Deacon Israel Sawyer should, and showed conclusively that she was not "all Randall," as had been supposed. Miranda was rather mollified by and pleased with the turn of events, although she did not intend to show it, or give anybody any reason to expect that this expression of hospitality was to serve for a precedent on any subsequent occasion.

"Well, I see you did only what you was obliged to do, Rebecca," she said, "and you worded your invitation as nice as anybody could have done. I wish your Aunt Jane and me wasn't both so worthless with these colds; but it only shows the good of havin' a clean house, with every room in order, whether open or shut, and enough victuals cooked so 't you can't be surprised and belittled by anybody, whatever happens. There was half a dozen there that might have entertained the Burches as easy as not, if they hadn't 'a' been too mean or lazy. Why didn't your missionaries come right along with you?"

"They had to go to the station for their valise and their children."

"Are there children?" groaned Miranda.

"Yes, Aunt Miranda, all born under Syrian skies."

"Syrian grandmother!" ejaculated Miranda (and it was not a fact). "How many?"

"I didn't think to ask; but I will get two rooms ready, and if there are any over I'll take 'em into my bed," said Rebecca, secretly hoping that this would be the case. "Now, as you're both half sick, couldn't you trust me just once to get ready for the company? You can come up when I call. Will you?"

"I believe I will," sighed Miranda reluctantly. "I'll lay down side o' Jane in our bedroom and see if I can get strength to cook supper. It's half-past three—don't you let me lay a minute past five. I kep' a good fire in the kitchen stove. I don't know, I'm sure, why I should have baked a pot o' beans in the middle of the week, but they'll come in handy. Father used to say there was nothing that went right to the spot with returned missionaries like pork 'n' beans 'n' brown bread. Fix up the two south chambers, Rebecca."

Rebecca, given a free hand for the only time in her life, dashed upstairs like a whirlwind. Every room in the brick house was as neat as wax, and she had only to pull up the shades, go over the floors with a whisk broom, and dust the furniture. The aunts could hear her scurrying to and fro, beating up pillows and feather-beds, flapping towels, jingling crockery, singing meanwhile in her clear voice:

> "In vain with lavish kindness
> The gifts of God are strown;
> The heathen in his blindness
> Bows down to wood and stone."

She had grown to be a handy little creature, and tasks she was capable of doing at all she did like a flash, so that when she called her aunts at five o'clock to pass judgment she had accomplished wonders. There were fresh towels on bureaus and washstands, the beds were fair and smooth, the pitchers were filled, and soap and matches were laid out; newspaper, kindling, and wood were in the boxes, and a large stick burned slowly in each air-tight stove. "I thought I'd better just take the chill off," she explained, "as they're right from Syria; and that reminds me I must look it up in the geography before they get here."

There was nothing to disapprove, so the two sisters went downstairs to make some slight changes in their dress. As they passed the parlour door Miranda thought she heard a crackle, and looked in. The shades were up; there was a cheerful blaze in the open stove in the front parlour, and a fire laid on the hearth in the back-room. Rebecca's own lamp, her second Christmas present from Mr. Aladdin, stood on a marble-topped table in the corner, the light that came softly through its rose-coloured shade transforming the stiff and gloomy ugliness of the room into a place where one could sit and love one's neighbour.

"For massy's sake, Rebecca!" called Miss Miranda up the stairs, "did you think we'd better open the parlour?"

Rebecca came out on the landing braiding her hair.

"We did on Thanksgiving and Christmas, and I thought this was about as great an occasion," she said. "I moved the wax flowers off the mantelpiece so they wouldn't melt, and put the shells, the coral, and the green stuffed bird on top of the what-not, so the

children wouldn't ask to play with them. Brother
Milliken's coming over to see Mr. Burch about business, and I shouldn't wonder if Brother and Sister
Cobb happened in. Don't go down cellar; I'll be
there in a minute to do the running."

Miranda and Jane exchanged glances.

"Ain't she the beatin'est creetur that ever was
born int' the world!" exclaimed Miranda; "but she
can turn off work when she's got a mind to!"

At quarter-past five everything was ready, and the
neighbours—those, at least, who were within sight of
the brick house (a prominent object in the landscape
when there were no leaves on the trees)—were curious
almost to desperation. Shades up in both parlours!
Shades up in the two south bedrooms! And fires—if
human vision was to be relied on—fires in about
every room. If it had not been for the kind offices
of a lady who had been at the meeting, and who
charitably called in at one or two houses and explained
the reason of all this preparation, there would have
been no sleep in many families.

The missionary party arrived promptly, and there
were but two children, seven or eight having been
left with the brethren in Portland to diminish travelling expenses. Jane escorted them all upstairs, while
Miranda watched the cooking of the supper; but
Rebecca promptly took the two little girls away from
their mother, divested them of their wraps, smoothed
their hair, and brought them down to the kitchen to
smell the beans.

There was a bountiful supper, and the presence of
the young people robbed it of all possible stiffness.
Aunt Jane helped clear the table and put away the

food, while Miranda entertained in the parlour; but Rebecca and the infant Burches washed the dishes and held high carnival in the kitchen, doing only trifling damage—breaking a cup and plate that had been cracked before, emptying a silver spoon with some dish-water out of the back-door (an act never permitted at the brick house), and putting coffee-grounds in the sink. All evidences of crime having been removed by Rebecca, and damages repaired in all possible cases, the three entered the parlour, where Mr. and Mrs. Cobb and Deacon and Mrs. Milliken had already appeared.

It was such a pleasant evening! Occasionally they left the heathen in his blindness bowing down to wood and stone, not for long, but just to give them-selves (and him) time enough to breathe, and then the Burches told strange, beautiful, marvellous things. The two smaller children sang together, and Rebecca, at the urgent request of Mrs. Burch, seated herself at the tinkling old piano and gave " Wild roved an Indian girl, bright Alfarata," with considerable spirit and style.

At eight o'clock she crossed the room, handed a palm-leaf fan to her Aunt Miranda, ostensibly that she might shade her eyes from the lamplight; but it was a piece of strategy that gave her an opportunity to whisper, " How about cookies?"

" Do you think it's worth while?" sibilated Miss Miranda in answer.

" The Perkinses always do."

" All right. You know where they be."

Rebecca moved quietly towards the door, and the young Burches cataracted after her as if they could not bear a second's separation. In five minutes they returned, the little ones bearing plates of thin caraway wafers—hearts, diamonds, and circles daintily sugared, and flecked with caraway-seed raised in the garden behind the house. These were a speciality of Miss Jane's, and Rebecca carried a tray with six tiny crystal glasses filled with dandelion wine, for which Miss Miranda had been famous in years gone by. Old Deacon Israel had always had it passed, and he had bought the glasses himself in Boston. Miranda admired them greatly, not only for their beauty, but because they held so little. Before their advent the dandelion wine had been served in sherry glasses.

As soon as these refreshments—commonly called a "colation" in Riverboro—had been genteelly partaken of, Rebecca looked at the clock, rose from her chair in the children's corner, and said cheerfully: "Come, time for little missionaries to be in bed!"

Everybody laughed at this—the big missionaries most of all—as the young people shook hands and disappeared with Rebecca.

XX

A CHANGE OF HEART

"THAT niece of yours is the most remarkable girl I have seen in years," said Mr. Burch when the door closed.

"She seems to be turnin' out smart enough lately;

but she's consid'able heedless," answered Miranda,
"an' most too lively."

"We must remember that it is deficient, not
excessive, vitality that makes the greatest trouble in
this world," returned Mr. Burch.

"She'd make a wonderful missionary," said Mrs.
Burch, "with her voice, and her magnetism, and her
gift of language."

"If I was to say which of the two she was best
adapted for, I'd say she'd make a better heathen,"
remarked Miranda curtly.

"My sister don't believe in flattering children,"
hastily interpolated Jane, glancing toward Mrs.
Burch, who seemed somewhat shocked, and was
about to open her lips to ask if Rebecca was not a
"professor."

Mrs. Cobb had been looking for this question
all the evening, and dreaded some allusion to her
favourite as gifted in prayer. She had taken an
instantaneous and illogical dislike to the Rev. Mr.
Burch in the afternoon because he called upon
Rebecca to "lead." She had seen the pallor creep
into the girl's face, the hunted look in her eyes, and
the trembling of the lashes on her cheeks, and realized
the ordeal through which she was passing. Her
prejudice against the minister had relaxed under his
genial talk and presence, but feeling that Mrs. Burch
was about to tread on dangerous ground, she hastily
asked her if one had to change cars many times from
Riverboro to Syria. She felt that it was not a
particularly appropriate question, but it served her
turn.

Deacon Milliken meantime said to Miss Sawyer:

"Mirandy, do you know who Rebecky reminds me of?"

"I can guess pretty well," she replied.

"Then you've noticed it too. I thought at first, seein' she favoured her father so on the outside, that she was the same all through; but she ain't: she's like your father, Israel Sawyer."

"I don't see how you make that out," said Miranda, thoroughly astonished.

"It struck me this afternoon when she got up to give your invitation in meetin'. It was kind o' cur'ous, but she set in the same seat he used to when he was leader o' the Sabbath-school. You know his old way of holdin' his chin up and throwing his head back a leetle when he got up to say anything? Well, she done the very same thing; there was more 'n one spoke of it."

The callers left before nine, and at that hour (an impossibly dissipated one for the brick house) the family retired for the night. As Rebecca carried Mrs. Burch's candle upstairs, and found herself thus alone with her for a minute, she said shyly: "Will you, please, tell Mr. Burch that I'm not a member of the church? I didn't know what to do when he asked me to pray this afternoon. I hadn't the courage to say I had never done it out loud, and didn't know how. I couldn't think, and I was so frightened I wanted to sink into the floor. It seemed bold and wicked for me to pray before all those old church members, and make believe I was better than I really was. But then, again, wouldn't God think I was wicked not to be willing to pray when a minister asked me to?"

The candle-light fell on Rebecca's flushed, sensitive

face. Mrs. Burch bent and kissed her good-night. "Don't be troubled," she said. "I'll tell Mr. Burch, and I guess God will understand."

Rebecca waked before six the next morning so full of household cares that sleep was impossible. She went to the window and looked out : it was still dark, and a blustering, boisterous day.

"Aunt Jane told me she should get up at half-past six, and have breakfast at half-past seven," she thought. "But I dare say they are both sick with their colds, and Aunt Miranda will be fidgety with so many in the house. I believe I'll creep down and start things for a surprise."

She put on a wadded wrapper and slippers, and stole quietly down the tabooed front-stairs, carefully closed the kitchen-door behind her so that no noise should awaken the rest of the household, busied herself for a half-hour with the early morning routine she knew so well, and then went back to her room to dress before calling the children.

Contrary to expectation, Miss Jane, who the evening before felt better than Miranda, grew worse in the night, and was wholly unable to leave her bed in the morning. Miranda grumbled without ceasing during the progress of her hasty toilet, blaming everybody in the universe for the afflictions she had borne and was to bear during the day; she even castigated the Missionary Board that had sent the Burches to Syria, and gave it as her unbiassed opinion that those who went to foreign lands for the purpose of saving heathen should stay there and save 'em, and not go gallivantin' all over the earth with a passel o' children, visitin' folks that didn't want 'em and never asked 'em.

Jane lay anxiously and restlessly in bed with a feverish headache, wondering how her sister could manage without her.

Miranda walked stiffly through the dining-room, tying a shawl over her head to keep the draughts away, intending to start the breakfast fire and then call Rebecca down, set her to work, and tell her, meanwhile, a few plain facts concerning the proper way of representing the family at a missionary meeting.

She opened the kitchen-door and stared vaguely about her, wondering whether she had strayed into the wrong house by mistake.

The shades were up, and there was a roaring fire in the stove; the tea-kettle was singing and bubbling as it sent out a cloud of steam, and pushed over its capacious nose was a half-sheet of note-paper with "Compliments of Rebecca" scrawled on it. The coffee-pot was scalding, the coffee was measured out in a bowl, and broken eggshells for the settling process were standing near. The cold potatoes and corned beef were in the wooden tray, and "Regards of Rebecca" stuck on the chopping-knife. The brown loaf was out, the white loaf was out, the toast-rack was out, the doughnuts were out, the milk was skimmed, the butter had been brought from the dairy.

Miranda removed the shawl from her head and sank into the kitchen-rocker, ejaculating under her breath: "She is the beatin'est child! I declare she's all Sawyer!"

The day and the evening passed off with credit and

honour to everybody concerned, even to Jane, who had the discretion to recover instead of growing worse and acting as a damper to the general enjoyment. The Burches left with lively regrets, and the little missionaries, bathed in tears, swore eternal friendship with Rebecca, who pressed into their hands at parting a poem composed before breakfast:

TO MARY AND MARTHA BURCH

Born under Syrian skies,
  'Neath hotter suns than ours,
The children grew and bloomed,
  Like little tropic flowers.

When they first saw the light,
  'Twas in a heathen land.
Not Greenland's icy mountains,
  Nor India's coral strand,

But some mysterious country
  Where men are nearly black,
And where of true religion
  There is a painful lack.

Then let us haste in helping
  The Missionary Board,
Seek dark-skinned unbelievers,
  And teach them of their Lord.

REBECCA ROWENA RANDALL.

It can readily be seen that this visit of the returned missionaries to Riverboro was not without somewhat far-reaching results. Mr. and Mrs. Burch themselves looked back upon it as one of the rarest pleasures of their half-year at home. The neighbourhood extracted considerable eager conversation from it; argument, rebuttal, suspicion, certainty, retrospect, and prophecy.

Deacon Milliken gave ten dollars towards the conversion of Syria to Congregationalism, and Mrs. Milliken had a spell of sickness over her husband's rash generosity.

It would be pleasant to state that Miranda Sawyer was an entirely changed woman afterwards, but that is not the fact. The tree that has been getting a twist for twenty years cannot be straightened in the twinkling of an eye. It is certain, however, that, although the difference to the outward eye was very small, it nevertheless existed, and she was less censorious in her treatment of Rebecca, less harsh in her judgments, more hopeful of final salvation for her. This had come about largely from her sudden vision that Rebecca, after all, inherited something from the Sawyer side of the house instead of belonging, mind, body, and soul, to the despised Randall stock. Everything that was interesting in Rebecca, and every evidence of power, capability, or talent afterwards displayed by her, Miranda ascribed to the brick-house training, and this gave her a feeling of honest pride—the pride of a master workman who has built success out of the most unpromising material; but never, to the very end, even when the waning of her bodily strength relaxed her iron grip and weakened her power of repression, never once did she show that pride or make a single demonstration of affection.

Poor misplaced, belittled Lorenzo de Medici Randall, thought ridiculous and good-for-naught by his associates because he resembled them in nothing! If Riverboro could have been suddenly emptied into a larger community, with different and more flexible opinions, he was, perhaps, the only personage in the

M

entire population who would have attracted the
smallest attention. It was fortunate for his daughter
that she had been dowered with a little practical ability
from her mother's family; but if Lorenzo had never
done anything else in the world, he might have glorified himself that he had prevented Rebecca from
being all Sawyer. Failure as he was, complete and
entire, he had generously handed down to her all that
was best in himself, and prudently retained all that
was unworthy. Few fathers are capable of such
delicate discrimination.

The brick house did not speedily become a sort of
wayside inn, a place of innocent revelry and joyous
welcome; but the missionary company was an entering
wedge, and Miranda allowed one spare bed to be
made up "in case anything should happen," while
the crystal glasses were kept on the second from the
top, instead of the top shelf, in the china closet.
Rebecca had had to stand on a chair to reach them;
now she could do it by stretching; and this is symbolic
of the way in which she unconsciously scaled the walls
of Miss Miranda's dogmatism and prejudice.

Miranda went so far as to say that she wouldn't
mind if the Burches came every once in a while, but
she was afraid he'd spread abroad the fact of his visit,
and missionaries' families would be underfoot the
whole continual time. As a case in point she grace-
fully cited the fact that if a tramp got a good meal at
anybody's back-door 'twas said that he'd leave some
kind of sign, so that other tramps would know where
they were likely to receive the same treatment.

It is to be feared that there is some truth in this
homely illustration, and Miss Miranda's dread as to

her future responsibilities had some foundation, though not of the precise sort she had in mind. The soul grows into lovely habits as easily as into ugly ones, and the moment a life begins to blossom into beautiful words and deeds, that moment a new standard of conduct is established, and your eager neighbours look to you for a continuous manifestation of the good cheer, the sympathy, the ready wit, the comradeship, or the inspiration you once showed yourself capable of. Bear figs for a season or two, and the world outside the orchard is very unwilling you should bear thistles.

The effect of the Burches' visit on Rebecca is not easily described. Nevertheless, as she looked back upon it from the vantage-ground of after-years she felt that the moment when Mr. Burch asked her to "lead in prayer" marked an epoch in her life.

If you have ever observed how courteous and gracious and mannerly you feel when you don a beautiful new frock; if you have ever noticed the feeling of reverence stealing over you when you close your eyes, clasp your hands, and bow your head; if you have ever watched your sense of repulsion toward a fellow-creature melt a little under the exercise of daily politeness—you may understand how the adoption of the outward and visible sign has some strange influence in developing the inward and spiritual state of which it is the expression.

It is only when one has grown old and dull that the soul is heavy and refuses to rise. The young soul is ever wingèd; a breath stirs it to an upward flight. Rebecca was asked to bear witness to a state of mind or feeling of whose existence she had only the vaguest consciousness. She obeyed; and as she uttered words they became true in the uttering—as she voiced aspirations they settled into realities.

As "dove that to its window flies," her spirit soared towards a great light, dimly discovered at first, but brighter as she came closer to it. To become sensible of oneness with the Divine heart before any sense of separation has been felt, this is surely the most beautiful way for the child to find God.

XXI

THE SKY-LINE WIDENS

THE time so long and eagerly waited for had come, and Rebecca was a student at Wareham. Persons who had enjoyed the social bewilderments and advantages of foreign courts, or had mingled freely in the intellectual circles of great universities, might not have looked upon Wareham as an extraordinary experience; but it was as much of an advance upon Riverboro as that village had been upon Sunnybrook Farm. Rebecca's intention was to complete the four years' course in three, as it was felt by all the parties concerned that, when she had attained the ripe age of seventeen, she must be ready to earn her own living, and help in the education of the younger children. While she was wondering how this could be successfully accomplished, some of the other girls were cogitating as to how they could meander through the four years, and come out at the end knowing no more than at the beginning. This would seem a difficult, wellnigh an impossible task; but it can be achieved, and has been, at other seats of learning than modest little Wareham.

Rebecca was to go to and fro on the cars daily from September to Christmas, and then board in Wareham during the three coldest months. Emma Jane's parents had always thought that a year or two in the Edgewood High School (three miles from River-boro) would serve every purpose for their daughter, and send her into the world with as fine an intellectual polish as she could well sustain. Emma Jane had hitherto heartily concurred in this opinion, for, if there was any one thing that she detested, it was the learning of lessons. One book was as bad as another in her eyes, and she could have seen the libraries of the world sinking into ocean depths and have eaten her dinner cheerfully the while; but matters assumed a different complexion when she was sent to Edgewood and Rebecca to Wareham. She bore it for a week—seven endless days of absence from the beloved object, whom she could see only in the evenings when both were busy with their lessons. Sunday offered an opportunity to put the matter before her father, who proved obdurate. He didn't believe in education, and thought she had full enough already. He never intended to keep up "blacksmith-ing" for good when he leased his farm and came into Riverboro, but proposed to go back to it presently, and by that time Emma Jane would have finished school, and would be ready to help her mother with the dairy work.

Another week passed. Emma Jane pined visibly

and audibly. Her colour faded, and her appetite (at table) dwindled almost to nothing.

Her mother alluded plaintively to the fact that the Perkinses had a habit of going into declines; that she'd always feared that Emma Jane's complexion was too beautiful to be healthy; that some men would be proud of having an ambitious daughter, and be glad to give her the best advantages; that she feared the daily journeys to Edgewood were going to be too much for her own health, and Mr. Perkins would have to hire a boy to drive Emma Jane; and, finally, that when a girl had such a passion for learning as Emma Jane, it seemed almost like wickedness to cross her will.

Mr. Perkins bore this for several days, until his temper, digestion, and appetite were all sensibly affected; then he bowed his head to the inevitable, and Emma Jane flew, like a captive set free, to the loved one's bower. Neither did her courage flag, although it was put to terrific tests when she entered the academic groves of Wareham. She passed in only two subjects, but went cheerfully into the preparatory department with her five " conditions," intending to let the stream of education play gently over her mental surfaces, and not get any wetter than she could help. It is not possible to blink the truth that Emma Jane was dull; but a dogged, unswerving loyalty, and the gift of devoted, unselfish loving—these, after all, are talents of a sort, and may possibly be of as much value in the world as a sense of numbers or a faculty for languages.

Wareham was a pretty village with a broad main street shaded by great maples and elms. It had an apothecary, a blacksmith, a plumber, several shops of one sort and another, two churches, and many boarding-houses; but all its interests gathered about its seminary and its academy. These seats of learning were neither better nor worse than others of their kind, but differed much in efficiency, according as the principal who chanced to be at the head was a man of power and inspiration or the reverse. There were boys and girls gathered from all parts of the county and State, and they were of every kind and degree as to birth, position in the world, wealth or poverty. There was an opportunity for a deal of foolish and imprudent behaviour, but on the whole surprisingly little advantage was taken of it. Among the third and fourth year students there was a certain amount of going to and from the trains in couples; some carrying of heavy books up the hill by the sterner sex for their feminine schoolmates, and occasional bursts of silliness on the part of heedless and precocious girls, among whom was Huldah Meserve. She was friendly enough with Emma Jane and Rebecca, but grew less and less intimate as time went on. She was extremely pretty, with a profusion of auburn hair and a few very tiny freckles, to which she constantly alluded, as no one could possibly detect them without noting her porcelain skin and her curling lashes. She had merry eyes, a somewhat too plump figure for her years, and was popularly supposed to have a fascinating way with her. Riverboro being poorly furnished with beaux, she intended to have as good a time during her four years at Wareham as circumstances would permit. Her idea of pleasure was an ever-changing circle of admirers to fetch and carry for her, the more

publicly the better; incessant chaff and laughter and
vivacious conversation, made eloquent and effective
by arch looks and telling glances. She had a habit of
confiding her conquests to less fortunate girls and
bewailing the incessant havoc and damage she was
doing—a damage she avowed herself as innocent of,
in intention, as any new-born lamb. It does not take
much of this sort of thing to wreck an ordinary friendship, so before long Rebecca and Emma Jane sat in
one end of the railway train in going to and from
Riverboro, and Huldah occupied the other with her
court. Sometimes this was brilliant beyond words,
including a certain youthful Monte Cristo, who on
Fridays expended thirty cents on a round trip ticket
and travelled from Wareham to Riverboro merely to
be near Huldah; sometimes, too, the circle was
reduced to the popcorn-and-peanut boy of the train,
who seemed to serve every purpose in default of
better game.

Rebecca was in the normally unconscious state that
belonged to her years; boys were good comrades, but
no more; she liked reciting in the same class with
them—everything seemed to move better; but from
vulgar and precocious flirtations she was protected by
her ideals. There was little in the lads she had met
thus far to awaken her fancy, for it habitually fed on
better meat. Huldah's schoolgirl romances, with
their wealth of commonplace detail, were not the stuff
her dreams were made of, when dreams did flutter
across the sensitive plate of her mind.

Among the teachers at Wareham was one who
influenced Rebecca profoundly, Miss Emily Maxwell,
with whom she studied English literature and com-

position. Miss Maxwell, as the niece of one of Maine's ex-governors and the daughter of one of Bowdoin's professors, was the most remarkable personality in Wareham, and that her few years of teaching happened to be in Rebecca's time was the happiest of all chances. There was no indecision or delay in the establishment of their relations; Rebecca's heart flew like an arrow to its mark, and her mind, meeting its superior, settled at once into an abiding attitude of respectful homage.

It was rumoured that Miss Maxwell "wrote," which word, when uttered in a certain tone, was understood to mean not that a person had command of penmanship, Spencerian or otherwise, but that she had appeared in print.

"You'll like her; she writes," whispered Huldah to Rebecca the first morning at prayers, where the faculty sat in an imposing row on the front seats. "She writes; and I call her stuck up."

Nobody seemed possessed of exact information with which to satisfy the hungry mind, but there was believed to be at least one person in existence who had seen, with his own eyes, an essay by Miss Maxwell in a magazine. This height of achievement made Rebecca somewhat shy of her, but she looked her admiration, something that most of the class could never do with the unsatisfactory organs of vision given them by Mother Nature. Miss Maxwell's glance was always meeting a pair of eager dark eyes; when she said anything particularly good, she looked for approval to the corner of the second bench, where every shade of feeling she wished to evoke was reflected on a certain sensitive young face.

One day, when the first essay of the class was under discussion, she asked each new pupil to bring her some composition written during the year before, that she might judge the work, and know precisely with what material she had to deal. Rebecca lingered after the others, and approached the desk shyly.

"I haven't any compositions here, Miss Maxwell, but I can find one when I go home on Friday. They are packed away in a box in the attic."

"Carefully tied with pink and blue ribbons?" asked Miss Maxwell, with a whimsical smile.

"No," answered Rebecca, shaking her head decidedly; "I wanted to use ribbons, because all the other girls did, and they looked so pretty, but I used to tie my essays with twine strings on purpose; and the one on 'Solitude' I fastened with an old shoe-lacing just to show it what I thought of it."

"'Solitude'!" laughed Miss Maxwell, raising her eyebrows. "Did you choose your own subject?"

"No; Miss Dearborn thought we were not old enough to find good ones."

"What were some of the others?"

"'Fireside Reveries,' 'Grant as a Soldier,' 'Reflections on the Life of P. T. Barnum,' 'Buried Cities'; I can't remember any more now. They were all bad, and I can't bear to show them; I can write poetry easier and better, Miss Maxwell."

"Poetry!" she exclaimed. "Did Miss Dearborn require you to do it?"

"Oh no; I always did it, even at the farm. Shall I bring all I have? It isn't much."

Rebecca took the blank-book in which she kept copies of her effusions and left it at Miss Maxwell's door, hoping that she might be asked in and thus obtain a private interview; but a servant answered her ring, and she could only walk away, disappointed.

A few days afterwards she saw the black-covered book on Miss Maxwell's desk, and knew that the dreaded moment of criticism had come, so she was not surprised to be asked to remain after class.

The room was quiet; the red leaves rustled in the breeze and flew in at the open window, bearing the first compliments of the season. Miss Maxwell came and sat by Rebecca's side on the bench.

"Did you think these were good?" she asked, giving her the verses.

"Not so very," confessed Rebecca; "but it's hard to tell all by yourself. The Perkinses and the Cobbs always said they were wonderful, but when Mrs. Cobb told me she thought they were better than Mr. Longfellow's I was worried, because I knew that couldn't be true."

This ingenuous remark confirmed Miss Maxwell's opinion of Rebecca as a girl who could hear the truth and profit by it.

"Well, my child," she said smilingly, "your friends were wrong and you were right; judged by the proper tests, they are pretty bad."

"Then I must give up all hope of ever being a writer!" sighed Rebecca, who was tasting the bitterness of hemlock and wondering if she could keep the tears back until the interview was over.

"Don't go so fast," interrupted Miss Maxwell. "Though they don't amount to anything as poetry, they show a good deal of promise in certain directions. You almost never make a mistake in rhyme or metre, and this shows you have a natural sense of what is right; a 'sense of form,' poets would call it. When you grow older, have a little more experience —in fact, when you have something to say, I think you may write very good verses. Poetry needs knowledge and vision, experience and imagination, Rebecca. You have not the first three yet, but I rather think you have a touch of the last."

"Must I never try any more poetry, not even to amuse myself?"

"Certainly you may; it will only help you to write better prose. Now for the first composition. I am going to ask all the new students to write a letter giving some description of the town and a hint of the school life."

"Shall I have to be myself?" asked Rebecca.

"What do you mean?"

"A letter from Rebecca Randall to her sister Hannah at Sunnybrook Farm, or to her Aunt Jane at the brick house, Riverboro, is so dull and stupid, if it is a real letter; but if I could make believe I was a different girl altogether, and write to somebody who would be sure to understand everything I said, I could make it nicer."

"Very well; I think that's a delightful plan," said Miss Maxwell; "and whom will you suppose yourself to be?"

"I like heiresses very much," replied Rebecca contemplatively. "Of course I never saw one, but interesting things are always happening to heiresses, especially to the golden-haired kind. My heiress wouldn't be vain and haughty like the wicked sisters in Cinderella; she would be noble and generous. She would give up a grand school in Boston because she wanted to come here where her father lived when he was a boy, long before he made his fortune. The father is dead now, and she has a guardian, the best and kindest man in the world; he is rather old, of course, and sometimes very quiet and grave, but sometimes when he is happy he is full of fun, and then Evelyn is not afraid of him. Yes, the girl shall be called Evelyn Abercrombie, and her guardian's name shall be Mr. Adam Ladd."

"Do you know Mr. Ladd?" asked Miss Maxwell in surprise.

"Yes, he's my very best friend," cried Rebecca delightedly. "Do you know him, too?"

"Oh yes; he is a trustee of these schools, you know, and often comes here. But if I let you 'suppose' any more, you will tell me your whole letter, and then I shall lose a pleasant surprise."

What Rebecca thought of Miss Maxwell we already know; how the teacher regarded the pupil may be gathered from the following letter written two or three months later:

"WAREHAM,
"*December* 1.

"MY DEAR FATHER,

"As you well know, I have not always been an enthusiast on the subject of teaching. The task of cramming knowledge into these self-sufficient, inefficient youngsters of both sexes discourages me at times. The more stupid they are, the less they are aware of it. If my department were geography or mathematics, I believe I should feel that I was accom-

plishing something, for in those branches application
and industry work wonders; but in English literature
and composition one yearns for brains, for appreciation, for imagination. Month after month I toil on,
opening oyster after oyster, but seldom finding a
pearl. Fancy my joy this term when, without any
violent effort at shell-splitting, I came upon a rare
pearl—a black one, but of satin skin and beautiful
lustre! Her name is Rebecca, and she looks not unlike Rebekah at the well in our family Bible, her hair
and eyes being so dark as to suggest a strain of Italian
or Spanish blood. She is nobody in particular. Man
has done nothing for her. She has no family to speak
of, no money, no education worthy the name, has had
no advantages of any sort; but Dame Nature flung
herself into the breach and said:

> " 'This child I to myself will take;
> She shall be mine, and I will make
> A Lady of my own.'

Blessed Wordsworth! How he makes us understand!
And the pearl never heard of him until now! Think
of reading 'Lucy' to a class, and when you finish,
seeing a fourteen-year-old pair of lips quivering with
delight, and a pair of eyes brimming with compre-
hending tears!

"You poor darling! You, too, know the dis-
couragement of sowing lovely seed in rocky earth,
in sand, in water, and (it almost seems sometimes) in
mud, knowing that if anything comes up at all it will
be some poor starveling plant. Fancy the joy of finding
a real mind—of dropping seed in a soil so warm, so
fertile, that one knows there are sure to be foliage,

blossoms, and fruit all in good time! I wish I were not so impatient and so greedy of results. I am not fit to be a teacher; no one is who is so scornful of stupidity as I am. . . . The pearl writes quaint, countrified little verses—doggerel they are; but somehow or other she always contrives to put in one line, one thought, one image, that shows you she is, quite unconsciously to herself, in possession of the secret. . . . Good-bye; I'll bring Rebecca home with me some Friday, and let you and mother see her for yourself.

"Your affectionate daughter,
"EMILY."

XXII

CLOVER BLOSSOMS AND SUNFLOWERS

"How d'ye do, girls?" said Huldah Meserve, peeping in at the door. "Can you stop studying a minute and show me your room? Say, I've just been down to the store and bought me these gloves, for I was bound I wouldn't wear mittens this winter; they're simply too countrified. It's your first year here, and you're younger than I am, so I s'pose you don't mind, but I simply suffer if I don't keep up some kind of style. Say, your room is simply too 'cute for words! I don't believe any of the others can begin to compare with it! I don't know what gives it that simply gorgeous look—whether it's the full curtains, or that elegant screen, or Rebecca's lamp—but you certainly do have a faculty for fixing up. I like a pretty room,

too, but I never have a minute to attend to mine;
I'm always so busy on my clothes that half the time
I don't get my bed made up till noon; and, after all,
having no callers but the girls, it don't make much
difference. When I graduate, I'm going to fix up
our parlour at home so it'll be simply regal. I've
learned decalcomania, and after I take up lustre-
painting, I shall have it simply stiff with drapes and
tidies and plaques and sofa-pillows, and make mother
let me have a fire, and receive my friends there evenings. May I dry my feet at your register? I can't
bear to wear rubbers unless the mud or the slush is
simply knee-deep; they make your feet look so
awfully big. I had such a fuss getting this pair of
French-heeled boots that I don't intend to spoil the
looks of them with rubbers any oftener than I can
help. I believe boys notice feet quicker than anything. Elmer Webster stepped on one of mine yesterday, when I accidentally had it out in the aisle, and
when he apologized after class, he said he wasn't so
much to blame, for the foot was so little he really
couldn't see it! Isn't he perfectly great? Of course,
that's only his way of talking, for, after all, I only
wear a number two; but these French heels and
pointed toes do certainly make your foot look smaller,
and it's always said a high instep helps, too. I used
to think mine was almost a deformity, but they say
it's a great beauty. Just put your feet beside mine,
girls, and look at the difference; not that I care much,
but just for fun."

"My feet are very comfortable where they are,"
responded Rebecca dryly. "I can't stop to measure
insteps on algebra days. I've noticed your habit of

keeping a foot in the aisle ever since you had those new shoes, so I don't wonder it was stepped on."

"Perhaps I am a little mite conscious of them, because they're not so very comfortable at first, till you get them broken in. Say, haven't you got a lot of new things?"

"Our Christmas presents, you mean," said Emma Jane. "The pillow-cases are from Mrs. Cobb, the rug from Cousin Mary in North Riverboro, the scrap-basket from Living and Dick. We gave each other the bureau and cushion covers, and the screen is mine from Mr. Ladd."

"Well, you were lucky when you met him! Gracious! I wish I could meet somebody like that. The way he keeps it up, too! It just hides your bed, doesn't it? And I always say that a bed takes the style off any room, specially when it's not made up, though you have an alcove, and it's the only one in the whole building. I don't see how you managed to get this good room when you're such new scholars," she finished discontentedly.

"We shouldn't have, except that Ruth Berry had to go away suddenly on account of her father's death. This room was empty, and Miss Maxwell asked if we might have it," returned Emma Jane.

"The great and only Max is more stiff and standoffish than ever this year," said Huldah. "I've simply given up trying to please her, for there's no justice in her; she is good to her favourites; but she doesn't pay the least attention to anybody else, except to make sarcastic speeches about things that are none of her business. I wanted to tell her yesterday it was her place to teach me Latin, not manners."

"I wish you wouldn't talk against Miss Maxwell to me," said Rebecca hotly. "You know how I feel."

"I know; but I can't understand how you can abide her."

"I not only abide her, I love her!" exclaimed Rebecca. "I wouldn't let the sun shine too hot on her, or the wind.blow too cold. I'd like to put a marble platform in her class-room, and have her sit in a velvet chair behind a golden table."

"Well, don't have a fit, because she can sit where she likes for all of me. I've got something better to think of;" and Huldah tossed her head.

"Isn't this your study hour?" asked Emma Jane, to stop possible discussion.

"Yes; but I lost my Latin grammar yesterday. I left it in the hall half an hour while I was having a regular scene with Herbert Dunn. I haven't spoken to him for a week, and gave him back his class pin. He was simply furious. Then, when I came back to the hall, the book was gone. I had to go down town for my gloves, and to the principal's office to see if the grammar had been handed in, and that's the reason I'm so fine."

Huldah was wearing a woollen dress that had once been grey, but had been dyed a brilliant blue. She had added three rows of white braid and large white pearl buttons to her grey jacket in order to make it a little more "dressy." Her grey felt hat had a white feather on it, and a white tissue veil with large black dots made her delicate skin look brilliant. Rebecca thought how lovely the knot of red hair looked under the hat behind, and how the colour of the front had been dulled by incessant frizzing with curling-irons.

Her open jacket disclosed a galaxy of souvenirs pinned to the background of bright blue—a small American flag, a button of the Wareham Rowing Club, and one or two society pins. These decorations proved her popularity in very much the same way as do the cotillion favours hanging on the bedroom walls of the fashionable belle. She had been pinning and unpinning, arranging and disarranging her veil, ever since she entered the room, in the hope that the girls would ask her whose ring she was wearing this week; but although both had noticed the new ornament instantly, wild horses could not have drawn the question from them, her desire to be asked was too obvious. With her gay plumage, her "nods and becks and wreathèd smiles," and her cheerful cackle, Huldah closely resembled the parrot in Wordsworth's poem :

> "Arch, volatile, a sportive bird,
>   By social glee inspired;
> Ambitious to be seen or heard,
>   And pleased to be admired!"

"Mr. Morrison thinks the grammar will be returned, and lent me another," Huldah continued. "He was rather snippy about my leaving a book in the hall. There was a perfectly elegant gentleman in the office, a stranger to me. I wish he was a new teacher, but there's no such luck. He was too young to be the father of any of the girls and too old to be a brother, but he was handsome as a picture, and had on an awful stylish suit of clothes. He looked at me about every minute I was in the room. It made me so embarrassed, I couldn't hardly answer Mr. Morrison's questions straight."

" You'll have to wear a mask pretty soon, if you're going to have any comfort, Huldah," said Rebecca. " Did he offer to lend you his class pin, or has it been so long since he graduated that he's left off wearing it? And tell us now whether the principal asked for a lock of your hair to put in his watch?"

This was all said merrily and laughingly, but there were times when Huldah could scarcely make up her mind whether Rebecca was trying to be witty or whether she was jealous; but she generally decided it was merely the latter feeling, rather natural in a girl who had little attention.

" He wore no jewellery but a cameo scarf-pin and a perfectly gorgeous ring—a queer kind of one that wound round and round his finger. Oh dear, I must run! Where has the hour gone? There's the study bell!"

Rebecca had pricked up her ears at Huldah's speech. She remembered a certain strange ring, and it belonged to the only person in the world (save Miss Maxwell) who appealed to her imagination, Mr. Aladdin. Her feeling for him and that of Emma Jane was a mixture of romantic and reverent admiration for the man himself, and the liveliest gratitude for his beautiful gifts. Since they first met him, not a Christmas had gone by without some remembrance for them both—remembrances chosen with the rarest taste and forethought. Emma Jane had seen him only twice, but he had called several times at the brick house, and Rebecca had learned to know him better. It was she, too, who always wrote the notes of acknowledgment and thanks, taking infinite pains to make Emma Jane's quite different from her own.

Sometimes he had written from Boston and asked her the news of Riverboro, and she had sent him pages of quaint and childlike gossip, interspersed on two occasions with poetry, which he read and reread with infinite relish. If Huldah's stranger should be Mr. Aladdin, would he come to see her? and could she and Emma Jane show him their beautiful room with so many of his gifts in evidence?

When the girls had established themselves in Wareham as real boarding pupils, it seemed to them existence was as full of joy as it well could hold. This first winter was, in fact, the most tranquilly happy of Rebecca's school-life—a winter long to be looked back upon. She and Emma Jane were room-mates, and had put their modest possessions together to make their surroundings pretty and homelike. The room had, to begin with, a cheerful red ingrain carpet and a set of maple furniture. As to the rest, Rebecca had furnished the ideas, and Emma Jane the materials and labour, a method of dividing responsibilities that seemed to suit the circumstances admirably. Mrs. Perkins' father had been a storekeeper, and on his death had left the goods of which he was possessed to his married daughter. The molasses, vinegar, and kerosene, had lasted the family for five years, and the Perkins' attic was still a treasure-house of ginghams, cottons, and "Yankee notions." So at Rebecca's instigation Mrs. Perkins had made full curtains and lambrequins of unbleached muslin, which she had trimmed and looped back with bands of Turkey-red cotton. There were two table-covers to match, and each of the girls had her study corner. Rebecca, after much coaxing, had been allowed to bring over her precious lamp, which would have given a luxurious air to any apartment, and when Mr. Aladdin's last Christmas presents were added— the Japanese screen for Emma Jane and the little shelf of English poets for Rebecca—they declared that it was all quite as much fun as being married and going to house-keeping.

The day of Huldah's call was Friday, and on Fridays from three to half-past four Rebecca was free to take a pleasure to which she looked forward the entire week. She always ran down the snowy path through the pine-woods at the back of the seminary, and coming out on a quiet village street, went directly to the large white house where Miss Maxwell lived. The maid-of-all-work answered her knock; she took off her hat and cape and hung them in the hall, put her rubber shoes and umbrella carefully in the corner, and then opened the door of paradise. Miss Maxwell's sitting-room was lined on two sides with bookshelves, and Rebecca was allowed to sit before the fire and browse among the books to her heart's delight for an hour or more. Then Miss Maxwell would come back from her class, and there would be a precious half-hour of chat before Rebecca had to meet Emma Jane at the station and take the train for Riverboro, where her Saturdays and Sundays were spent, and where she was washed, ironed, mended, and examined, approved and reproved, warned and advised in quite sufficient quantity to last her the succeeding week.

On this Friday she buried her face in the blooming geraniums on Miss Maxwell's plant-stand, selected "Romola" from one of the bookcases, and sank into a seat by the window with a sigh of infinite content. She glanced at the clock now and then, remembering the day on which she had been so immersed in "David Copperfield" that the Riverboro train had no place in her mind. The distracted Emma Jane had refused to leave without her, and had run from the station to look for her at Miss Maxwell's. There was but one later train, and that went only to a place three miles the other side of Riverboro, so that the two girls appeared at their respective homes long after dark, having had a weary walk in the snow.

When she had read for half an hour she glanced out of the window and saw two figures issuing from the path through the woods. The knot of bright hair and the coquettish hat could belong to but one person; and her companion, as the couple approached, proved to be none other than Mr. Aladdin. Huldah was lifting her skirts daintily and picking safe stepping-places for the high-heeled shoes, her cheeks glowing, her eyes sparkling under the black and white veil.

Rebecca slipped from her post by the window to the rug before the bright fire and leaned her head on the seat of the great easy-chair. She was frightened at the storm in her heart, at the suddenness with which it had come on as well as at the strangeness of an entirely new sensation. She felt all at once as if she could not bear to give up her share of Mr. Aladdin's friendship to Huldah—Huldah so bright, saucy, and pretty; so gay and ready, and such good company. She had always joyfully admitted Emma Jane into the precious partnership, but perhaps unconsciously to herself she had realized that Emma Jane had never held anything but a secondary place in Mr. Aladdin's regard; yet who was she herself, after all, that she could hope to be first?

Suddenly the door opened softly and somebody looked in, somebody who said : " Miss Maxwell told me I should find Miss Rebecca Randall here."

Rebecca started at the sound and sprang to her feet, saying joyfully, " Mr. Aladdin! Oh! I knew you were in Wareham, and I was afraid you wouldn't have time to come and see us."

" Who is ' us'? The aunts are not here, are they? Oh, you mean the rich blacksmith's daughter, whose name I can never remember. Is she here?"

" Yes, and my room-mate," answered Rebecca, who thought her own knell of doom had sounded, if he had forgotten Emma Jane's name.

The light in the room grew softer, the fire crackled cheerily, and they talked of many things, until the old sweet sense of friendliness and familiarity crept back into Rebecca's heart. Adam had not seen her for several months, and there was much to be learned about school matters as viewed from her own standpoint; he had already inquired concerning her progress from Mr. Morrison.

" Well, little Miss Rebecca," he said, rousing himself at length, " I must be thinking of my drive to Portland. There is a meeting of railway directors there to-morrow, and I always take this opportunity of visiting the school and giving my valuable advice concerning its affairs educational and financial."

" It seems funny for you to be a school trustee," said Rebecca contemplatively. " I can't seem to make it fit."

" You are a remarkably wise young person, and I

quite agree with you," he answered; "the fact is," he added soberly, "I accepted the trusteeship in memory of my poor little mother, whose last happy years were spent here."

"That was a long time ago!"

"Let me see, I am thirty-two—only thirty-two, despite an occasional grey hair. My mother was married a month after she graduated, and she lived only until I was ten; yes, it is a long way back to my mother's time here, though the school was fifteen or twenty years old then, I believe. Would you like to see my mother, Miss Rebecca?"

The girl took the leather case gently and opened it to find an innocent, pink-and-white daisy of a face, so confiding, so sensitive, that it went straight to the heart. It made Rebecca feel old, experienced, and maternal. She longed on the instant to comfort and strengthen such a tender young thing.

"Oh, what a sweet, sweet, flowery face!" she whispered softly.

"The flower had to bear all sorts of storms," said Adam gravely. "The bitter weather of the world bent its slender stalk, bowed its head, and dragged it to the earth. I was only a child, and could do nothing to protect and nourish it, and there was no one else to stand between it and trouble. Now I have success and money and power, all that would have kept her alive and happy, and it is too late. She died for lack of love and care, nursing and cherishing, and I can never forget it. All that has come to me seems now and then so useless, since I cannot share it with her!"

This was a new Mr. Aladdin, and Rebecca's heart gave a throb of sympathy and comprehension. This explained the tired look in his eyes, the look that peeped out now and then, under all his gay speech and laughter.

"I'm so glad I know," she said, "and so glad I could see her just as she was when she tied that white muslin hat under her chin and saw her yellow curls and her sky-blue eyes in the glass. Mustn't she have been happy! I wish she could have been kept so, and had lived to see you grow up strong and good. My mother is always sad and busy, but once when she looked at John I heard her say, 'He makes up for everything.' That's what your mother would have thought about you if she had lived, and perhaps she does as it is."

"You are a comforting little person, Rebecca," said Adam, rising from his chair.

As Rebecca rose, the tears still trembling on her lashes, he looked at her suddenly as with new vision.

"Good-bye!" he said, taking her slim brown hands in his, adding, as if he saw her for the first time, "Why, little Rose-Red-Snow-White is making way for a new girl! Burning the midnight oil and doing four years' work in three is supposed to dull the eye and blanch the cheek, yet Rebecca's eyes are bright, and she has a rosy colour! Her long braids are looped one on the other so that they make a black letter U behind, and they are tied with grand bows at the top! She is so tall that she reaches almost to my shoulder. This will never do in the world! How will Mr. Aladdin get on without his comforting little friend? He doesn't like grown-up young ladies in long trains and wonderful fine clothes; they frighten and bore him!"

"Oh, Mr. Aladdin!" cried Rebecca eagerly, taking his jest quite seriously, "I am not fifteen yet, and it will be three years before I'm a young lady; please don't give me up until you have to!"

"I won't; I promise you that," said Adam. "Rebecca," he continued, after a moment's pause, "who is that young girl with a lot of pretty red hair and very citified manners? She escorted me down the hill; do you know whom I mean?"

"It must be Huldah Meserve; she is from Riverboro."

Adam put a finger under Rebecca's chin and looked into her eyes—eyes as soft, as clear, as unconscious and childlike as they had been when she was ten. He remembered the other pair of challenging blue eyes that had darted coquettish glances through half-dropped lids, shot arrowy beams from under archly-lifted brows, and said gravely: "Don't form yourself on her, Rebecca. Clover blossoms that grow in the fields beside Sunnybrook mustn't be tied in the same bouquet with gaudy sunflowers; they are too sweet and fragrant and wholesome."

XXIII

THE HILL DIFFICULTY

THE first happy year at Wareham, with its widened sky-line, its larger vision, its greater opportunity, was over and gone. Rebecca had studied during the

summer vacation, and had passed, on her return in
the autumn, certain examinations which would enable
her, if she carried out the same programme the next
season, to complete the course in three instead of four
years. She came off with no flying colours—that
would have been impossible in consideration of her
inadequate training; but she did wonderfully well in
some of the required subjects, and so brilliantly in
others that the average was respectable. She would
never have been a remarkable scholar under any circumstances, perhaps, and she was easily outstripped
in mathematics and the natural sciences by a dozen
girls, but in some inexplicable way she became, as
the months went on, the foremost figure in the school.
When she had entirely forgotten the facts which
would enable her to answer a question fully and conclusively, she commonly had some original theory
to expound; it was not always correct, but it was
generally unique and sometimes amusing. She was
only fair in Latin or French grammar, but when it
came to translation, her freedom, her choice of words,
and her sympathetic understanding of the spirit of
the text made her the delight of her teachers and the
despair of her rivals.

" She can be perfectly ignorant of a subject," said
Miss Maxwell to Adam Ladd, " but entirely intel-
ligent the moment she has a clue. Most of the
other girls are full of information and as stupid as
sheep."

Rebecca's gifts had not been discovered, save by
the few, during the first year, when she was adjusting
herself quietly to the situation. She was distinctly
one of the poorer girls; she had no fine dresses to

attract attention, no visitors, no friends in the town.
She had more study hours, and less time, therefore,
for the companionship of other girls, gladly as she
would have welcomed the gaiety of that side of school
life. Still, water will find its own level in some way,
and by the spring of the second year she had naturally
settled into the same sort of leadership which had
been hers in the smaller community of Riverboro.
She was unanimously elected assistant editor of the
Wareham School Pilot, being the first girl to assume
that enviable though somewhat arduous and thankless
position, and when her maiden number went to the
Cobbs, Uncle Jerry and Aunt Sarah could hardly eat
or sleep for pride.

"She'll always get votes," said Huldah Meserve
when discussing the election, "for whether she knows
anything or not, she looks as if she did, and whether
she's capable of filling an office or not, she looks as
if she was. I only wish I was tall and dark, and had
the gift of making people believe I was great things,
like Rebecca Randall. There's one thing: though the
boys call her handsome, you notice they don't trouble
her much with attention."

It was a fact that Rebecca's attitude towards the
opposite sex was still somewhat indifferent and
oblivious, even for fifteen and a half! No one could
look at her and doubt that she had potentialities of
attraction latent within her somewhere, but that side
of her nature was happily biding its time. A human
being is capable only of a certain amount of activity
at a given moment, and it will inevitably satisfy first
its most pressing needs, its most ardent desires, its
chief ambitions. Rebecca was full of small anxieties

and fears, for matters were not going well at the brick house, and were anything but hopeful at the home farm. She was overbusy and overtaxed and her thoughts were naturally drawn towards the difficult problems of daily living.

It had seemed to her during the autumn and winter of that year as if her Aunt Miranda had never been, save at the very first, so censorious and fault-finding. One Saturday Rebecca ran upstairs, and, bursting into a flood of tears, exclaimed: "Aunt Jane, it seems as if I never could stand her continual scoldings. Nothing I can do suits Aunt Miranda. She's just said it will take me my whole life to get the Randall out of me, and I'm not convinced that I want it all out, so there we are!"

Aunt Jane, never demonstrative, cried with Rebecca as she attempted to soothe her.

"You must be patient," she said, wiping first her own eyes and then Rebecca's. "I haven't told you, for it isn't fair you should be troubled when you're studying so hard, but your Aunt Miranda isn't well. One Monday morning about a month ago she had a kind of faint spell; it wasn't bad, but the doctor is afraid it was a shock, and if so, it's the beginning of the end. Seems to me she's failing right along, and that's what makes her so fretful and easy vexed. She has other troubles, too, that you don't know anything about, and if you're not kind to your Aunt Miranda now, child, you'll be dreadful sorry some time."

All the temper faded from Rebecca's face, and she stopped crying to say penitently: "Oh, the poor, dear thing! I won't mind a bit what she says now. She's just asked me for some milk-toast, and I was dreading to take it to her, but this will make everything different. Don't worry yet, Aunt Jane, for perhaps it won't be as bad as you think."

So when she carried the toast to her aunt a little later it was in the best gilt-edged china bowl, with a fringed napkin on the tray, and a sprig of geranium lying across the salt-cellar.

"Now, Aunt Miranda," she said cheerily, "I expect you to smack your lips and say this is good. It's not Randall, but Sawyer, milk-toast."

"You've tried all kinds on me one time an' another," Miranda answered. "This tastes real kind o' good; but I wish you hadn't wasted that nice geranium."

"You can't tell what's wasted," said Rebecca philosophically. "Perhaps that geranium has been hoping this long time it could brighten somebody's supper, so don't disappoint it by making believe you don't like it. I've seen geraniums cry—in the very early morning."

The mysterious trouble to which Jane had alluded was a very real one, but it was held in profound secrecy. Twenty-five hundred dollars of the small Sawyer property had been invested in the business of a friend of their father's, and had returned them a regular annual income of a hundred dollars. The family friend had been dead for some five years, but his son had succeeded to his interests, and all went on as formerly. Suddenly there came a letter saying that the firm had gone into bankruptcy, that the business had been completely wrecked, and that the Sawyer money had been swept away with everything else.

The loss of one hundred dollars a year is a very trifling matter, but it made all the difference between comfort and self-denial to the two old spinsters. Their manner of life had been so rigid and careful that it was difficult to economize any further, and the blow had fallen just when it was most inconvenient, for Rebecca's school and boarding expenses, small as they were, had to be paid promptly and in cash.

"Can we possibly go on doing it? Shan't we have to give up and tell her why?" asked Jane tearfully of the elder sister.

"We have put our hand to the plough, and we can't turn back," answered Miranda in her grimmest tone. "We have taken her away from her mother and offered her an education, and we've got to keep our word. She's Aurelia's only hope for years to come, to my way o' thinkin'. Hannah's beau takes all her time 'n' thought, and when she gits a husband her mother'll be out o' sight and out o' mind. John, instead of farmin', thinks he must be a doctor—as if folks wasn't gettin' unhealthy enough these days without turnin' out more young doctors to help 'em into their graves. No, Jane; we'll skimp 'n' do without, 'n' plan to git along on our interest money somehow, but we won't break into our principal, whatever happens."

"Breaking into the principal" was, in the minds of most thrifty New England women, a sin only second to arson, theft, or murder; and though the rule was occasionally carried too far for common sense—as in this case, where two elderly women of sixty might reasonably have drawn something from their little hoard in time of special need—it doubtless wrought more of good than evil in the community.

Rebecca, who knew nothing of their business affairs, merely saw her aunts grow more and more saving, pinching here and there, cutting off this and that relentlessly. Less meat and fish were bought; the woman who had lately been coming two days a week for washing, ironing, and scrubbing was dismissed; the old bonnets of the season before were brushed up and retrimmed; there were no drives to Moderation or trips to Portland. Economy was carried to its very extreme; but though Miranda was wellnigh as gloomy and uncompromising in her manner and conversation as a woman could well be, she at least never twitted her niece of being a burden. So Rebecca's share of the Sawyers' misfortunes consisted only in wearing her old dresses, hats and jackets, without any apparent hope of a change.

There was, however, no concealing the state of things at Sunnybrook, where chapters of accidents had unfolded themselves in a sort of serial story that had run through the year. The potato crop had failed; there were no apples to speak of; the hay had been poor; Aurelia had turns of dizziness in her head; Mark had broken his ankle. As this was his fourth offence, Miranda inquired how many bones there were in the human body "so 't they'd know when Mark got through breakin' 'em." The time for paying the interest on the mortgage, that incubus that had crushed all the joy out of the Randall household, had come and gone, and there was no possibility, for the first time in fourteen years, of paying the required forty-eight dollars. The only bright spot in

the horizon was Hannah's engagement to Will Melville, a young farmer whose land adjoined Sunnybrook, who had a good house, was alone in the world,
and his own master. Hannah was so satisfied with
her own unexpectedly radiant prospects that she
hardly realized her mother's anxieties; for there are
natures which flourish in adversity and deteriorate
when exposed to sudden prosperity. She had made
a visit of a week at the brick house; and Miranda's
impression, conveyed in privacy to Jane, was that
Hannah was close as the bark of a tree, and consid'-
able selfish too; that when she'd clim' as fur as she
could in the world, she'd kick the ladder out from
under her, everlastin' quick; that, on being sounded
as to her ability to be of use to the younger children
in the future, she said she guessed she'd done her
share a'ready, and she wan't goin' to burden Will with
her poor relations. "She's Susan Randall through and
through!" ejaculated Miranda. "I was glad to see
her face turned towards Temperance. If that mortgage
is ever cleared from the farm, 'twon't be Hannah
that'll do it: it'll be Rebecca or me!"

XXIV

ALADDIN RUBS HIS LAMP

"Your esteemed contribution entitled 'Wareham
Wildflowers,' has been accepted for the *Pilot*, Miss
Perkins," said Rebecca, entering the room where

Emma Jane was darning the firm's stockings. "I stayed to tea with Miss Maxwell, but came home early to tell you."

"You are joking, Becky!" faltered Emma Jane, looking up from her work.

"Not a bit; the senior editor read it and thought it highly instructive. It appears in the next issue."

"Not in the same number with your poem about the golden gates that close behind us when we leave school?"—and Emma Jane held her breath as she awaited the reply.

"Even so, Miss Perkins."

"Rebecca," said Emma Jane, with the nearest approach to tragedy that her nature would permit, "I don't know as I shall be able to bear it; and if anything happens to me, I ask you solemnly to bury that number of the *Pilot* with me."

Rebecca did not seem to think this the expression of an exaggerated state of feeling, inasmuch as she replied, "I know; that's just the way it seemed to me at first, and even now, whenever I'm alone and take out the *Pilot* back numbers to read over my contributions, I almost burst with pleasure; and it's not that they are good either, for they look worse to me every time I read them."

"If you would only live with me in some little house when we get older," mused Emma Jane, as, with her darning-needle poised in air, she regarded the opposite wall dreamily, "I would do the housework and cooking, and copy all your poems and stories, and take them to the post-office, and you needn't do anything but write. It would be perfectly elergant!"

"I'd like nothing better, if I hadn't promised to keep house for John," replied Rebecca.

"He won't have a house for a good many years, will he?"

"No," sighed Rebecca ruefully, flinging herself down by the table and resting her head on her hand. "Not unless we can contrive to pay off that detestable mortgage. The day grows farther off instead of nearer, now that we haven't paid the interest this year."

She pulled a piece of paper towards her, and scribbling idly on it, read aloud in a moment or two:

"Will you pay a little faster?" said the mortgage to the farm;
    "I confess I'm very tired of this place."
"The weariness is mutual," Rebecca Randall cried;
    "I would I'd never gazed upon your face!"

"A note has a 'face,'" observed Emma Jane, who was gifted in arithmetic; "I didn't know that a mortgage had."

"Our mortgage has," said Rebecca revengefully. "I should know him if I met him in the dark. Wait, and I'll draw him for you. It will be good for you to know how he looks, and then when you have a husband and seven children you won't allow him to come anywhere within a mile of your farm."

The sketch when completed was of a sort to be shunned by a timid person on the verge of slumber. There was a tiny house on the right, and a weeping family gathered in front of it. The mortgage was depicted as a cross between a fiend and an ogre, and held an axe uplifted in his red right hand. A figure with streaming black locks was staying the blow, and this, Rebecca explained complacently, was intended as a likeness of herself, though she was rather vague as to the method she should use in attaining her end.

"He's terrible," said Emma Jane, "but awfully wizened and small."

"It's only a twelve hundred dollar mortgage," said Rebecca, "and that's called a small one. John saw a man once that was mortgaged for twelve thousand."

"Shall you be a writer or an editor?" asked Emma Jane presently, as if one had only to choose and the thing were done.

"I shall have to do what turns up first, I suppose."

"Why not go out as a missionary to Syria, as the Burches are always coaxing you to? The Board would pay your expenses."

"I can't make up my mind to be a missionary," Rebecca answered. "I'm not good enough in the first place, and I don't 'feel a call,' as Mr. Burch says you must. I would like to do something for somebody, and make things move, somewhere; but I don't want to go thousands of miles away teaching people how to live when I haven't learned myself. It isn't as if the heathen really needed me; I'm sure they'll come out all right in the end."

"I can't see how, if all the people who ought to go out to save them stay at home as we do," argued Emma Jane.

"Why, whatever God is, and wherever He is, He must always be there, ready and waiting. He can't move about and miss people. It may take the heathen a little longer to find Him, but God will make allowances, of course. He knows if they live in such hot climates it must make them lazy and slow; and the parrots and tigers and snakes and bread-fruit trees distract their minds; and having no books, they can't think as well; but they'll find God somehow, some time."

"What if they die first?" asked Emma Jane.

"Oh, well, they can't be blamed for that; they don't die on purpose," said Rebecca, with a comfortable theology.

In these days Adam Ladd sometimes went to Temperance on business connected with the proposed branch of the railroad familiarly known as the "York and Yank 'em," and while there he gained an inkling of Sunnybrook affairs. The building of the new road was not yet a certainty, and there was a difference of opinion as to the best route from Temperance to Plumville. In one event the way would lead directly through Sunnybrook, from corner to corner, and Mrs. Randall would be compensated; in the other, her interests would not be affected either for good or ill, save as all land in the immediate neighbourhood might rise a little in value.

Coming from Temperance to Wareham one day, Adam had a long walk and talk with Rebecca, whom he thought looking pale and thin, though she was holding bravely to her self-imposed hours of work. She was wearing a black cashmere dress that had been her Aunt Jane's second-best. We are familiar with the heroine of romance whose foot is so exquisitely shaped that the coarsest shoe cannot conceal its perfections, and one always cherishes a doubt of the statement; yet it is true that Rebecca's peculiar and

individual charm seemed wholly independent of
accessories. The lines of her figure, the rare colour-
ing of skin and hair and eyes, triumphed over shabby
clothing, though, had the advantage of artistic apparel
been given her, the little world of Wareham would
probably at once have dubbed her a beauty. The long
black braids were now disposed after a quaint fashion
of her own. They were crossed behind, carried up to
the front, and crossed again, the tapering ends finally
brought down and hidden in the thicker part at the
neck. Then a purely feminine touch was given to the
hair that waved back from the face—a touch that
rescued little crests and wavelets from bondage and
set them free to take a new colour in the sun.

Adam Ladd looked at her in a way that made her
put her hands over her face and laugh through them
shyly as she said: "I know what you are thinking,
Mr. Aladdin—that my dress is an inch longer than
last year, and my hair different; but I'm not nearly
a young lady yet—truly I'm not. Sixteen is a month
off still, and you promised not to give me up till my
dress trails. If you don't like me to grow old, why
don't you grow young? Then we can meet in the
halfway house and have nice times. Now that I think
about it," she continued, "that's just what you've
been doing all along. When you bought the soap, I
thought you were Grandfather Sawyer's age; when
you danced with me at the flag-raising, you seemed
like my father; but when you showed me your
mother's picture, I felt as if you were my John,
because I was so sorry for you."

"That will do very well," smiled Adam—"unless
you go so swiftly that you become my grandmother

before I really need one. You are studying too hard,
Miss Rebecca Rowena!"

"Just a little," she confessed. "But vacation comes
soon, you know."

"And are you going to have a good rest and try
to recover your dimples? They are really worth pre-
serving."

A shadow crept over Rebecca's face and her eyes
suffused. "Don't be kind, Mr. Aladdin; I can't bear
it; it's—it's not one of my dimply days!" and she
ran in at the seminary gate, and disappeared with a
farewell wave of her hand.

Adam Ladd wended his way to the principal's office
in a thoughtful mood. He had come to Wareham to
unfold a plan that he had been considering for several
days. This year was the fiftieth anniversary of the
founding of the Wareham schools, and he meant to
tell Mr. Morrison that, in addition to his gift of a
hundred volumes to the reference library, he intended
to celebrate it by offering prizes in English composition, a subject in which he was much interested. He
wished the boys and girls of the two upper classes to
compete; the award to be made to the writers of the
two best essays. As to the nature of the prizes, he
had not quite made up his mind, but they would be
substantial ones, either of money or of books.

This interview accomplished, he called upon Miss
Maxwell, thinking as he took the path through the
woods: "Rose-Red-Snow-White needs the help; and
since there is no way of my giving it to her without
causing remark, she must earn it, poor little soul! I
wonder if my money is always to be useless where
most I wish to spend it."

He had scarcely greeted his hostess, when he said:
"Miss Maxwell, doesn't it strike you that our friend
Rebecca looks wretchedly tired?"

"She does indeed; and I am considering whether I
can take her away with me. I always go South for the
spring vacation, travelling by sea to Old Point Comfort, and rusticating in some quiet spot near by. I
should like nothing better than to have Rebecca for
a companion."

"The very thing!" assented Adam heartily. "But
why should you take the whole responsibility? Why
not let me help? I am greatly interested in the child,
and have been for some years."

"You needn't pretend you discovered her," interrupted Miss Maxwell warmly, "for I did that myself."

"She was an intimate friend of mine long before
you ever came to Wareham," laughed Adam; and he
told Miss Maxwell the circumstances of his first meeting with Rebecca. "From the beginning I've tried to
think of a way I could be useful in her development,
but no reasonable solution seemed to offer itself."

"Luckily, she attends to her own development,"
answered Miss Maxwell. "In a sense she is independent of everything and everybody; she follows
her saint without being conscious of it. But she needs
a hundred practical things that money would buy for
her, and, alas! I have a slender purse."

"Take mine, I beg; and let me act through you,"
pleaded Adam. "I could not bear to see even a young
tree trying its best to grow without light or air—
how much less a gifted child! I interviewed her aunts
a year ago, hoping I might be permitted to give her

a musical education. I assured them it was a most ordinary occurrence, and that I was willing to be repaid later on if they insisted; but it was no use. The elder Miss Sawyer remarked that no member of her family ever had been 'on the town,' and she guessed they wouldn't begin at this late day."

"I rather like that uncompromising New England grit," exclaimed Miss Maxwell; "and so far I don't regret one burden that Rebecca has borne or one sorrow that she has shared. Necessity has only made her brave; poverty has only made her daring and self-reliant. As to her present needs, there are certain things only a woman ought to do for a girl, and I should not like to have you do them for Rebecca; I should feel that I was wounding her pride and self-respect, even though she were ignorant. But there is no reason why I may not do them if necessary, and let you pay her travelling expenses. I would accept those for her without the slightest embarrassment, but I agree that the matter would better be kept private between us."

"You are a real fairy godmother!" exclaimed Adam, shaking her hand warmly. "Would it be less trouble for you to invite her room-mate, too—the pink-and-white inseparable?"

"No, thank you; I prefer to have Rebecca all to myself," said Miss Maxwell.

"I can understand that," replied Adam absent-mindedly. "I mean, of course, that one child is less trouble than two. There she is now."

Here Rebecca appeared in sight, walking down the quiet street with a lad of sixteen. They were in animated conversation, and were apparently reading something aloud to each other, for the black head and the curly brown one were both bent over a sheet of letter paper. Rebecca kept glancing up at her companion, her eyes sparkling with appreciation.

"Miss Maxwell," said Adam, "I am a trustee of this institution; but, upon my word, I don't believe in coeducation!"

"I have my own occasional hours of doubt," she answered; "but surely its disadvantages are reduced to a minimum with—children. That is a very impressive sight which you are privileged to witness, Mr. Ladd. The folk in Cambridge often gloated on the spectacle of Longfellow and Lowell arm-in-arm. The little school world of Wareham palpitates with excitement when it sees the senior and the junior editors of the *Pilot* walking together."

XXV

ROSES OF JOY

THE day before Rebecca started for the South with Miss Maxwell she was in the library with Emma Jane and Huldah, consulting dictionaries and encyclopædias. As they were leaving they passed the locked cases containing the library of fiction, open to the teachers and townspeople, but forbidden to the students.

They looked longingly through the glass, getting some little comfort from the titles of the volumes, as hungry children imbibe emotional nourishment from

the pies and tarts inside a confectioner's window.
Rebecca's eyes fell upon a new book in the corner,
and she read the name aloud with delight: "'The
Rose of Joy.' Listen, girls! isn't that lovely? 'The
Rose of Joy.' It looks beautiful, and it sounds beauti-
ful. What does it mean, I wonder?"

"I guess everybody has a different rose," said
Huldah shrewdly. "I know what mine would be,
and I'm not ashamed to own it. I'd like a year in a
city, with just as much money as I wanted to spend,
horses and splendid clothes, and amusements every
minute of the day; and I'd like, above everything, to
live with people that wear low necks." (Poor Huldah
never took off her dress without bewailing the fact
that her lot was cast in Riverboro, where her pretty
white shoulders could never be seen.)

"That would be fun—for a while, anyway," Emma
Jane remarked. "But wouldn't that be pleasure more
than joy? Oh, I've got an idea!"

"Don't shriek so!" said the startled Huldah. "I
thought it was a mouse."

"I don't have them very often," apologized Emma
Jane—"ideas, I mean. This one shook me like a
stroke of lightning. Rebecca, couldn't it be success?"

"That's good," mused Rebecca. "I can see that
success would be joy, but it doesn't seem to me like a
rose, somehow. I was wondering if it could be love."

"I wish we could have a peep at the book; it must
be perfectly elergant," said Emma Jane. "But now
you say it is love, I think that's the best guess yet."

All day long the four words haunted and possessed
Rebecca; she said them over to herself continually.
Even the prosaic Emma Jane was affected by them,

for in the evening she said: "I don't expect you to believe it, but I have another idea; that's two in one day. I had it while I was putting cologne on your head. The rose of joy might be helpfulness."

"If it is, then it is always blooming in your dear little heart, you darlingest, kind Emmie, taking such good care of your troublesome Becky!"

"Don't dare to call yourself troublesome! You're —you're—you're my rose of joy, that's what you are!" And the two girls hugged each other affectionately.

In the middle of the night Rebecca touched Emma Jane on the shoulder softly. "Are you very fast asleep, Emmie?" she whispered.

"Not so very," answered Emma Jane drowsily.

"I've thought of something new. If you sang, or painted, or wrote—not a little, but beautifully, you know—wouldn't the doing of it just as much as you wanted give you the rose of joy?"

"It might if it was a real talent," answered Emma Jane, "though I don't like it so well as love. If you have another thought, Becky, keep it till morning."

"I did have one more inspiration," said Rebecca when they were dressing next morning, "but I didn't wake you. I wondered if the rose of joy could be sacrifice. But I think sacrifice would be a lily, not a rose, don't you?"

The journey southward, the first glimpse of the ocean, the strange new scenes, the ease and delicious freedom, the intimacy with Miss Maxwell, almost intoxicated Rebecca. In three days she was not only herself again, she was another self, thrilling with delight, anticipation, and realization. She had always had such eager hunger for knowledge, such thirst for love, such passionate longing for the music, the beauty, the poetry of existence. She had always been straining to make the outward world conform to her inward dreams, and now life had grown all at once rich and sweet, wide and full. She was using all her natural, God-given outlets, and Emily Maxwell marvelled daily at the inexhaustible way in which the girl poured out and gathered in the treasures of thought and experience that belonged to her. She was a life-giver, altering the whole scheme of any picture she made a part of by contributing new values. Have you never seen the dull blues and greens of a room changed, transfigured by a burst of sunshine? That seemed to Miss Maxwell the effect of Rebecca on the groups of people with whom they now and then mingled; but they were commonly alone, reading to each other and having quiet talks. The prize essay was very much on Rebecca's mind. Secretly she thought she could never be happy unless she won it. She cared nothing for the value of it, and in this case almost nothing for the honour. She wanted to please Mr. Aladdin, and justify his belief in her.

" If I ever succeed in choosing a subject, I must ask if you think I can write well on it; and then I suppose I must work in silence and secret, never even reading the essay to you, nor talking about it."

Miss Maxwell and Rebecca were sitting by a little brook on a sunny spring day. They had been in a stretch of wood by the sea since breakfast, going every now and then for a bask on the warm white sand, and returning to their shady solitude when tired of the sun's glare.

"The subject is very important," said Miss Maxwell, "but I do not dare choose for you. Have you decided on anything yet?"

"No," Rebecca answered; "I plan a new essay every night. I've begun one on 'What is Failure?' and another on 'He and She.' That would be a dialogue between a boy and girl just as they were leaving school, and would tell their ideals of life. Then, do you remember you said to me one day, 'Follow your Saint'? I'd love to write about that. I didn't have a single thought in Wareham, and now I have a new one every minute, so I must try and write the essay here—think it out, at any rate, while I am so happy and free and rested. Look at the pebbles in the bottom of the pool, Miss Emily, so round and smooth and shining."

"Yes, but where did they get that beautiful polish, that satin skin, that lovely shape, Rebecca? Not in the still pool lying on the sands. It was never there that their angles were rubbed off and their rough surfaces polished, but in the strife and warfare of running waters. They have jostled against other pebbles, dashed against sharp rocks, and now we look at them and call them beautiful."

"If Fate had not made somebody a teacher,
    She might have been, oh! such a splendid preacher!"

rhymed Rebecca. "Oh, if I could only think and speak as you do!" she sighed. "I am so afraid I shall never get education enough to make a good writer."

"You could worry about plenty of other things to better advantage," said Miss Maxwell a little scornfully. "Be afraid, for instance, that you won't understand human nature; that you won't realize the beauty of the outer world; that you may lack sympathy, and thus never be able to read a heart; that your faculty of expression may not keep pace with your ideas—a thousand things, every one of them more important to the writer than the knowledge that is found in books. Æsop was a Greek slave who could not even write down his wonderful fables, yet all the world reads them."

"I didn't know that," said Rebecca, with a half-sob. "I didn't know anything until I met you!"

"You will only have had a high-school course, but the most famous universities do not always succeed in making men and women. When I long to go abroad and study I always remember that there were three great schools in Athens and two in Jerusalem, but the Teacher of all teachers came out of Nazareth, a little village hidden away from the bigger, busier world."

"Mr. Ladd says that you are almost wasted on Wareham," said Rebecca thoughtfully.

"He is wrong; my talent is not a great one, but no talent is wholly wasted unless its owner chooses to hide it in a napkin. Remember that of your own gifts, Rebecca; they may not be praised of men, but they may cheer, console, inspire, perhaps, when and where you least expect. The brimming glass that overflows its rim moistens the earth about it."

"Did you ever hear of 'The Rose of Joy'?" asked Rebecca after a long silence.

"Yes, of course; where did you see it?"

"On the outside of a book in the library."

"I saw it on the inside of a book in the library,"

smiled Miss Maxwell. " It is from Emerson, but I'm afraid you haven't quite grown up to it, Rebecca, and it is one of the things impossible to explain."

" Oh, try me, dear Miss Maxwell!" pleaded Rebecca. " Perhaps by thinking hard I can guess a little bit what it means."

" ' In the actual—this painful kingdom of time and chance—are Care, Canker, and Sorrow; with thought, with the Ideal, is immortal hilarity—the Rose of Joy; round it all the Muses sing,' " quoted Miss Maxwell.

Rebecca repeated it over and over again until she had learned it by heart; then she said, " I don't want to be conceited, but I almost believe I do understand it, Miss Maxwell. Not altogether, perhaps, because it is puzzling and difficult; but a little, enough to go on with. It's as if a splendid shape galloped past you on horseback; you are so surprised, and your eyes move so slowly you cannot half see it, but you just catch a glimpse as it whisks by, and you know it is beautiful. It's all settled: my essay is going to be called ' The Rose of Joy.' I've just decided. It hasn't any beginning, nor any middle, but there will be a thrilling ending, something like this—let me see: joy, boy, toy, ahoy, decoy, alloy :

> " Then come what will of weal or woe
>   (Since all gold hath alloy),
>   Thou'lt bloom unwithered in this heart,
>   My Rose of Joy!

Now I'm going to tuck you up in the shawl and give you the fir pillow, and while you sleep I am going down on the shore and write a fairy story for you. It's one of our ' supposing ' kind; it flies far, far into the future, and makes beautiful things happen that may never really all come to pass; but some of them will, you'll see; and then you'll take out the little fairy story from your desk and remember Rebecca."

"I wonder why these young things always choose subjects that would tax the powers of a great essayist," thought Miss Maxwell, as she tried to sleep. "Are they dazzled, captivated, taken possession of, by the splendour of the theme, and do they fancy they can write up to it? Poor little innocents, hitching their toy waggons to the stars! How pretty this particular innocent looks under her new sunshade."

Adam Ladd had been driving through Boston streets on a cold spring day, when nature and the fashion-mongers were holding out promises which seemed far from performance. Suddenly his vision was assailed by the sight of a rose-coloured parasol gaily unfurled in a shop window, signalling the passer-by and setting him to dream of summer sunshine. It reminded Adam of a New England appletree in full bloom, the outer covering of deep pink shining through the thin white lining, and a fluffy, fringe-like edge of mingled rose and cream dropping over the green handle. All at once he remembered one of Rebecca's early confidences—the little pink sunshade that had given her the only peep into the gay world of fashion that her childhood had ever known; her adoration of the flimsy bit of finery, and its tragic and sacrificial end. He entered the shop, bought the extravagant bauble, and expressed it to Wareham at once, not a single doubt of its appropriateness crossing the darkness of his masculine mind.

He thought only of the joy in Rebecca's eyes; of the poise of her head under the apple-blossom canopy. It was a trifle embarrassing to return an hour later and buy a blue parasol for Emma Jane Perkins, but it seemed increasingly difficult, as the years went on, to remember her existence at all the proper times and seasons.

This is Rebecca's fairy story, copied the next day, and given to Emily Maxwell just as she was going to her room for the night. She read it with tears in her eyes, and then sent it to Adam Ladd, thinking he had earned a share in it, and that he deserved a glimpse of the girl's budding imagination, as well as of her grateful young heart:

A FAIRY STORY

There was once a tired and rather poverty-stricken Princess who dwelt in a cottage on the great highway between two cities. She was not as unhappy as thousands of others; indeed, she had much to be grateful for; but the life she lived and the work she did were full hard for one who was fashioned slenderly.

Now the cottage stood by the edge of a great green forest where the wind was always singing in the branches and the sunshine filtering through the leaves.

And one day, when the Princess was sitting by the wayside quite spent by her labour in the fields, she saw a golden chariot rolling down the King's Highway, and in it a person who could be none other than somebody's Fairy Godmother on her way to the

Court. The chariot halted at her door, and, though
the Princess had read of such beneficent personages,
she never dreamed for an instant that one of them
could ever alight at her cottage.

"If you are tired, poor little Princess, why do you
not go into the cool, green forest and rest?" asked
the Fairy Godmother."

"Because I have no time," she answered. "I must
go back to my plough."

"Is that your plough leaning by the tree? and is
it not too heavy?"

"It is heavy," answered the Princess; "but I love
to turn the hard earth into soft furrows, and know
that I am making good soil wherein my seeds may
grow. When I feel the weight too much, I try to
think of the harvest."

The golden chariot passed on, and the two talked
no more together that day; nevertheless, the King's
messengers were busy, for they whispered one word
into the ear of the Fairy Godmother and another into
the ear of the Princess, though so faintly that neither
of them realized that the King had spoken.

The next morning a strong man knocked at the
cottage door, and, doffing his hat to the Princess,
said: "A golden chariot passed me yesterday, and
one within it flung me a purse of ducats, saying:
'Go out into the King's Highway, and search until
you find a cottage with a heavy plough leaning against
a tree near by. Enter, and say to the Princess whom
you will find there: "I will guide the plough, and
you must go and rest, or walk in the cool, green
forest, for this is the command of your Fairy Godmother."'"

And the same thing happened every day, and every day the tired Princess walked in the green wood. Many times she caught the glitter of the chariot, and ran into the Highway to give thanks to the Fairy Godmother; but she was never fleet enough to reach the spot. She could only stand with eager eyes and longing heart as the chariot passed by. Yet she never failed to catch a smile; and sometimes a word or two floated back to her—words that sounded like: "I would not be thanked. We are all children of the same King, and I am only his messenger."

Now, as the Princess walked daily in the green forest, hearing the wind singing in the branches, and seeing the sunlight filter through the latticework of green leaves, there came unto her thoughts that had lain asleep in the stifling air of the cottage and the weariness of guiding the plough. And by-and-bye she took a needle from her girdle and pricked the thoughts on the leaves of the trees, and sent them into the air to float hither and thither. And it came to pass that people began to pick them up, and, holding them against the sun, to read what was written on them; and this was because the simple little words on the leaves were only, after all, a part of one of the King's messages, such as the Fairy Godmother dropped continually from her golden chariot.

But the miracle of the story lies deeper than all this.

Whenever the Princess pricked the words upon the leaves she added a thought of her Fairy Godmother, and, folding it close within, sent the leaf out on the breeze to float hither and thither, and fall where it would. And many other little Princesses felt the same impulse and did the same thing. And as nothing is ever lost in the King's Dominion, so these thoughts and wishes and hopes, being full of love and gratitude, had no power to die, but took unto themselves other shapes, and lived on for ever. They cannot be seen, our vision is too weak; nor heard, our hearing is too dull; but they can sometimes be felt, and we know not what force is stirring our hearts to nobler aims.

The end of the story is not come, but it may be that some day, when the Fairy Godmother has a message to deliver in person straight to the King, he will say: "Your face I know, your voice, your thoughts, and your heart. I have heard the rumble of your chariot-wheels on the great Highway, and I knew that you were on the King's business. Here in my hand is a sheaf of messages from every quarter of my kingdom. They were delivered by weary and footsore travellers, who said that they could never have reached the gate in safety had it not been for your help and inspiration. Read them, that you may know when and where and how you sped the King's service."

And when the Fairy Godmother reads them, it may be that sweet odours will rise from the pages and half-forgotten memories will stir the air; but in the gladness of the moment nothing will be half so lovely as the voice of the King when he said: "Read, and know how you sped the King's service."

REBECCA ROWENA RANDALL.

XXVI

THE summer term at Wareham had ended, and Huldah Meserve, Dick Carter, and Living Perkins had finished school, leaving Rebecca and Emma Jane to represent Riverboro in the year to come. Delia Weeks was at home from Lewiston on a brief visit, and Mrs. Robinson was celebrating the occasion by a small and select party, the particular day having been set because strawberries were ripe and there was a rooster that wanted killing. Mrs. Robinson explained this to her husband, and requested that he eat his dinner on the carpenter's bench in the shed, as the party was to be a ladies' affair.

"All right; it won't be any loss to me," said Mr. Robinson. "Give me beans; that's all I ask. When a rooster wants to be killed, I want somebody else to eat him, not me!"

Mrs. Robinson had company only once or twice a year, and was generally much prostrated for several days afterwards, the struggle between pride and parsimony being quite too great a strain upon her. It was necessary, in order to maintain her standing in the community, to furnish a good "set out"; yet the extravagance of the proceeding goaded her from the first moment she began to stir the marble cake to the moment when the feast appeared upon the table.

The rooster had been boiling steadily over a slow fire since morning, but such was his power of resistance that his shape was as firm and handsome in the pot as on the first moment when he was lowered into it.

"He ain't goin' to give up!" said Alice, peering nervously under the cover, "and he looks like a scarecrow."

"We'll see whether he gives up or not when I take a sharp knife to him," her mother answered; "and as to his looks, a platter full o' gravy makes a sight o' difference with old roosters, and I'll put dumplings round the aidge; they're turrible fillin', though they don't belong with boiled chicken."

The rooster did indeed make an impressive showing, lying in his border of dumplings, and the dish was much complimented when it was borne in by Alice. This was fortunate, as the chorus of admiration ceased abruptly when the ladies began to eat the fowl.

"I was glad you could git over to Huldy's graduation, Delia," said Mrs. Meserve, who sat at the foot of the table and helped the chicken while Mrs. Robinson poured coffee at the other end. She was a fit mother for Huldah, being much the most stylish person in Riverboro; ill-health and dress were, indeed, her two chief enjoyments in life. It was rumoured that her elaborately curled "front-piece" had cost five dollars, and that it was sent into Portland twice a year to be dressed and frizzed; but it is extremely difficult to discover the precise facts in such cases, and a conscientious historian always prefers to warn a too credulous reader against imbibing as Gospel truth something that might be the basest perversion of it. As to Mrs. Meserve's appearance, have you ever, in earlier years, sought the comforting society of the cook and hung over the kitchen table while she rolled out sugar gingerbread? Perhaps then, in some unaccustomed moment of amiability, she made you a dough lady, cutting the outline deftly with her pastry-knife, and then, at last, placing the human stamp upon it by sticking in two black currants for eyes. Just call to mind the face of that sugar gingerbread lady, and you will have an exact portrait of Huldah's mother—Mis' Peter Meserve, she was generally called, there being several others.

"How 'd you like Huldy's dress, Delia?" she asked, snapping the elastic in her black jet bracelets after an irritating fashion she had.

"I thought it was about the handsomest of any," answered Delia; "and her composition was first-rate. It was the only real amusin' one there was, and she read it so loud and clear we didn't miss any of it; most o' the girls spoke as if they had hasty puddin' in their mouths."

"That was the composition she wrote for Adam Ladd's prize," explained Mrs. Meserve, "and they do say she'd 'a' come out first, 'stead o' fourth, if her subject had been dif'rent. There was three ministers and three deacons on the committee, and it was only natural they should choose a serious piece; hers was too lively to suit 'em."

Huldah's inspiring theme had been "Boys," and she certainly had a fund of knowledge and experience that fitted her to write most intelligently upon it. It was vastly popular with the audience, who enjoyed the rather cheap jokes and allusions with which it coruscated; but judged from a purely literary standpoint, it left much to be desired.

"Rebecca's piece wa'n't read out loud, but the one that took the boy's prize was; why was that?" asked Mrs. Robinson.

"Because she wa'n't graduatin'," explained Mrs. Cobb, "and couldn't take part in the exercises; it'll be printed, with Herbert Dunn's, in the school paper."

"I'm glad o' that, for I'll never believe it was better 'n Huldy's till I read it with my own eyes; it seems as if the prize ought to 'a' gone to one of the seniors."

"Well, no, Marthy, not if Ladd offered it to any of the two upper classes that wanted to try for it," argued Mrs. Robinson. "They say they asked him to give out the prizes, and he refused up and down. It seems odd, his bein' so rich and travellin' about all over the country, that he was too modest to git up on that platform."

"My Huldy could 'a' done it and not winked an eyelash," observed Mrs. Meserve complacently, a remark which there seemed no disposition on the part of any of the company to controvert.

"It was complete, though, the governor happening to be there to see his niece graduate," said Delia Weeks. "Land! he looked elegant! They say he's only six feet, but he might 'a' been sixteen, and he certainly did make a fine speech."

"Did you notice Rebecca, how white she was, and how she trembled when she and Herbert Dunn stood there while the governor was praisin' 'em? He'd read her composition, too, for he wrote the Sawyer girls a letter about it." This remark was from the sympathetic Mrs. Cobb.

"I thought 'twas kind o' foolish, his makin' so

much of her when it wa'n't her graduation," objected Mrs. Meserve; "layin' his hand on her head 'n' all that, as if he was a Pope pronouncin' benediction. But there! I'm glad the prize come to Riverboro, 't any rate, and a han'somer one never was give out from the Wareham platform. I guess there ain't no end to Adam Ladd's money. The fifty dollars would 'a' been good enough, but he must needs go and put it into those elegant purses."

"I set so fur back I couldn't see 'em fairly," complained Delia, "and now Rebecca has taken hers home to show her mother."

"It was kind of a gold net bag with a chain," said Mrs. Perkins, "and there was five ten-dollar gold pieces in it. Herbert Dunn's was put in a fine leather wallet."

"How long is Rebecca goin' to stay at the farm?" asked Delia.

"Till they get over Hannah's bein' married, and get the house to runnin' without her," answered Mrs. Perkins. "It seems as if Hannah might 'a' waited a little longer. Aurelia was set against her goin' away while Rebecca was at school, but she's obstinate as a mule, Hannah is, and she just took her own way in spite of her mother. She's been doin' her sewin' for a year; the awfullest coarse cotton-cloth she had, but she's nearly blinded herself with fine stitchin' and rufflin' and tuckin'. Did you hear about the quilt she made? It's white, and has a big bunch o' grapes in the centre, quilted by a thimble-top. Then there's a row of circle-borderin' round the grapes, and she done them the size of a spool. The next border was done with a sherry glass, and the last with a port glass, an' all outside o' that was solid stitchin' done in straight rows; she's goin' to exhibit it at the county fair."

"She'd better 'a' been takin' in sewin' and earnin' money, 'stead o' blindin' her eyes on such foolishness as quilted counterpanes," said Mrs. Cobb. "The next thing you know that mortgage will be foreclosed on Mis' Randall, and she and the children won't have a roof over their heads."

"Don't they say there's a good chance of the railroad goin' through her place?" asked Mrs. Robinson. "If it does, she'll git as much as the farm is worth, and more. Adam Ladd's one of the stock-holders, and everything is a success he takes holt of. They're fightin' it in Augusty, but I'd back Ladd agin any o' them legislaters if he thought he was in the right."

"Rebecca'll have some new clothes now," said Delia, "and the land knows she needs 'em. Seems to me the Sawyer girls are gittin' turrible near!"

"Rebecca won't have any new clothes out o' the prize-money," remarked Mrs. Perkins, "for she sent it away the next day to pay the interest on that mortgage."

"Poor little girl!" exclaimed Delia Weeks.

"She might as well help along her folks as spend it on foolishness," affirmed Mrs. Robinson. "I think she was mighty lucky to get it to pay the interest with, but she's probably like all the Randalls; it was easy come, easy go, with them."

"That's more than could be said of the Sawyer stock," retorted Mrs. Perkins; "seems like they enjoyed savin' more 'n anything in the world, and it's gainin' on Mirandy sence her shock."

"I don't believe it was a shock; it stands to reason

she'd never 'a' got up after it and been so smart as
she is now. We had three o' the worst shocks in our
family that there ever was on this river, and I know
every symptom of 'em better 'n the doctors." And
Mrs. Peter Meserve shook her head wisely.

"Mirandy's smart enough," said Mrs. Cobb, "but
you notice she stays right to home, and she's more
close-mouthed than ever she was; never took a mite o'
pride in the prize, as I could see, though it pretty
nigh drove Jeremiah out o' his senses. I thought I
should 'a' died o' shame when he cried 'Hooray!' and
swung his straw hat when the governor shook hands
with Rebecca. It's lucky he couldn't get fur into the
church and had to stand back by the door, for, as it
was, he made a spectacle of himself. My suspicion is"
—and here every lady stopped eating and sat up
straight—"that the Sawyer girls have lost money.
They don't know a thing about business, 'n' never
did, and Mirandy's too secretive and contrairy to ask
advice."

"The most o' what they've got is in gov'ment
bonds, I always heard, and you can't lose money on
them. Jane hed the timber land left her, an' Mirandy
had the brick house. She probably took it awful hard
that Rebecca's fifty dollars had to be swallowed up in
a mortgage, 'stead of goin' towards school expenses.
The more I think of it, the more I think Adam Ladd
intended Rebecca should have that prize when he gave
it." The mind of Huldah's mother ran towards the
idea that her daughter's rights had been assailed.

"Land, Marthy, what foolishness you talk!" exclaimed Mrs. Perkins. "You don't suppose he could
tell what composition the committee was going to

choose; and why should he offer another fifty dollars for a boy's prize, if he wa'n't interested in helpin' along the school? He's give Emma Jane about the same present as Rebecca every Christmas for five years; that's the way he does."

"Some time he'll forget one of 'em and give to the other, or drop 'em both and give to some new girl," said Delia Weeks, with an experience born of fifty years of spinsterhood.

"Like as not," assented Mrs. Peter Meserve, "though it's easy to see he ain't the marryin' kind. There's men that would marry once a year if their wives would die fast enough, and there's men that seems to want to live alone."

"If Ladd was a Mormon, I guess he could have every woman in North Riverboro that's a suitable age, accordin' to what my cousins say," remarked Mrs. Perkins.

"'Tain't likely he could be ketched by any North Riverboro girl," demurred Mrs. Robinson; "not when he prob'bly has had the pick o' Boston. I guess Marthy hit it when she said there's men that ain't the marryin' kind."

"I wouldn't trust any of 'em when Miss Right comes along!" laughed Mrs. Cobb genially. "You never can tell what 'n' who's goin' to please 'em. You know Jeremiah's contrairy horse, Buster? He won't let anybody put the bit into his mouth if he can help it. He'll fight Jerry, and fight me, till he has to give in. Rebecca didn't know nothin' about his tricks, and the other day she went int' the barn to hitch up. I followed right along, knowing she'd have trouble with the headstall, and I declare if she wa'n't pattin'

Buster's nose and talkin' to him, and when she put her
little fingers into his mouth he opened it so fur I
thought he'd swaller her, for sure. He jest smacked
his lips over the bit as if 'twas a lump o' sugar. 'Land!
Rebecca,' I says, 'how 'd you persuade him to take the
bit?' 'I didn't,' she says; 'he seemed to want it;
perhaps he's tired of his stall and wants to get out in
the fresh air.' "

XXVII

"THE VISION SPLENDID"

A YEAR had elapsed since Adam Ladd's prize had been
discussed over the teacups in Riverboro. The months
had come and gone, and at length the great day had
dawned for Rebecca—the day to which she had been
looking forward for five years as the first goal to be
reached on her little journey through the world.
School-days were ended, and the mystic function
known to the initiated as "graduation" was about to
be celebrated; it was even now heralded by the sun
dawning in the eastern sky. Rebecca stole softly out
of bed, crept to the window, threw open the blinds,
and welcomed the rosy light that meant a cloudless
morning. Even the sun looked different somehow,
larger, redder, more important than usual; and if it
were really so, there was no member of the graduating class who would have thought it strange or unbecoming, in view of all the circumstances. Emma
Jane stirred on her pillow, woke, and seeing Rebecca
at the window, came and knelt on the floor beside

her. "It's going to be pleasant!" she sighed grate-fully. "If it wasn't wicked, I could thank the Lord, I'm so relieved in mind! Did you sleep?"

"Not much; the words of my class poem kept run-ning through my head, and the accompaniments of the songs; and worse than anything, Mary Queen of Scots' prayer in Latin—it seemed as if

> "'Adoro, imploro,
>   Ut liberes me!'

were burned into my brain."

No one who is unfamiliar with life in rural neigh-bourhoods can imagine the gravity, the importance, the solemnity of this last day of school. In the matter of preparation, wealth of detail, and general excite-ment, it far surpasses a wedding; for that is com-monly a simple affair in the country, sometimes even beginning and ending in a visit to the parsonage. Nothing quite equals graduation in the minds of the graduates themselves, their families, and the younger students, unless it be the inauguration of a governor at the State Capitol. Wareham, then, was shaken to its very centre on this day of days. Mothers and fathers of the scholars, as well as relatives to the remotest generation, had been coming on the train and driving into the town since breakfast-time; old pupils, both married and single, with and without families, streamed back to the dear old village. The two livery stables were crowded with vehicles of all sorts, and lines of buggies and waggons were drawn up along the sides of the shady roads, the horses switching their tails in luxurious idleness. The streets were filled with people wearing their best clothes, and the fashions included not only "the latest thing," but the well-preserved relic of a bygone day. There were all sorts and conditions of men and women, for there were sons and daughters of store-keepers, lawyers, butchers, doctors, shoemakers, pro-fessors, ministers, and farmers at the Wareham schools, either as boarders or day scholars. In the seminary building there was an excitement so deep and profound that it expressed itself in a kind of hushed silence, a transient suspension of life, as those most interested approached the crucial moment. The feminine graduates-to-be were seated in their own bedrooms, dressed with a completeness of detail to which all their past lives seemed to have been but a prelude. At least, this was the case with their bodies; but their heads, owing to the extreme heat of the day, were one and all ornamented with leads, or papers, or dozens of little braids, to issue later in every sort of curl known to the girl of that period. Rolling the hair on leads or papers was a favourite method of attaining the desired result, and though it often en-tailed a sleepless night, there were those who gladly paid the price. Others, in whose veins the blood of martyrs did not flow, substituted rags for leads and pretended that they made a more natural and less woolly curl. Heat, however, will melt the proudest head and reduce to fiddling strings the finest product of the waving-pin; so anxious mothers were stationed over their offspring, waving palm-leaf fans, it having been decided that the supreme instant when the town clock struck ten should be the one chosen for releasing the prisoners from their self-imposed tortures.

Dotted or plain Swiss muslin was the favourite

garb, though there were those who were steaming in white cashmere or alpaca, because in some cases such frocks were thought more useful afterwards. Blue and pink waist ribbons were lying over the backs of chairs, and the girl who had a Roman sash was praying that she might be kept from vanity and pride.

The way to any graduating dress at all had not seemed clear to Rebecca until a month before. Then, in company with Emma Jane, she visited the Perkins' attic, found piece after piece of white butter muslin or cheesecloth, and decided that, at a pinch, it would do. The " rich blacksmith's daughter " cast the thought of dotted Swiss behind her, and elected to follow Rebecca in cheesecloth as she had in higher matters, straightway devising costumes that included such drawing of threads, such hemstitching and pin-tucking, such insertions of fine thread tatting, that, in order to be finished, Rebecca's dress was given out in sections—the sash to Hannah, waist and sleeves to Mrs. Cobb, and skirt to Aunt Jane. The stitches that went into the despised material, worth only three or four pennies a yard, made the dresses altogether lovely, and as for the folds and lines into which they fell, they could have given points to satins and brocades.

The two girls were waiting in their room alone, Emma Jane in rather a tearful state of mind. She kept thinking that it was the last day that they would be together in this altogether sweet and close intimacy. The beginning of the end seemed to have dawned, for two positions had been offered Rebecca by Mr. Morrison the day before: one in which she would play for singing and calisthenics, and superintend the piano practice of the younger girls in a boarding-school; the other an assistant's place in the Edgewood High School. Both were very modest as to salary, but the former included educational advantages that Miss Maxwell thought might be valuable.

Rebecca's mood had passed from that of excitement into a sort of exaltation, and when the first bell rang through the corridors announcing that in five minutes the class would proceed in a body to the church for the exercises, she stood motionless and speechless at the window with her hand on her heart.

"It is coming, Emmie," she said presently; "do you remember, in 'The Mill on the Floss,' when Maggie Tulliver closed the golden gates of childhood behind her? I can almost see them swing, almost hear them clang; and I can't tell whether I am glad or sorry."

"I shouldn't care how they swung or clanged," said Emma Jane, "if only you and I were on the same side of the gate; but we shan't be, I know we shan't!"

"Emmie, don't dare to cry, for I'm just on the brink myself. If only you were graduating with me! that's my only sorrow. There, I hear the rumble of the wheels! People will be seeing our grand surprise now. Hug me once for luck, dear Emmie; a careful hug, remembering our butter-muslin frailty."

Ten minutes later Adam Ladd, who had just arrived from Portland, and was wending his way to the church, came suddenly into the main street and stopped short under a tree by the wayside, riveted to the spot by a scene of picturesque loveliness such as his eyes had seldom witnessed before. The class of which Rebecca was president was not likely to follow accepted customs. Instead of marching two by two from the seminary to the church, they had elected to proceed thither by royal chariot. A haycart had been decked with green vines and bunches of long-stemmed field daisies, those gay darlings of New England meadows. Every inch of the rail, the body, even the spokes, all were twined with yellow and green and white. There were two white horses, flower-trimmed reins, and in the floral bower, seated on maple boughs, were the twelve girls of the class, while the ten boys marched on either side of the vehicle, wearing button-hole bouquets of daisies, the class flower.

Rebecca drove, seated on a green-covered bench that looked not unlike a throne. No girl clad in white muslin, no happy girl of seventeen, is plain; and the twelve little country maids, from the vantage-ground of their setting, looked beautiful as the June sunlight filtered down on their uncovered heads, showing their bright eyes, their fresh cheeks, their smiles, and their dimples.

Rebecca, Adam thought, as he took off his hat and saluted the pretty panorama—Rebecca, with her tall slenderness, her thoughtful brow, the fire of young joy in her face, her fillet of dark braided hair, might have been a young Muse or Sibyl; and the flowery hayrack, with its freight of blooming girlhood, might have been painted as an allegorical picture of "The Morning of Life." It all passed him, as he stood under the elms in the old village street where his mother had walked half a century ago, and he was turning with the crowd towards the church when he heard a little sob. Behind a hedge in the garden near where he was standing was a forlorn person in white, whose neat nose, chestnut hair, and blue eyes he seemed to know. He stepped inside the gate and said: "What's wrong, Miss Emma?"

"Oh, is it you, Mr. Ladd? Rebecca wouldn't let me cry for fear of spoiling my looks, but I must have just one chance before I go in. I can be as homely as I like, after all, for I only have to sing with the school. I'm not graduating; I'm just leaving. Not that I mind that; it's only being separated from Rebecca that I never can stand."

The two walked along together, Adam comforting the disconsolate Emma Jane, until they reached the old meeting-house where the commencement exercises were always held. The interior, with its decorations of yellow, green, and white, was crowded, the air hot and breathless, the essays and songs and recitations precisely like all others that have been since the world began. One always fears that the platform may sink under the weight of youthful platitudes uttered on such occasions; yet one can never be properly critical, because the sight of the boys and girls themselves— those young and hopeful makers of to-morrow—disarms one's scorn. We yawn desperately at the essays, but our hearts go out to the essayists, all the same, for "the vision splendid" is shining in their eyes, and there is no fear of "th' inevitable yoke" that the years are so surely bringing them.

Rebecca saw Hannah and her husband in the audience; dear old John and Cousin Ann also, and felt a pang at the absence of her mother, though she had known there was no possibility of seeing her; for poor Aurelia was kept at Sunnybrook by cares of children and farm, and lack of money either for the journey or for suitable dress. The Cobbs she saw too. No one, indeed, could fail to see Uncle Jerry, for he shed tears more than once, and in the intervals between the essays descanted to his neighbours concerning the marvellous gifts of one of the graduating class whom he had known ever since she was a child; in fact, had driven her from Maplewood to Riverboro when she left her home, and he had told mother that same night that there wa'n't nary rung on the ladder o' fame that that child wouldn't mount before she got through with it."

The Cobbs, then, had come, and there were other Riverboro faces, but where was Aunt Jane in her black silk made over-especially for this occasion? Aunt Miranda had not intended to come, she knew; but where, on this day of days, was her beloved Aunt Jane? However, this thought, like all others, came and went in a flash, for the whole morning was like a series of magic-lantern pictures crossing and recrossing her field of vision. She played, she sang, she recited Queen Mary's Latin prayer like one in a dream, only brought to consciousness by meeting Mr. Aladdin's eyes as she spoke the last line. Then at the end of the programme came her class poem, "Makers of To-morrow"; and there, as on many a former occasion, her personality played so great a part that she seemed to be uttering Miltonic sentiments instead of school-girl verse. Her voice, her eyes, her body breathed conviction, earnestness, emotion; and when she left the platform the audience felt that they had listened to a masterpiece. Most of her hearers knew little of Carlyle or Emerson, or they might have remembered that the one said, "We are all poets when we read a poem well," and the other, "'Tis the good reader makes the good book."

It was over! The diplomas had been presented, and each girl, after giving furtive touches to her hair, sly tweaks to her muslin skirts, and caressing pats to her sash, had gone forward to receive the roll of parchment with a bow that had been the subject of anxious thought for weeks. Rounds of applause greeted each graduate at this thrilling moment, and Jeremiah Cobb's behaviour when Rebecca came forward was the talk of Wareham and Riverboro for days. Old Mrs. Webb avowed that he, in the space of two hours, had worn out her pew more—the carpet, the cushions, and wood-work—than she had by sitting in it forty years. Yes, it was over, and after the crowd had thinned a little Adam Ladd made his way to the platform.

Rebecca turned from speaking to some strangers and met him in the aisle. "Oh, Mr. Aladdin, I am so glad you could come! Tell me" and she looked at him half shyly, for his approval was dearer to her, and more difficult to win, than that of the others—"tell me, Mr. Aladdin, were you satisfied?"

"More than satisfied!" he said. "Glad I met the child, proud I know the girl, longing to meet the woman!"

XXVIII

"TH' INEVITABLE YOKE"

REBECCA'S heart beat high at this sweet praise from her hero's lips, but before she had found words to thank him, Mr. and Mrs. Cobb, who had been modestly biding their time in a corner, approached her, and she introduced them to Mr. Ladd.

"Where, where is Aunt Jane?" she cried, holding Aunt Sarah's hand on one side and Uncle Jerry's on the other.

"I'm sorry, lovey, but we've got bad news for you."

"Is Aunt Miranda worse? She is; I can see it by your looks;" and Rebecca's colour faded.

"She had a second stroke yesterday morning jest when she was helpin' Jane lay out her things to come here to-day. Jane said you wa'n't to know anything about it till the exercises was all over, and we promised to keep it secret till then."

"I will go right home with you, Aunt Sarah. I must just run to tell Miss Maxwell, for after I had packed up to-morrow I was going to Brunswick with her. Poor Aunt Miranda! And I have been so gay and happy all day, except that I was longing for mother and Aunt Jane."

"There ain't no harm in bein' gay, lovey; that's what Jane wanted you to be. And Miranda's got her speech back, for your aunt has just sent a letter sayin' she's better; and I'm goin' to set up to-night, so you can stay here and have a good sleep, and get your things together comfortably to-morrow."

"I'll pack your trunk for you, Becky dear, and attend to all our room things," said Emma Jane, who had come towards the group and heard the sorrowful news from the brick house.

They moved into one of the quiet side-pews, where Hannah and her husband and John joined them. From time to time some straggling acquaintance or old schoolmate would come up to congratulate Rebecca and ask why she had hidden herself in a corner. Then some member of the class would call to her excitedly, reminding her not to be late at the picnic luncheon, or begging her to be early at the class party in the evening. All this had an air of unreality to Rebecca. In the midst of the happy excitement of the last two days, when "blushing honours" had been falling thick upon her, and behind the delicious exaltation of the morning, had been the feeling that the condition was a transient one, and that the burden, the struggle, the anxiety, would soon loom again on the horizon. She longed to steal away into the woods with dear old John, grown so manly and handsome, and get some comfort from him.

Meantime Adam Ladd and Mr. Cobb had been having an animated conversation.

"I s'pose up to Boston girls like that one are as thick as blackb'ries?" Uncle Jerry said, jerking his head interrogatively in Rebecca's direction.

"They may be," smiled Adam, taking in the old man's mood; "only I don't happen to know one."

"My eyesight bein' poor 's the reason she looked han'somest of any girl on the platform, I s'pose."

"There's no failure in my eyes," responded Adam; "but that was how the thing seemed to me."

"What did you think of her voice? Anything extry about it?"

"Made the others sound poor and thin, I thought."

"Well, I'm glad to hear your opinion, you bein' a travelled man, for mother says I'm foolish 'bout Rebecky, and hev been sense the fust. Mother scolds me for spoilin' her, but I notice mother ain't fur behind when it comes to spoilin'. Land! it made me sick, thinkin' o' them parents travellin' miles to see their young ones graduate, and then when they got here hevin' to compare 'em with Rebecky. Good-bye, Mr. Ladd. Drop in some day when you come to Riverboro."

"I will," said Adam, shaking the old man's hand cordially; "perhaps to-morrow, if I drive Rebecca home, as I shall offer to do. Do you think Miss Sawyer's condition is serious?"

"Well, the doctor don't seem to know; but, anyhow, she's paralyzed, and she'll never walk fur again, poor soul! She ain't lost her speech; that'll be a comfort to her."

Adam left the church, and in crossing the common came upon Miss Maxwell doing the honours of the institution as she passed from group to group of strangers and guests. Knowing that she was deeply interested in all Rebecca's plans, he told her, as he drew her aside, that the girl would have to leave Wareham for Riverboro the next day.

"That is almost more than I can bear!" exclaimed Miss Maxwell, sitting down on a bench and stabbing the greensward with her parasol. "It seems to me Rebecca never has any respite. I had so many plans for her this next month in fitting her for her position, and now she will settle down to housework again, and to the nursing of that poor, sick, cross old aunt."

"If it had not been for the cross old aunt, Rebecca would still have been at Sunnybrook; and from the standpoint of educational advantages, or, indeed, advantages of any sort, she might as well have been in the backwoods," returned Adam.

"That is true. I was vexed when I spoke, for I thought an easier and happier day was dawning for my prodigy and pearl."

"*Our* prodigy and pearl," corrected Adam.

"Oh yes!" she laughed. "I always forget that it pleases you to pretend you discovered Rebecca."

"I believe, though, that happier days are dawning for her," continued Adam. "It must be a secret for the present, but Mrs. Randall's farm will be bought by the new railroad. We must have right-of-way through the land, and the station will be built on her property. She will receive six thousand dollars, which, though not a fortune, will yield her three or four hundred dollars a year if she will allow me to invest it for her. There is a mortgage on the land; that paid, and Rebecca self-supporting, the mother ought to push the education of the oldest boy, who is a fine, ambitious fellow. He should be taken away from farm work and settled at his studies."

"We might form ourselves into a Randall Protective Agency, Limited," mused Miss Maxwell. "I confess I want Rebecca to have a career."

"I don't," said Adam promptly.

"Of course you don't. Men have no interest in the careers of women. But I know Rebecca better than you."

"You understand her mind better, but not necessarily her heart. You are considering her for the moment as prodigy; I am thinking of her more as pearl."

"Well," sighed Miss Maxwell whimsically, "prodigy or pearl, the Randall Protective Agency may pull Rebecca in opposite directions, but, nevertheless, she will follow her saint."

"That will content me," said Adam gravely.

"Particularly if the saint beckons your way." And Miss Maxwell looked up and smiled provokingly.

Rebecca did not see her Aunt Miranda till she had been at the brick house for several days. Miranda steadily refused to have anyone but Jane in the room until her face had regained its natural look, but her door was always ajar, and Jane fancied she liked to hear Rebecca's quick, light step. Her mind was perfectly clear now, and, save that she could not move, she was most of the time quite free from pain, and alert in every nerve to all that was going on within or without the house. "Were the windfall apples being picked up for sauce? Were the potatoes thick in the hills? Was the corn tosselin' out? Were they cuttin' the upper field? Were they keepin' fly-paper laid out everywheres? Were there any ants in the dairy? Was the kindlin' wood holdin' out? Had the bank sent the cowpons?"

Poor Miranda Sawyer! Hovering on the verge

of the great beyond—her body "struck," and no longer under control of her iron will—no divine visions floated across her tired brain; nothing but petty cares and sordid anxieties. Not all at once can the soul talk with God, be He ever so near. If the heavenly language never has been learned, quick as is the spiritual sense in seizing the facts it needs, then the poor soul must use the words and phrases it has lived on and grown into day by day. Poor Miss Miranda!—held fast within the prison walls of her own nature, blind in the presence of revelation because she had never used the spiritual eye, deaf to angelic voices because she had not used the spiritual ear.

There came a morning when she asked for Rebecca. The door was opened into the dim sickroom, and Rebecca stood there with the sunlight behind her, her hands full of sweet-peas. Miranda's pale, sharp face, framed in its nightcap, looked haggard on the pillow, and her body was pitifully still under the counterpane.

"Come in," she said; "I ain't dead yet. Don't mess up the bed with them flowers, will ye?"

"Oh no! they're going in a glass pitcher," said Rebecca, turning to the washstand as she tried to control her voice and stop the tears that sprang to her eyes.

"Let me look at ye; come closer! What dress are ye wearin'?" said the old aunt in her cracked, weak voice.

"My blue calico."

"Is your cashmere holdin' its colour?"

"Yes, Aunt Miranda."

"Do you keep it in a dark closet hung on the wrong side, as I told ye?"

"Always."

"Has your mother made her jelly?"

"She hasn't said."

"She always had the knack o' writin' letters with nothin' in 'em. What's Mark broke sence I've been sick?"

"Nothing at all, Aunt Miranda."

"Why, what's the matter with him? Gittin' lazy, ain't he? How's John turnin' out?"

"He's going to be the best of us all."

"I hope you don't slight things in the kitchen because I ain't there. Do you scald the coffee-pot and turn it upside down on the winder-sill?"

"Yes, Aunt Miranda."

"It's always 'Yes' with you, and 'Yes' with Jane," groaned Miranda, trying to move her stiffened body; "but all the time I lay here knowin' there's things done the way I don't like 'em."

There was a long pause, during which Rebecca sat down by the bedside and timidly touched her aunt's hand, her heart swelling with tender pity at the gaunt face and closed eyes.

"I was dreadful ashamed to have you graduate in cheesecloth, Rebecca, but I couldn't help it nohow. You'll hear the reason some time, and know I tried to make it up to ye. I'm afraid you was a laughin'-stock!"

"No," Rebecca answered. "Ever so many people said our dresses were the very prettiest; they looked like soft lace. You're not to be anxious about anything. Here I am, all grown up and graduated—

number three in a class of twenty-two, Aunt Miranda
—and good positions offered me already. Look at
me! big and strong and young, all ready to go into
the world and show what you and Aunt Jane have
done for me. If you want me near, I'll take the Edgewood school, so that I can be here nights and Sundays to help; and if you get better, then I'll go to
Augusta, for that's a hundred dollars more, with
music lessons and other things beside."

"You listen to me," said Miranda quaveringly
"take the best place, regardless o' my sickness. I'd
like to live long enough to know you'd paid off that
mortgage, but I guess I shan't."

Here she ceased abruptly, having talked more than
she had for weeks; and Rebecca stole out of the room,
to cry by herself and wonder if old age must be so
grim, so hard, so unchastened and unsweetened, as it
slipped into the valley of the shadow.

The days went on, and Miranda grew stronger
and stronger. Her will seemed unassailable, and
before long she could be moved into a chair by the
window, her dominant thought being to arrive at
such a condition of improvement that the doctor need
not call more than once a week, instead of daily,
thereby diminishing the bill that was mounting to
such a terrifying sum that it haunted her thoughts
by day and dreams by night.

Little by little hope stole back into Rebecca's
young heart. Aunt Jane began to "clear starch" her
handkerchiefs and collars and purple muslin dress,
so that she might be ready to go to Brunswick at
any moment when the doctor pronounced Miranda
well on the road to recovery. Everything beautiful

was to happen in Brunswick if she could be there by
August, everything that heart could wish or imagination conceive, for she was to be Miss Emily's very
own visitor, and sit at table with college professors
and other great men.

At length the day dawned when the few clean,
simple dresses were packed in the hair-trunk, together
with her beloved coral necklace, her cheesecloth
graduating dress, her class pin, Aunt Jane's lace cap,
and the one new hat, which she tried on every night
before going to bed. It was of white chip with a
wreath of cheap white roses and green leaves, and
cost between two and three dollars, an unprecedented
sum in Rebecca's experience. The effect of its glories
when worn with her nightdress was dazzling enough,
but if ever it appeared in conjunction with the cheesecloth gown Rebecca felt that even reverend professors
might regard it with respect. It is probable, indeed,
that any professorial gaze lucky enough to meet a pair
of dark eyes shining under that white rose garland
would never have stopped at respect!

Then, when all was ready and Abijah Flagg at the
door, came a telegram from Hannah: "Come at once.
Mother has had bad accident."

In less than an hour Rebecca was started on her
way to Sunnybrook, her heart palpitating with fear as
to what might be awaiting her at her journey's end.

Death, at all events, was not there to meet her, but
something that looked at first only too much like it.
Her mother had been standing on the haymow super-
intending some changes in the barn, had been seized
with giddiness, they thought, and slipped. The right
knee was fractured and the back strained and hurt,

but she was conscious and in no immediate danger, so Rebecca wrote when she had a moment to send Aunt Jane the particulars.

"I don' know how 'tis," grumbled Miranda, who was not able to sit up that day; "but from a child I could never lay abed without Aurelia's gettin' sick too. I don' know's she could help fallin', though it ain't any place for a woman—a haymow; but if it hadn't been that, 'twould 'a' been somethin' else. Aurelia was born unfortunate. Now she'll probably be a cripple, and Rebecca 'll have to nurse her instead of earning a good income somewheres else."

"Her first duty's to her mother," said Aunt Jane; "I hope she'll always remember that."

"Nobody remembers anything they'd ought to—at seventeen," responded Miranda. "Now that I'm strong again, there's things I want to consider with you, Jane—things that are on my mind night and day. We've talked 'em over before; now we'll settle 'em. When I'm laid away, do you want to take Aurelia and the children down here to the brick house? There's an awful passel of 'em—Aurelia, Jenny, and Fanny; but I won't have Mark. Hannah can take him; I won't have a great boy stompin' out the carpets and ruinin' the furniture, though I know when I'm dead I can't hinder ye, if you make up your mind to do anything."

"I shouldn't like to go against your feelings, especially in laying out your money, Miranda," said Jane.

"Don't tell Rebecca I've willed her the brick house. She won't git it till I'm gone, and I want to take my time 'bout dyin' and not be hurried off by them that's goin' to profit by it; nor I don't want to be thanked, neither. I s'pose she'll use the front stairs as common as the back, and like as not have water brought into the kitchen; but mebbe when I've been dead a few years I shan't mind. She sets such store by you, she'll want you to have your home here as long 's you live; but any way, I've wrote it down that way. Though Lawyer Burns's wills don't hold more 'n half the time, he's cheaper, but I guess it comes out jest the same in the end. I wa'n't goin' to have the fust man Rebecca picks up for a husband turnin' you ou'doors."

There was a long pause, during which Jane knit silently, wiping the tears from her eyes from time to time, as she looked at the pitiful figure lying weakly on the pillows. Suddenly Miranda said slowly and feebly:

"I don' know, after all, but you might as well take Mark; I s'pose there's tame boys as well as wild ones. There ain't a mite o' sense in havin' so many children, but it's a turrible risk splittin' up families and farmin' 'em out here 'n' there; they'd never come to no good, an' everybody would keep rememberin' their mother was a Sawyer. Now, if you'll draw the curtin, I'll try to sleep."

XXIX

Two months had gone by—two months of steady, fagging work: of cooking, washing, ironing; of mending and caring for the three children, although Jenny was fast becoming a notable little housewife— quick, ready, and capable. There were months in which there had been many a weary night of watching by Aurelia's bedside, of soothing and bandaging and rubbing, of reading and nursing, even of feeding and bathing. The ceaseless care was growing less now, and the family breathed more freely, for the mother's sigh of pain no longer came from the stifling bed-room, where during a hot and humid August Aurelia had lain, suffering with every breath she drew. There would be no question of walking for many a month to come; but blessings seemed to multiply when the blinds could be opened and the bed drawn near the window, when mother, with pillows behind her, could at least sit and watch the work going on, could smile at the past agony, and forget the weary hours that had led to her present comparative ease and comfort.

No girl of seventeen can pass through such an ordeal and come out unchanged; no girl of Rebecca's temperament could go through it without some inward repining and rebellion. She was doing tasks in which she could not be fully happy—heavy and trying tasks, which perhaps she could never do with complete success or satisfaction, and, like promise of nectar to thirsty lips, was the vision of joys she had

had to put aside for the performance of dull daily
duty. How brief, how fleeting, had been those
splendid visions when the universe seemed open for
her young strength to battle and triumph in! How
soon they had faded into the light of common day!
At first sympathy and grief were so keen she thought
of nothing but her mother's pain. No consciousness
of self interposed between her and her filial service.
Then, as the weeks passed, little blighted hopes began
to stir and ache in her breast, defeated ambitions
raised their heads as if to sting her, unattainable
delights teased her by their very nearness—by the
narrow line of separation that lay between her and
their realization. It is easy for the moment to tread
the narrow way, looking neither to the right nor left,
upborne by the sense of right-doing; but that first
joy of self-denial—the joy that is like fire in the
blood—dies away, the path seems drearier, and the
footsteps falter. Such a time came to Rebecca, and
her bright spirit flagged when the letter was received
saying that her position in Augusta had been filled.
There was a mutinous leap of the heart then, a beating of wings against the door of the cage, a longing
for the freedom of the big world outside. It was the
stirring of the powers within her, though she called
it by no such grand name. She felt as if the wind of
destiny were blowing her flame hither and thither,
burning, consuming her, but kindling nothing. All
this meant one stormy night in her little room at
Sunnybrook; but the clouds blew over, the sun shone
again, a rainbow stretched across the sky, while " hope
clad in April green " smiled into her upturned face
and beckoned her on, saying:

" Grow old along with me;
  The best is yet to be."

Threads of joy ran in and out of the grey tangled web of daily living. There was the attempt at odd moments to make the bare little house less bare by bringing in out-of-doors, taking a leaf from Nature's book, and noting how she conceals ugliness wherever she finds it. Then there was the satisfaction of being mistress of the poor domain; of planning, governing, deciding; of bringing order out of chaos; of implanting gaiety in the place of inert resignation to the inevitable. Another element of comfort was the children's love, for they turned to her as flowers to the sun, drawing confidently on her fund of stories, serene in the conviction that there was no limit to Rebecca's power of make-believe. In this and in yet greater things, little as she realized it, the law of compensation was working in her behalf, for in those anxious days mother and daughter found and knew each other as never before. A new sense was born in Rebecca as she hung over her mother's bed of pain and unrest—a sense that comes only of ministering, a sense that grows only when the strong bend toward the weak. As for Aurelia, words could never have expressed her dumb happiness when the real revelation of motherhood was vouchsafed her. In all the earlier years, when her babies were young, carking cares and anxieties darkened the fireside with their brooding wings. Then Rebecca had gone away, and in the long months of absence her mind and soul had grown out of her mother's knowledge, so that now, when Aurelia had time and strength to study her child, she was like some enchanting changeling.

Aurelia and Hannah had gone on in the dull round
and the common task growing duller and duller; but
now, on a certain stage of life's journey, who should
appear but this bewildering being, who gave wings
to thoughts that had only crept before, who brought
colour and grace and harmony into the dun-brown
texture of existence.

You might harness Rebecca to the heaviest plough,
and while she had youth on her side she would always
remember the green earth under her feet and the blue
sky over her head. Her physical eye saw the cake
she was stirring and the loaf she was kneading; her
physical ear heard the kitchen fire crackling and the
tea-kettle singing, but ever and anon her fancy
mounted on pinions, rested itself, renewed its
strength in the upper air. The bare little farmhouse
was a fixed fact, but she had many a palace into which
she now and then withdrew—palaces peopled with
stirring and gallant figures belonging to the world of
romance: palaces not without their heavenly appari-
tions, too, breathing celestial counsel. Every time she
retired to her citadel of dreams she came forth radiant
and refreshed, as one who has seen the evening star,
or heard sweet music, or smelled the Rose of Joy.

Aurelia could have understood the feeling of
a narrow-minded and conventional hen who has
brought a strange, intrepid duckling into the world;
but her situation was still more wonderful, for she
could only compare her sensations to those of some
quiet, brown Dorking who has brooded an ordinary
egg and hatched a bird of paradise. Such an idea had
crossed her mind more than once during the past fortnight, and it flashed to and fro this mellow October

morning when Rebecca came into the room with her arms full of golden-rod and flaming autumn leaves.

"Just a hint of the fall styles, mother," she said, slipping the stem of a gorgeous red and yellow sapling between the mattress and the foot of the bed. "This was leaning over the pool, and I was afraid it would be vain if I left it there too long looking at its beautiful reflection, so I took it away from danger. Isn't it wonderful? How I wish I could carry one to poor Aunt Miranda to-day! There's never a flower in the brick house when I'm away."

It was a marvellous morning. The sun had climbed into a world that held in remembrance only a succession of golden days and starlit nights. The air was fragrant with ripening fruit, and there was a mad little bird on a tree outside the door nearly bursting his throat with joy of living. He had forgotten that summer was over, that winter must ever come; and who could think of cold winds, bare boughs, or frozen streams on such a day? A painted moth came in at the open window and settled on the tuft of brilliant leaves. Aurelia heard the bird, and looked from the beauty of the glowing bush to her tall, splendid daughter, standing like young Spring with golden Autumn in her arms.

Then suddenly she covered her eyes and cried, "I can't bear it! Here I lie chained to this bed, interfering with everything you want to do. It's all wasted—all my saving and doing without, all your hard study, all Miranda's outlay—everything that we thought was going to be the making of you!"

"Mother, mother, don't talk so—don't think so!" exclaimed Rebecca, sitting down impetuously on the

floor by the bed, and dropping the golden-rod by her
side. "Why, mother, I'm only a little past seventeen!
This person in a purple calico apron, with flour on her
nose, is only the beginnings of me. Do you remember
the young tree that John transplanted? We had a dry
summer and a cold winter, and it didn't grow a bit,
nor show anything of all we did for it; then there was
a good year, and it made up for lost time. This is
just my little 'rooting season,' mother; but don't go
and believe my day is over, because it hasn't begun!
The old maple by the well that's in its hundredth year
had new leaves this summer, so there must be hope
for me at seventeen!"

"You can put a brave face on it," sobbed Aurelia,
"but you can't deceive me. You've lost your place;
you'll never see your friends here, and you're nothing
but a drudge!"

"I look like a drudge," said Rebecca mysteriously,
with laughing eyes, "but I really am a princess. You
mustn't tell, but this is only a disguise; I wear it for
reasons of state. The king and queen who are at
present occupying my throne are very old and totter-
ing, and are going to abdicate shortly in my favour.
It's rather a small kingdom, I suppose, as kingdoms
go, so there isn't much struggle for it in royal circles;
and you mustn't expect to see a golden throne set
with jewels. It will probably be only of ivory, with
a nice screen of peacock feathers for a background.
But you shall have a comfortable chair very near it,
with quantities of slaves to do what they call in novels
your 'lightest bidding.'"

Aurelia smiled in spite of herself, and though not
perhaps wholly deceived, she was comforted.

"I only hope you won't have to wait too long for your thrones and your kingdoms, Rebecca," she said, "and that I shall have a sight of them before I die. But life looks very hard and rough to me, what with your Aunt Miranda a cripple at the brick house, me another here at the farm, you tied hand and foot, first with one and then with the other, to say nothing of Jenny and Fanny and Mark. You've got something of your father's happy disposition, or it would weigh on you as it does on me."

"Why, mother," cried Rebecca, clasping her knees with her hands—"why, mother, it's enough joy just to be here in the world on a day like this—to have the chance of seeing, feeling, doing, becoming! When you were seventeen, mother, wasn't it good just to be alive? You haven't forgotten?"

"No," said Aurelia, "but I wasn't so much alive as you are, never in the world."

"I often think," Rebecca continued, walking to the window and looking out at the trees—"I often think how dreadful it would be if I were not here at all. If Hannah had come, and then, instead of me, John; John and Jenny and Fanny and the others, but no Rebecca—never any Rebecca! To be alive makes up for everything. There ought to be fears in my heart, but there aren't; something stronger sweeps them out—something like a wind. Oh, see! there is Will driving up the lane, mother, and he ought to have a letter from the brick house."

XXX

WILL MELVILLE drove up to the window, and, tossing a letter into Rebecca's lap, went off to the barn on an errand.

"Sister's no worse, then," sighed Aurelia gratefully, "or Jane would have telegraphed. See what she says."

Rebecca opened the envelope, and read in one flash of an eye the whole brief page:

"Your Aunt Miranda passed away an hour ago. Come at once if your mother is out of danger. I shall not have the funeral till you are here. She died very suddenly and without any pain. Oh, Rebecca, I long for you so!

"AUNT JANE."

The force of habit was too strong; and even in the hour of death Jane had remembered that a telegram was twenty-five cents, and that Aurelia would have to pay half a dollar for its delivery.

Rebecca burst into a passion of tears as she cried: "Poor, poor Aunt Miranda! She is gone without taking a bit of comfort in life, and I couldn't say good-bye to her! Poor lonely Aunt Jane! What can I do, mother? I feel torn in two between you and the brick house."

"You must go this very instant," said Aurelia, starting from her pillows. "If I was to die while

266

you were away, I would say the very same thing.
Your aunts have done everything in the world for you
—more than I've ever been able to do—and it is your
turn to pay back some o' their kindness and show
your gratitude. The doctor says I've turned the
corner, and I feel I have. Jenny can make out somehow, if Hannah 'll come over once a day."

"But, mother, I *can't* go! Who'll turn you in
bed?" exclaimed Rebecca, walking the floor and
wringing her hands distractedly.

"It don't make any difference if I don't get
turned," replied Aurelia stoically. "If a woman of
my age and the mother of a family hasn't got sense
enough not to slip off haymows, she'd ought to suffer.
Go put on your black dress and pack your bag. I'd
give a good deal if I was able to go to my sister's
funeral, and prove that I've forgotten and forgiven
all she said when I was married. Her acts were softer
'n' her words, Mirandy's were, and she's made up to
you for all she ever sinned against me 'n' your father.
And oh, Rebecca!" she continued with quivering
voice, "I remember so well when we were little girls
together, and she took such pride in curling my hair;
and another time, when we were grown up, she lent
me her best blue muslin. It was when your father had
asked me to lead the grand march with him at the
Christmas dance; and I found out afterwards she
thought he'd intended to ask her."

Here Aurelia broke down and wept bitterly, for
the recollection of the past had softened her heart,
and brought the comforting tears even more effectu-
ally than the news of her sister's death.

There was only an hour for preparation. Will

would drive Rebecca to Temperance and send Jenny back from school. He volunteered also to engage a woman to sleep at the farm in case Mrs. Randall should be worse at any time in the night.

Rebecca flew down over the hill to get a last pail of spring water; and as she lifted the bucket from the crystal depths, and looked out over the glowing beauty of the autumn landscape, she saw a company of surveyors with their instruments making calculations, and laying lines that apparently crossed Sunnybrook at the favourite spot where Mirror Pool lay clear and placid, the yellow leaves on its surface no yellower than its sparkling sands.

She caught her breath. "The time has come," she thought. "I am saying good-bye to Sunnybrook, and the golden gates that almost swung together that last day in Wareham will close for ever now. Goodbye, dear brook and hills and meadows; you are going to see life, too, so we must be hopeful, and say to one another :

> "Grow old along with me;
> The best is yet to be."

Will Melville had seen the surveyors too, and had heard in the Temperance post-office that morning the probable sum that Mrs. Randall would receive from the railway company. He was in good spirits at his own improved prospects, for his farm was so placed that its value could be only increased by the new road; he was also relieved in mind that his wife's family would no longer be in dire proverty directly at his doorstep, so to speak. John could now be hurried forward, and forced into the position of head of the family several years sooner than had been anticipated, so Hannah's husband was obliged to exercise great self-control, or he would have whistled while he was driving Rebecca to the Temperance station. He could not understand her sad face or the tears that rolled silently down her cheeks from time to time, for Hannah had always represented her Aunt Miranda as an irascible, parsimonious old woman, who would be no loss to the world whenever she should elect to disappear from it.

"Cheer up, Becky!" he said, as he left her at the depôt. "You'll find your mother sitting up when you come back; and the next thing you know the whole family 'll be moving to some nice little house wherever your work is. Things will never be so bad again as they have been this last year; that's what Hannah and I think." And he drove away to tell his wife the news.

Adam Ladd was in the station and came up to Rebecca instantly, as she entered the door looking very unlike her bright self.

"The Princess is sad this morning," he said, taking her hand. "Aladdin must rub the magic lamp; then the slave will appear, and these tears be dried in a trice."

He spoke lightly, for he thought her trouble was something connected with affairs at Sunnybrook, and that he could soon bring the smiles by telling her that the farm was sold and that her mother was to receive a handsome price in return. He meant to remind her, too, that though she must leave the home of her youth, it was too remote a place to be a proper dwelling either for herself or for her lonely mother

and the three younger children. He could hear her
say, as plainly as if it were yesterday, "I don't
think one ever forgets the spot where one lived as a
child." He could see the quaint little figure sitting on
the piazza at North Riverboro and watch it disappear
in the lilac-bushes when he gave the memorable order
for three hundred cakes of Rose-Red and Snow-
White soap.

A word or two soon told him that her grief was
of another sort, and her mood was so absent, so
sensitive and tearful, that he could only assure her
of his sympathy and beg that he might come soon to
the brick house to see with his own eyes how she
was faring.

Adam thought, when he had put her on the train
and taken his leave, that Rebecca was, in her sad
dignity and gravity, more beautiful than he had ever
seen her—all-beautiful and all-womanly. But in that
moment's speech with her he had looked into her eyes,
and they were still those of a child; there was no
knowledge of the world in their shining depths, no
experience of men or women, no passion nor comprehension of it. He turned from the little country
station to walk in the woods by the wayside until his
own train should be leaving, and from time to time
he threw himself under a tree to think and dream and
look at the glory of the foliage. He had brought a
new copy of "The Arabian Nights" for Rebecca,
wishing to replace the well-worn old one that had
been the delight of her girlhood; but meeting her at
such an inauspicious time, he had absently carried it
away with him. He turned the pages idly until he
came to the story of "Aladdin and the Wonderful

Lamp," and presently, in spite of his thirty-four years, the old tale held him spell-bound as it did in the days when he first read it as a boy. But there were certain paragraphs that especially caught his eye and arrested his attention, paragraphs that he read and reread, finding in them he knew not what secret delight and significance. These were the quaintly-turned phrases describing the effect on the once poor Aladdin of his wonderful riches, and those descanting upon the beauty and charm of the Sultan's daughter, the Princess Badroulboudour:

Not only those who knew Aladdin when he played in the streets like a vagabond did not know him again; those who had seen him but a little while before hardly knew him, so much were his features altered; such were the effects of the lamp, as to procure by degrees to those who possessed it perfections agreeable to the rank the right use of it advanced them to.

The Princess was the most beautiful brunette in the world; her eyes were large, lively, and sparkling; her looks sweet and modest; her nose was of a just proportion and without a fault; her mouth small, her lips of a vermilion red, and charmingly agreeable symmetry; in a word, all the features of her face were perfectly regular. It is not, therefore, surprising that Aladdin, who had never seen, and was a stranger to, so many charms, was dazzled. With all these perfections the Princess had so delicate a shape, so majestic an air, that the sight of her was sufficient to inspire respect.

" Adorable Princess," said Aladdin to her, accost-

*ing her, and saluting her respectfully, "if I have the
misfortune to have displeased you by my boldness in
aspiring to the possession of so lovely a creature, I
must tell you that you ought to blame your bright
eyes and charms, not me."*

*"Prince," answered the Princess, "it is enough for
me to have seen you, to tell you that I obey without
reluctance."*

XXXI

AUNT MIRANDA'S APOLOGY

WHEN Rebecca alighted from the train at Maplewood
and hurried to the post-office where the stage was
standing, what was her joy to see Uncle Jerry Cobb
holding the horses' heads!

"The reg'lar driver's sick," he explained, "and
when they sent for me, thinks I to myself, my drivin'
days is over; but Rebecky won't let the grass grow
under her feet when she gits her Aunt Jane's letter,
and like as not I'll ketch her to-day; or, if she gits
delayed, to-morrow for certain. So here I be jest as
I was more 'n six years ago. Will you be a real lady
passenger, or will ye sit up in front with me?"

Emotions of various sorts were all struggling
together in the old man's face, and the two or three
bystanders were astounded when they saw the handsome, stately girl fling herself on Mr. Cobb's dusty
shoulder crying like a child. "Oh, Uncle Jerry!"
she sobbed—"dear Uncle Jerry! It's all so long ago,

and so much has happened, and we've grown so old, and so much is going to happen, that I'm fairly frightened."

"There, there, lovey!" the old man whispered comfortably; "we'll be all alone on the stage, and we'll talk things over 's we go along the road, an' mebbe they won't look so bad."

Every mile of the way was as familiar to Rebecca as to Uncle Jerry; every watering-trough, grindstone, red barn, weather-vane, duck-pond, and sandy brook. And all the time she was looking backward to the day, seemingly so long ago, when she sat on the box-seat for the first time, her legs dangling in the air, too short to reach the footboard. She could smell the big bouquet of lilacs, see the pink-flounced parasol, feel the stiffness of the starched buff calico and the hated prick of the black and yellow porcupine quills.

The drive was taken almost in silence, but it was a sweet, comforting silence to both Uncle Jerry and the girl.

Then came the sight of Abijah Flagg shelling beans in the barn, and then the Perkins' attic windows with a white cloth fluttering from them. She could spell Emma Jane's loving thought and welcome in that little waving flag—a word and a message sent to her just at the first moment when Riverboro chimneys rose into view—something to warm her heart till they could meet.

The brick house came next, looking just as of yore, though it seemed to Rebecca as if death should have cast some mysterious spell over it. There were the rolling meadows, the stately elms, all yellow and brown now; the glowing maples, the garden-beds

bright with asters, and the hollyhocks rising tall
against the parlour windows; only in place of the
cheerful pinks and reds of the nodding stalks, with
their gay rosettes of bloom, was a crape scarf holding
the blinds together, and another on the sitting-room
side, and another on the brass knocker of the brown-
painted door.

"Stop, Uncle Jerry! Don't turn in at the side.
Hand me my satchel, please. Drop me in the road,
and let me run up the path by myself; then drive
away quickly."

At the noise and rumble of the approaching stage
the house door opened from within just as Rebecca
closed the gate behind her. Aunt Jane came down
the stone steps, a changed woman, frail and broken
and white. Rebecca held out her arms, and the old
aunt crept into them feebly, as she did on that day
when she opened the grave of her buried love and
showed the dead face, just for an instant, to a child.
Warmth and strength and life flowed into the aged
frame from the young one.

"Rebecca," she said, raising her head, " before you
go in to look at her, do you feel any bitterness over
anything she ever said to you?"

Rebecca's eyes blazed reproach, almost anger, as
she said chokingly: "Oh, Aunt Jane! could you
believe it of me? I am going in with a heart brimful
of gratitude!"

" She was a good woman, Rebecca; she had a quick
temper and a sharp tongue, but she wanted to do
right, and she did it as near as she could. She never
said so, but I'm sure she was sorry for every hard
word she spoke to you; she didn't take 'em back in

life, but she acted so 't you'd know her feeling when she was gone."

"I told her before I left that she'd been the making of me, just as mother says," sobbed Rebecca.

"She wasn't that," said Jane. "God made you in the first place, and you've done considerable yourself to help Him along; but she gave you the wherewithal to work with, and that ain't to be despised, specially when anybody gives up her own luxuries and pleasures to do it. Now let me tell you something, Rebecca. Your Aunt Mirandy's willed all this to you —the brick house and buildings and furniture, and the land all round the house, as far 's you can see."

Rebecca threw off her hat and put her hand to her heart, as she always did in moments of intense excitement. After a moment's silence she said: "Let me go in alone; I want to talk to her; I want to thank her; I feel as if I could make her hear and feel and understand!"

Jane went back into the kitchen to the inexorable tasks that death has no power, even for a day, to blot from existence. He can stalk through dwelling after dwelling, leaving despair and desolation behind him, but the table must be laid, the dishes washed, the beds made, by somebody.

Ten minutes later Rebecca came out from the Great Presence looking white and spent, but chastened and glorified. She sat in the quiet doorway, shaded from the little Riverboro world by the overhanging elms. A wide sense of thankfulness and peace possessed her, as she looked at the autumn landscape, listened to the rumble of a waggon on the bridge, and heard the call of the river as it dashed to the sea. She put up her hand softly and touched first the shining brass knocker and then the red bricks, glowing in the October sun.

It was home: her roof, her garden, her green acres, her dear trees; it was shelter for the little family at Sunnybrook; her mother would have once more the companionship of her sister and the friends of her girlhood; the children would have teachers and playmates.

And she? Her own future was close-folded still —folded and hidden in beautiful mists; but she leaned her head against the sun-warmed door, and closing her eyes, whispered, just as if she had been a child saying her prayers: "God bless Aunt Miranda! God bless the brick house that was! God bless the brick house that is to be!"